The *New York Times* calls
The Next Great Paulie Fink
"A FUNNY AND FAST-PACED ROMP."

★ "A story with **massive heart**, Benjamin's follow-up to
The Thing About Jellyfish proves this writer's incredible **wit**,
charm, and ability to navigate **deep questions** while tapping
directly into the middle school mindset.... A book to make
readers **think, question, reach, laugh**, and **strive harder**."
—*Kirkus Reviews*, starred review

★ "A **witty, tender**, and **utterly engaging** modern school
story that draws on the wisdom of the ages."
—*School Library Journal*, starred review

★ "**Genuinely original**, the novel offers **thoughtful**
perspectives on friendship, accepting change, and the many
rewarding guises of storytelling, as well as a **fully gratifying**
ending that the characters don't see coming."
—*Publishers Weekly*, starred review

★ "A **gorgeous tapestry**.... A **beautiful, powerful** novel
about embracing one's own great self."
—*Shelf Awareness*, starred review

"An **inspirational** story about finding your place
in an unfamiliar community and learning that
normal is not always better."
—*The Denver Post*

"**A middle school story to top all middle school stories**."
—*The Buffalo News*

THE NEXT GREAT PAULIE FINK

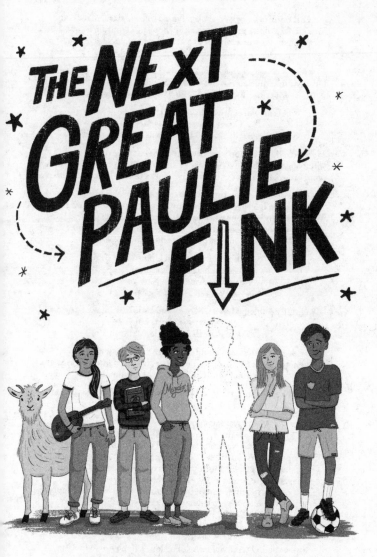

ALI BENJAMIN

LITTLE, BROWN AND COMPANY
New York Boston

Copyright © 2019 by Ali Benjamin
Discussion Guide copyright © 2020 by Little, Brown and Company
Interior illustrations © 2019 by Sarah J. Coleman

Cover art copyright © 2020 by Maeve Norton
Cover design by Angelie Yap
Cover copyright © 2020 by Hachette Book Group, Inc.

Little, Brown and Company
Hachette Book Group
1290 Avenue of the Americas, New York, NY 10104
Visit us at LBYR.com

Originally published in hardcover and ebook by Little, Brown and Company in April 2019
First Trade Paperback Edition: March 2020

Little, Brown and Company is a division of Hachette Book Group, Inc. The Little, Brown name and logo are trademarks of Hachette Book Group, Inc.

The publisher is not responsible for websites (or their content) that are not owned by the publisher.

The Library of Congress has cataloged the hardcover edition as follows:
Names: Benjamin, Ali, author.
Title: The Next Great Paulie Fink / Ali Benjamin.
Description: First edition. | New York ; Boston : Little, Brown and Company, 2019. | Summary: Led by new student Caitlyn, seventh-graders at a tiny rural school in Vermont create a reality-show inspired competition to determine who will replace the school's legendary class clown, Paulie Fink.
Identifiers: LCCN 2018032813| ISBN 9780316380881 (hardcover) | ISBN 9780316380898 (ebook) | ISBN 9780316381529 (library ebook edition)
Subjects: | CYAC: Schools—Fiction. | Behavior—Fiction. | Contests—Fiction. | Luck—Fiction. | Friendship—Fiction.
Classification: LCC PZ7.1.B453 Nex 2019 | DDC [Fic]—dc23
LC record available at https://lccn.loc.gov/2018032813

ISBNs: 978-0-316-38087-4 (pbk.), 978-0-316-54184-8 (Barnes & Noble), 978-0-316-38089-8 (ebook)

Printed in the United States of America

LSC-C

10 9 8 7 6 5 4 3 2

Now goddess, child of Zeus,
tell the old story for our modern times.
Find the beginning.

—Homer, *The Odyssey*

THE
OFFICIAL RECORD
OF THE SEARCH
FOR THE
NEXT GREAT
PAULIE FINK

THE CONTESTANTS

Gabby Amisi
Timothy Boggs
Thomas Boggs
Henry Cardinali
Willow Das
Fiona Fawnstock
Sam Moyes
Lydia Shea
Diego Silva
Yumi Watanabe-Peterson

THE JUDGE

Caitlyn Breen

THE KICKOFF

[Recording on]

SEPTEMBER 25, four weeks ADP
(After the Disappearance of Paulie)

FIONA:

Come on, Caitlyn. What are you waiting for? We've elected you leader. Just start this thing already!

CAITLYN:

Okay...uh...what am I supposed to say?

FIONA:

Anything! Who cares? Just make it sound official. And try to sound excited for a change.

CAITLYN:

Okay, so this is the official record of the Search for the Next Great Paulie Fink. This reality-TV-style competition is being conducted by the Mitchell School's seventh grade, aka the Originals, aka the cave, aka this den of stinking goats...

FIONA:

Hey! Be nice. Actually, never mind. We elected you because you're *not* nice. Go ahead.

CAITLYN:

The competition will be run and documented by me, Caitlyn Breen, the eleventh and most recent member of Mitchell's seventh grade. But I'd like to state for the record that it's ridiculous you all want me to be in charge. A month ago, I'd never even heard the name Paulie Fink, and I'd never met any of you, and—

ORIGINALS:

Cait-lyn! Cait-lyn! Cait-lyn!

CAITLYN:

—now here I am running an entire show, or whatever the heck this is, and will you *please* stop chanting like that?

ORIGINALS:

Cait-lyn! Cait-lyn! Cait-lyn!

CAITLYN:

Listen, if I'm going to do this, I need to hear more stories about this mysterious Paulie Fink. But I can't start if you don't stop making so much noise. So can you be quiet for a change? Please?

Okay, thank you. Now, who wants to go first?

CAITLYN:

Okay, it's recording, Diego. Go ahead.

DIEGO:

Hey ho, Diego Silva, king of the soccer field here. Master attacker, wizard of kicks, genius of speed and agility—

CAITLYN:

Diego. Stick to the topic, okay? We're here to talk about Paulie Fink.

DIEGO:

Right. Diego Silva here, coming in live to talk about the one and only Paulie Fink. And I'm here to tell you: That kid was a god.

Oh, don't roll your eyes like that, Caitlyn! I don't mean he was *God*. I mean, duh. Obviously he wasn't that. He was *a* god, which is totally different. I also don't mean god like all those Brazilian soccer gods. Nah, Paulie couldn't play soccer to save his life. I mean the kind of gods that Mags talks about in humanities class. The ones who sat up on Mount Olympus. In a way, those gods were like normal people—they messed up constantly, and they drove each other bonkers, and sometimes they played wild pranks. But they also had powers that regular people didn't have, and they created chaos for everyone else.

That's what Paulie was like. He messed up big-time. Sometimes he played wicked-funny tricks. And everything he did always led to chaos for the rest of us.

The kid was legendary. I'm pretty sure that's the word. Paulie Fink was totally legendary.

Interview: Mr. Farabi

Paulie Fink? Brilliant, that kid.

Not that he was always a joy to have in class, mind you. But as the school's science and math teacher, I found it hard not to appreciate his...um...*innovative thinking*.

I mean, the banana-peel debacle? Mini-geddon? His food wars with Principal Glebus? Wait, you haven't heard those stories? Ask your classmates. I think you'll see that every one of his stunts had a certain element of genius.

I don't mean genius like Marie Curie or Neil deGrasse Tyson or Stephen Hawking. He wasn't like any sort of genius that's going to appear in your textbooks. Paulie Fink was more of what you'd call...an evil genius.

There was something about his eyes. Even when he was in trouble, even when Ms. Glebus was wagging that craggy finger in his face, his eyes were always kind of sparkly, like he had a disco ball back there, twirling around inside his brain.

And then he just up and disappeared. No warning. No good-bye. First day of seventh grade, Paulie just wasn't there.

Poof.

Gone.

See ya, wouldn't want to be ya.

And no offense, Caitlyn, but it's not like you were any sort of replacement. In fact, the first time I saw *your* eyes, I was all, *Now there's a girl who's never laughed. Not once in her entire stinkin' life.*

A DAY
WITHOUT
PAULIE

How It Begins

If the whole thing really had been a TV show, like everyone kept pretending it was, there are a million places the first episode could have started.

Like, maybe a good place to start would have been back in June, when I came home toward the end of sixth grade, and Mom greeted me with three fateful words: *Caitlyn, we're moving.* Not *Would you like to…?* Or *What would you think if…?* Or *Would you ever consider…?* Not a question at all. By the time she brought up the subject, she'd already accepted her new job as director of the Mitchell Urgent Care Center, given notice at the hospital where she'd worked as a nurse practitioner since forever, and taken out a lease on a tiny house in Mitchell, Vermont.

Which is to say, the middle of absolutely nowhere.

But that's just one place where the show could start. There are other options. Like on the drive here, when we passed the big green sign: WELCOME TO THE GREEN MOUNTAIN STATE. I saw nothing but trees and fields in all directions, and suddenly it hit me: *This is really happening.* I had to pretend to sleep just so I could press my face into a rumpled old sweatshirt against the window and cry without Mom noticing. By the time I opened my eyes again, we were passing an abandoned factory, the words OXTHORPE TEXTILES, MITCHELL, VERMONT still faintly visible on the bricks.

Or maybe the show would begin the first time I pulled up in front of my new school. The sign said it was a school, anyway—THE MITCHELL SCHOOL, K–7—but it sure didn't look like any school I'd ever seen. This place was more like a haunted mansion: a huge wooden house with broken shutters, peeling paint, and a tangle of weedy vines snaking up the exterior. Near the front door, there was a bell, like a miniature version of the Liberty Bell, with a sign that read, THE GOOD DAY BELL: RING IF YOU HAD A GOOD DAY.

I remember thinking, *The Good Day Bell. Stupidest thing I've ever seen in my life.*

It's strange how hard it is to choose just one beginning for this show. There are so many different ways to tell a single story. But I guess if I had to pick, I'd start the show a few minutes after I first saw that Good Day Bell. I'd begin in a classroom that doesn't look like a classroom, inside a school that doesn't look like a school, in a town where I never wanted to be living.

Let's pause in that classroom to look around. Chances are, it's not like any you've ever seen. There's a marble fireplace and a gold-framed portrait of some old man. A stained-glass window featuring a bunch of half-naked flying babies. An enormous chandelier dangling from a cracked ceiling above a heavy wooden table. And around that table: ten seventh graders, all frozen in place.

They're staring, twenty eyes fixed on something in the doorway. Whatever it is they see there, they don't like it. Not one bit.

If we'd begun this show even ten seconds earlier, these very same kids would have been cheering their heads off. The applause began as soon as they heard a rap on the classroom door. They expected something fantastic when they heard that knock. They whooped and high-fived, shouted *yeah*s and *woohoo*s, and it's possible there was even a very enthusiastic *Let the games begin!*

Sorry, though. This show doesn't begin with cheers. It begins only after the door opens all the way. That's when the room goes instantly, eerily silent.

Look at those faces, how quickly the kids moved from excitement to disappointment. All of them: the pink-haired girl with a tiny guitar in her lap. The kid in the soccer jersey, one leg jutting casually to the side. The scrawny boy pushing up blue-framed glasses that are way too big for his face. There are three kids in headbands with pom-pom ears, two identical boys in camouflage, a girl in a lavender sweatshirt, the word MEGASTAR emblazoned across the front, and a small freckled girl in a bright red pantsuit, like it's Halloween and she's decided to dress as a middle-aged senator.

Different kids, different sizes, different shades, different styles. Yet they seem united in their feeling about what's appeared in the doorway. Whatever they expected, whatever they were cheering for, it's not *this*.

And what *are* they looking at? Well, I'm sorry to say that it's me, Caitlyn Breen.

Hi. I'm Caitlyn. I'm the New Kid here at Mitchell. I like when everything's in its place, because that's how I know I have a place. I do not like when kids stare at me, making me feel like they can see right through me, all the way to my softest insides. So this, right here, is probably the most horrifying moment of my life.

Oh, and those ten kids who are staring at me right now? This is the Mitchell School's entire seventh grade, right here—me, plus these ten strangers, who seem to despise me already, even as they're seeing me for the very first time.

The girl in the red pantsuit tilts her head to the side. Eyes on me, she wrinkles her nose.

"Well, *you're* not Paulie Fink," she says.

**Email sent to my mom back in late June, 61 days BDP
(Before the Disappearance of Paulie)**

TO: WENDY BREEN
FROM: PRINCIPAL GLEBUS

Dear Wendy:

We have received Caitlyn's records, and we are delighted that she will be joining our seventh-grade class in the fall. As you can imagine, a school of our size in a location as remote as Mitchell doesn't see many new students. We barely have enough seventh graders to field a soccer team in the annual soccer game against Devlinshire Hills.

You mentioned that Caitlyn is making this move only reluctantly—I believe you said she was responding to the move "with all the enthusiasm of a feral cat being dipped in an ice-water bath." Please reassure Caitlyn that her new class is lively and friendly—if I'm being completely honest, I might describe them as lively to a fault. You'll see what I mean soon enough, I suppose.

A bit of history that will help you understand this school a little better: Two decades after Oxthorpe Textiles—once the largest employer in town—closed its doors, our school lacked sufficient funds to continue operating. It's a common story in rural towns like ours: schools closing after a steady decline in population and tax revenues, combined with rising costs. Mitchell's school building was even torn down. Mitchell children began attending school over in St. Johnsbury. The drive was nearly forty minutes each way, even in the best weather; in winter, it could be downright hazardous. Eight years ago, a group of dedicated parents decided to experiment by opening up a town academy. While the approach is still experimental, the town-academy model allows for the flexibility needed to educate such small numbers. It's often a rural community's last chance for keeping schools local.

Descendants of the Oxthorpes generously donated the family's old estate to the school. It hadn't been occupied for years, so it took both creativity and elbow grease to adapt the place for educational purposes. Classes are held in what used to be bedrooms and sitting rooms. We don't have a gym, and we had to knock out the servants' quarters to make room for bathrooms. But here we are!

We began with just a kindergarten. In year two, we had a kindergarten and a first grade. By year three, we were a K-through-second-grade school. This fall, those original kindergarten students will be in seventh grade.

Yes, you can tell Caitlyn her class is comprised of the Mitchell School's first-ever students. We call this group "the Originals" for that reason . . . though I suspect she'll find the name fits in other ways, too.

Looking forward to seeing you on the first day of school.

Alice Glebus
Principal, The Mitchell School

Interview: Timothy, Thomas, and Yumi

CAITLYN:

Okay, so I want you to think back to last month, the first day of seventh grade. Remember how you all started cheering when I knocked on the door?

TIMOTHY:

Yeah, that's because we thought Paulie had arrived. We couldn't wait to find out what he was going to do to kick off the new year.

THOMAS:

Just like he did last year, on the first day of sixth grade. Do you know about that one, Caitlyn?

YUMI:

She doesn't know anything about Paulie. Remember? That's the whole point of these interviews.

THOMAS:

Right. Okay, so when we got to the sixth-grade classroom on the first day, there was a note taped to the door in Paulie's handwriting. It said GLEBUS IS GIVING OUT CANDY IN HER OFFICE. HURRY, BEFORE THE OTHER GRADES EAT IT ALL!

TIMOTHY:

And Caitlyn, you probably know that sixth graders crave candy the way zombies crave brains...

YUMI:

That metaphor is highly disturbing. But also oddly poetic.

TIMOTHY:

It's also a fact. So we all went tearing through the building and burst into Glebus's office, like, "Yo, Glebus, where's the candy at?"

THOMAS:

Spoiler alert: There was no candy. Just Glebus, standing in front of that desk of hers, looking furious. Her desk is huge—way too wide to fit anywhere but in the corner. Anyway, she started lecturing us, going all, "You're in sixth grade now...remember you're the role models for all the younger children..."

TIMOTHY:

...when all of a sudden, behind her, one of the desk drawers popped open. Out of the blue, almost like a ghost had opened it.

THOMAS:

Glebus didn't think anything about it at first. She turned around and closed the drawer. But as soon as she did, a *different* drawer opened. She shut that one, too. Then, *bam*, it happened again. And again.

YUMI:

Finally, it dawned on Glebus to look *behind* her desk.

TIMOTHY:

That's when Paulie Fink popped up. He'd wedged himself into the gap between the desk and the wall, and he'd been pushing open the drawers from behind.

YUMI:

Like everything Paulie did, it was highly juvenile. But also highly entertaining.

THOMAS:

Anyway, on the first day *this* year, we figured Paulie was late because he'd been up to no good. We couldn't wait to find out what had happened.

TIMOTHY:

But then it turned out *you* were standing there, Caitlyn. And you looked like someone was forcing you to eat boogers—

THOMAS:

Dipped in decades-old mayonnaise.

I'm Not Him

Well, you're *not Paulie Fink.* That's what the girl in the pant-suit just said.

I look around the classroom, trying to take it all in: the confused faces, the haunted-house vibe, the fact that this is everyone, the whole seventh grade. From behind a teacher's desk, a woman rises. She's small, but what she lacks in height she's apparently decided to make up for in layers of fabric— flowy pants, tunic, mile-long scarf.

She swishes over to me. "You must be Caitlyn! I'm Miss Magruder, though most kids call me Mags." Then she turns to the class. "Everybody, this is Caitlyn. She just moved to Mitchell, isn't that a thrill?"

And just like that, I'm officially the New Kid.

Every year at my old school, there were always a hand-ful of New Kids. Teachers always introduced them by say-ing things like *I know you will give so-and-so a great welcome. I'm sure you'll let them know how happy we are to have them join us.* But most of the time, we *weren't* happy to have them join us. We were too busy trying to figure out who they were and how they fit in. If the New Kid wore a *Star Trek* T-shirt, we knew that by lunchtime she'd be sitting with the sci-fi geeks in the cafeteria. If it was an athletic-looking boy in basketball shorts, he'd sit with the jocks. The whole thing reminded me of one of those coin-sorting machines: You take a jar of jumbled-up change, dump it all into the machine, and within about twenty seconds all the dimes are neatly stacked, and all the nickels, and all the pennies and quarters, too. That's what middle school feels like: a giant sorting machine.

Which means that right now, everyone's trying to figure out where *I* fit.

My new class stares. I swallow. Soccer Boy hiccups. Then one of the identical kids in camouflage shouts, "But where's Paulie?"

"Yeah," says his twin. "Why isn't Paulie here yet?"

Then everyone starts shouting that name.

"Yeah, where is Paulie?"

"You think Paulie got in trouble already?"

"Uh-oh, what'd Paulie do!?"

Then Pantsuit Girl stands up, jams her fist in the air. *"Paul-ie!"* she chants. *"Paul-ie! Paul-ie! Paul-ie!"*

And suddenly they're all chanting, like sports fans demanding the star player be allowed in the game. They're looking at me as if I'm the one who's holding him back.

"Pau-lie! Pau-lie! Pau-lie!"

The girl with the pink hair and the tiny guitar even

starts strumming along, like she's writing music to go with their cheers.

Just for a moment, I let myself imagine that I'm not really here. That I'm back home, with my friends. I can picture the seventh-grade hallway at my old school: my friends waiting for me by the lockers. All of us huddled together, checking out kids' back-to-school haircuts and first-day outfits. Peering at our schedules to see which classes we'll have together.

I realize my friends *are* doing all that right now, at this very second. They're just doing it without me.

That's when I feel a swell in my throat, almost like my insides are flooding.

Sometimes this is how it is. Sometimes I go all swampy inside. My insides slosh and rise, and I know that if I'm not careful, I'm going to start crying. I've learned that there are three things you have to do when your insides get swampy:

1. *Stare at something. Anything. And then don't blink, not even once.* I choose the portrait hanging above the fireplace. It's some old man with bushy eyebrows and eyes like ice. There's a big gold plaque attached to the frame. It says JULIUS HEWITT MAYBERRY OXTHORPE, 1869–1931.

2. *Take a breath.* I use what Mom calls a "cleansing breath"—*in through the nose, out through the top of my head*—even though that is technically impossible.

3. *Turn to stone.* I imagine that all my swampy insides are hardening into something dense and cool, so strong I'll never cry again.

Everyone knows the first two tricks. But the third trick is all my own, and it's the one that works best of all. When your insides are made of stone, nothing can hurt you.

"*Paulie!*"

The teacher, Mags, must take some sort of pity on me, because she doesn't force the whole *I know you will give Caitlyn a great big welcome* thing. Instead, she points to a chair between Pantsuit Girl and Soccer Boy and tells me to take a seat.

When she finally quiets the class, Mags leans against the fireplace. "Originals, I have some news," she says. "For some reason, Paulie Fink is not on my class list this year. It looks like he's no longer enrolled at Mitchell."

Next to me, Pantsuit Girl leaps out of her seat again, this time so fast her chair crashes backward. She throws her arms out to the sides, practically smacking me in the forehead with the back of her hand. "What?!" she shouts. "I mean…WHAT?!"

"Sit down, please, Fiona," says Mags reasonably.

"But where *is* he?" asks Pink Hair. She's wearing a T-shirt that says THERE IS NO EARTH WITHOUT ART, and she's got a million woven bracelets on her arm.

Mags shakes her head. "I really don't know any details, Yumi. I double-checked as soon as I got the list, and apparently it's true. Paulie Fink is no longer a student here. I'm sure we'll find out more soon enough."

"Maybe this is one of his pranks," says one of the three kids in matching pom-pom ears, a girl with pink cheeks,

23

frizzy red hair, and a mouth full of braces. The other two pom-poms nod along. It's funny, because these three kids look nothing alike—in addition to the redhead, there's also a wispy girl in yoga clothes with perfect posture and a kid who could be either a girl or a boy, lean and wiry, with hair buzzed practically to stubble—but somehow you can tell they're a threesome. It's not just the pom-poms, either. It's the way they're leaning into one another. You can tell they've known each other forever.

"Yeah," the girl in the MEGASTAR sweatshirt pipes up. Her dark hair's piled into a high ponytail and spills out in every direction. "Maybe Paulie wants us to think he's missing, but it's all part of a dramatic setup!"

Again, everyone starts shouting.

"I mean, a person can't just vanish into thin air!"

"He'd tell us if he was really leaving, wouldn't he?"

"This place won't be the same without Paulie!"

Then the door cracks open and the room goes instantly silent again. By the looks on everyone's faces, I half expect the ghost of mean old Julius Oxthorpe to come drifting through the door.

Actually, that's not so far from what *does* happen. It's not a ghost that pokes its head into the classroom. It's a witch.

Witch in Yellow Boots

The witch peers around the room suspiciously. She's wearing a dark blazer, dark blouse, dark lipstick, and has dark hair cut into blunt bangs across her forehead. I can even see dark veins, like tiny fingers, throbbing on one temple.

"What's the commotion, Originals?" she asks. "I can hear you all the way downstairs in my office!"

"I just gave them the news about Paulie, Ms. Glebus," says Mags. "They're a little upset, that's all."

Sharp lines at the corners of the witch's mouth move toward the floor. She glares around the room until her eyes land on me. "You must be Caitlyn," she says, not a bit warmly. "I'm Ms. Glebus, Mitchell School principal." She steps all the way into the room to shake my hand, and that's when I notice something interesting. Her top half might be all witch, but her lower half looks like it belongs to a different person entirely. She's wearing raggedy jeans with mud-caked knees. They're tucked into bright yellow rubber boots. The whole effect is like one of those mix-and-match books, where you turn flaps to create different combinations of outfits.

I guess she sees me noticing her boots, because she says, sort of brusquely, "I spent much of the morning helping settle the goats."

I force a smile, because I figure she's trying to make some sort of joke. *Helping settle the goats.* Maybe because students are kids, and *kid* is a term that can mean either a child or a baby goat? *I dunno, Principal Glebus. You might want to work on your stand-up routine.*

Soccer Boy says, "Hey, Ms. Glebus, where's Paulie?"

"Student records are confidential, Diego," she answers curtly. "Even in a community as small as ours."

"Wait," says Fiona, who's out of her seat again. "You're not even going to tell us where he is? Are you *kidding* me?"

But Ms. Glebus is already out the door, gone as suddenly as she arrived.

When Mags finally settles everyone, she explains that in addition to being our homeroom teacher, she'll be teaching us a variety of subjects that are rolled up into something called humanities.

"Humanities combines history, mythology, philosophy, and language arts. It's about the stories people tell, the way they live, the things that they think about and value. Ultimately, it's a way of exploring the question *What does it mean to be human?* Last year, we studied ancient China and the Middle East. So we'll start this year in ancient Greece, beginning with mythology."

She starts talking about the gods and goddesses of Mount Olympus, and the boy in the big blue glasses interrupts. "There were twelve of them," he announces. "Zeus was the king of the gods. There was also Athena, goddess of wisdom, and Poseidon, god of the sea, and Ares, god of war, and—"

"That's right, Henry." Mags cuts him off. "But before we go into details about each one, it's important to understand that for the Greeks, these gods weren't remote. People believed that gods and goddesses intervened in the daily affairs of mortals..."

As Mags talks, Fiona leans across me like I'm not even there and whispers to Diego: "You noticed that, right? The way Glebus slithered out of the room, avoiding any questions about Paulie? She's a snake, that's what she is. She's a snake and...and...an *avoiderer.*"

Now Diego leans across me, too. "*Avoiderer?*" he teases.

"Oh, don't give me a hard time, Diego," Fiona snaps. "Not with this missing-Paulie crisis we're facing."

"It's just not a word, that's all," he says.

On the other side of Diego, pink-haired Yumi joins the conversation. "Well, technically, *avoiderer is* a word. It means avoiding a person who avoids."

Fiona rises from her seat for a high five. "Thank you, Yumi! Sisterhood is powerful, am I right?" But Yumi just ignores her and strums on her instrument instead.

"Yumi, no ukulele during class," Mags says. "And Fiona, if you can't sit quietly, I'm going to have to ask you to hang out with Ms. Glebus for the morning. As I was saying: The Greek myths were carried down, generation upon generation, in the form of stories…"

Diego leans across me again and whispers to Fiona: "Ha, you got in trouble in the first minute of class!"

"Did not!" Fiona insists, too loudly.

"Fiona," Mags warns.

Fiona sits up straight in her seat, but as soon as Mags turns away, Fiona whispers to Diego, "Mags said my name *twice* so far. It's only trouble when a teacher has to say your name three times."

Diego looks skeptical. "I'm not sure that's how it works…"

"It is *too* the way it works."

On the other side of Fiona, the MEGASTAR girl leans over. "Actually, I think Diego's right."

Fiona whips around to glare at MEGASTAR. "Don't you dare take his side, Gabby. You're supposed to be the *nice* one."

Mags stops talking. "*Fiona*," she says, exasperated.

Diego bangs the desk. "*Now* it's three times! Boom! *Official* trouble!"

"Who *cares* what sort of trouble I'm in?" hollers Fiona.

28

She looks around the classroom. "Our classmate has vanished! For all we know, we'll never see him again!"

That's when the whole class starts shouting a bunch of theories about what happened to this Paulie Fink kid. It's hard to hear over all the noise, but I'm pretty sure I catch "beamed up!" and "locked in Glebus's closet!"

Yumi rolls her eyes and starts plucking out a tune on her ukulele again. On the opposite side of the table, I see Henry, the know-it-all kid, open up a book called *1,001 Nature Facts*, as if none of this chaos is even happening. He furrows his brow in concentration, like he's studying for a test.

Me? I'm just sitting there like a big nobody. Like I'm not even in the room.

The Rules

I reach into the pocket of my hoodie for a folded piece of paper. I don't need to pull it out; I know what's on it by heart. Right before I moved, each of my friends had given me a piece of advice, which they compiled into a list. I hold it now between my fingers, like it's some sort of good-luck charm.

CAITLYN'S RULES OF LIFE

AKA HOW TO WIN SEVENTH GRADE

1. Make a great first impression. Remember, you never get a second chance!

2. When in doubt, stay quiet. People will think you're all mysterious and stuff. Also, it's easier not to make a mistake than it is to fix one.

3. Act as if you couldn't care less about anyone. The best way to make people care about you is to show zero interest in them.

4. Hahaha, remember that coin theory of yours? About how the point of middle school is to sort us all into clusters? Don't let anyone forget: you're the silver dollar!

5. Play to win! You got this!!!

6. **Whatever you do, don't do anything humiliating. Do not be an Anna Spang!**

Anna showed up a few weeks into sixth grade. As the teachers did their usual *I know you will welcome her* thing, her eyes darted over the room. We could just tell: Anna wouldn't be sitting with anyone in the cafeteria. In the coin-sorting machine that was middle school, she was a coin without a cluster.

That's how I feel right now. As I sit here clutching the list of rules in my pocket, everyone shouting past me and no one talking *to* me: I feel like a coin without any matches. I feel like Anna Spang.

Make a great first impression, the rules said. But apparently I've failed to make any impression at all.

Interview: Gabby

I am an expert in the art of making impressions. It's not that I make such a big impression on people myself. It's because I am *literally* the world's biggest fan of *The Search for the Next Great Megastar*. *Megastar* is the best reality show there is, and I should know—I've watched almost all of them: *American Hermit, Man vs. Toddler, Are You a Secret Superhero?, Extreme Scrapbooking, Stunt Grandmas, Project Photobomb, Dumpster-Diving Divas*, and a whole bunch of others.

Like I say, literal expert.

Here's one of the things I've learned from *Megastar*: You can't always know who a character is based on the first impression. Sure, some—like Jadelicious, who is the greatest Megastar of all time—make a bang right from the start. Others sneak up on you and surprise you.

But every time a new character joins the show? Or gets eliminated? Things change. Sometimes for better, sometimes for worse. And when one character disappears, like Paulie? And another comes waltzing through the door, like you, Caitlyn?

It's like my grandma says: "Get out that big pink piggy bank, girl. Change is coming fast."

Interview: Fiona

CAITLYN:

You were pretty upset that first day. About Paulie not being here. It was almost like you couldn't focus on anything else.

FIONA:

Heck yeah, I was upset! Paulie was the only kid at this school who ever got in more trouble than I did.

You don't understand, Caitlyn. My whole life, my mom always said that I needed to listen for my name. If I heard it more than three times in a class period, it meant it was a big-trouble kind of day. And let me tell you, I heard my name a LOT. *Fiona, sit still. Fiona, don't draw on books. Fiona, don't scoop the sand out of the sand table. Fiona, don't you dare leap off the slide just to see what it feels like to fly. Fiona, honey, now you're getting blood everywhere. Fiona Fiona Fiona Fiona.*

Back in third grade when we learned about tally marks, we all had to pick something in our lives to tally, so I tallied the number of times an adult called out my name in one day. Guess how many tally marks I made that day?

CAITLYN:

I don't know. Ten? Fifteen?

FIONA:

Fifty-seven! In a single day! I used to feel sort of bad about all the trouble I got into. And then I heard that expression *Well-behaved women seldom make history.*

Well. Let's just say I've always been on the fast track to make history. And when I do, I'm going to move to a big city, and once in a blue moon I'll come home to Mitchell in a limousine and everyone will be all, *Remember when you used to get in trouble all the time?* And I'll be like, *No. I really don't.*

CAITLYN:

Fiona, we were talking about Paulie Fink, remember?

FIONA:

I *am* talking about Paulie Fink! 'Cause guess what? One day in fourth grade, I counted again, and I only heard my name twenty-two times. To be honest, I don't think this is because I was any better behaved. It's because that was the year Paulie moved to town. All the teachers were so busy saying *his* name, they didn't have time to say mine. I guess you could say that Paulie launched my upswing.

CAITLYN:

So you're saying...that first day, you thought you kind of *needed* Paulie?

FIONA:

Well, I mean, it's not just me. Doesn't everybody need a little Paulie Fink in their life?

Dance Party

The whole first morning feels like a slow-moving, not-so-great dream. Mitchell vaguely *resembles* school—there are classes and kids and stuff—but only in the same way your own reflection looks when you stare into a fun-house mirror. Everything is distorted, the proportions all wrong. It gives me a dizzy, seasick sort of feeling.

Also, there's so much to figure out. First of all, there are my new classmates. In addition to Soccer Boy Diego, Pantsuit Girl Fiona, Pink Hair Yumi, Nice One Gabby, and Know-It-All Henry, I learn that the camouflage twins are Timothy and Thomas, and the threesome with the pom-pom ears are Lydia (frizzy red hair), Willow (wispy yoga girl), and Sam (buzz cut). I also learn that those pom-poms are actually supposed to be dragon ears, because they adore some stupid role-playing game involving mythical creatures.

But knowing their names doesn't tell me where they fit. Take Fiona, for example: Either that red suit is some kind of costume, or she's a total misfit, like Anna Spang. And if she's an Anna, then why does everyone else, even Diego, who's cute and sporty, keep talking to her? Don't they know about clusters here?

Then there are the million other ways that this school is different from my old one. Like, the Mitchell School is so small that we're going to spend the whole day moving back and forth between two main teachers: Mags and Mr. Farabi, who teaches math and science, but who *also* happens to be the gym teacher and soccer coach.

And when Mags tells us we're supposed to meet Mr. Farabi by the soccer field for science class—I check, and the schedule definitely says science—everyone acts like it's totally normal.

I follow the other kids through a maze of dim, dusty, wallpaper-covered hallways until we reach some French doors, and everyone bursts outside.

I expect to see the soccer field out there. Instead, I'm looking at a lawn full of broken statues, all these figures in draping robes. Most are missing limbs, or parts of their faces. A stone footpath winds its way through the statues, and the lawn is flanked on both sides by looming dark pines and drooping willows. I swear, if this were a movie and a bunch of people were gathering at a property like this, you just know that at any second, they'd start getting chased by mummies or something like that.

But this is where everything gets weirder. As everyone

heads down the path, Fiona calls out, "Dance party! Do the Diego!"

All of a sudden, the whole class is swaying their shoulders back and forth, arms loose. Then Diego shouts, "Do the Yumi!" and everyone begins twirling their arms in random circular motions above their heads. Yumi hollers, "Do the Fiona!" and they all start hopping up and down really fast, like hyperactive bunnies.

I turn to Gabby. *The nice one.* "What's happening?"

Gabby explains that everyone in the class has a signature dance. "When your name gets called, everyone does your dance. Then you get to pick the next name, see? Don't worry, you'll get your own move soon enough. In the meantime, just follow along."

I don't follow along. Instead, I think about the rules in my pocket. *Don't do anything humiliating.* Except they don't seem humiliated at all. They look like they're having fun.

Fiona shouts "Paulie!" Next thing I know, each kid is doing something different at the same time. Gabby explains that Paulie kept changing his dance, so his name means everyone can dance however they feel. Finally, Fiona says, "Never mind, I forgot he wasn't even here. How about... Timothy!" And then everyone's moving their arms like a sprinkler.

"We didn't do...this...back in New York," I say to Gabby.

She stops mid-sprinkle. "You're from New York? As in New York *City*?"

Actually, no. Mom and I lived pretty far from the city, and I've only visited Manhattan a couple of times in my life. But I find myself nodding. "Yeah," I say casually. Then I add, "The city," just to hear how that sounds.

"Did you ever see Jadelicious there?"

"Who?"

"You know, *Jadelicious*? *The Search for the Next Great Megastar*? The television show?"

"Never heard of it." This makes the second lie I've told in almost as many sentences. Of course I've heard of *Megastar*—it's one of the most popular reality-television shows of all time. Even though it's been off the air for a couple of years, I've watched a bunch of old episodes online. But I don't want to let Gabby know that.

"Never *heard* of it?" Gabby squawks. "Oh, you have to see it. It's a *great* show! Season two was the best one of all time. That's the season that Jadelicious won—nobody had ever even *heard* of Jadelicious before *Megastar*, and now she's got her own perfume and clothing lines, and her picture is in all the magazines."

Then she starts telling me about her favorite episodes. "I think my favorite is the one where Jadelicious is told she has to sing for the toughest audience in the world, and she thinks it's going to be some superstar, but instead she's brought into an auditorium filled with crying toddlers.

My grandma's favorite episode is where Jadelicious finally stands up to her archenemy, Rexx Rowdy. He's the *worst*."

While she's talking, I watch Fiona and Diego. They're cracking each other up as they dance. "Hey," I interrupt. "What's the deal with those two? Are they friends or enemies or what?"

Gabby tells me that they've been best friends since they were little, but they also fight all the time. "They're like, you know, frenemies, but in a good way."

"And what's with Fiona's weird suit?" I ask. A little too loudly, apparently.

"Hey, Fiona," shouts one of the twins. "The new kid wants to know what's up with your weird suit."

Fiona whirls around, puts her hands on her hips, and glares at me. "What do you mean, *weird suit?*"

"I mean—is it some sort of dare?"

Fiona stands up a little straighter. "Why would it be a *dare*? I dress this way because I am a strong and powerful woman."

Diego elbows her. "A strong and powerful woman who gets in trouble *all the time*."

She turns to Diego. "I keep trying to explain this to you, Diego. *Well-behaved women seldom make history.*" Then she returns her focus to me. "And for the record, my suit is *fierce*." She says it with such confidence that I wonder if it's possible that *she's* the silver dollar.

When in doubt, stay quiet. I don't say anything else—not

when everyone starts dancing again, not as we pass a playground filled with younger kids, not when that playground gives way to what looks like a toy junkyard. There's a truck with a missing wheel, a plastic pail with a broken handle, and the base of an old basketball hoop.

"Hey!" Fiona shouts, her voice suddenly bright, like she wasn't furious with me two seconds ago. She points to the far end of a scraggly soccer field. "There they are!"

I look where she's pointing, and that's when I remember Ms. Glebus's joke, the one that I assumed was a play on the word *kid*. *I spent much of the morning helping settle the goats.*

I guess it wasn't a joke. Because that's exactly what Fiona's pointing toward: a pen full of goats.

Real, live goats.

My New Archenemy

"Goats!" my classmates chant as they head toward the pen. *"Goats! Goats! Goats!"*

There's a man waiting next to the goat pen with a bucket in his hand. He's got a neat beard, a flannel shirt with a bow tie, pants the color of ketchup, and mud-crusted work boots. Lumberjack meets professor. Paul Bunyan meets golf pro. Like the rest of this place, it's hard to categorize him exactly. *So this is Mr. Farabi.*

He introduces himself to me quickly, then spreads his arms wide. "Welcome, Originals, to seventh-grade science!" Behind him, a dozen or so goats run all over the place bleating wildly behind a flimsy-looking portable fence. "Before I talk to you about science, or about these magnificent creatures making a ruckus behind me," Mr. Farabi says, "I want to talk about the annual soccer game we play against Devlinshire Hills."

The whole class starts to boo. Fiona mutters, "Those snoots!"

"As most of you know," Mr. Farabi continues, "your

41

soccer field has been shrinking each year, thanks to an ever-expanding population of buckthorn and honeysuckle bushes. Every year, we cut them back. And every single year, without fail, they respond to our efforts by growing back stronger and thicker. Last year, as you surely recall, it got to the point that our biggest—well, to be fair, our *only*—rivals refused to play on our field."

Everyone boos again, and Fiona leans over to me. "They demanded that we play on *their* fancy field instead," she says. "Said they didn't want to risk the *injuries*."

"Who?" I whisper back.

"*Devlinshire Hills*. They're snobs, and we hate them." Then, to the rest of the class, Fiona yells, "Don't we hate Devlinshire, guys?"

"Excuse me, but we don't *hate anyone*," says Mr. Farabi. He gives Fiona a hard look. "But this year, I would very much like to return the game to our home turf. I happen to know a little secret, too: Goats are nature's best bulldozers. Estimates are that a dozen goats—which is what we have here—can go through half an acre a month. We're scheduled to play Devlinshire on October 27. That's about two months away, which means if my calculations are correct, our hairy little friends here should have the edges of this field cleared just in time for you to take on Devlinshire right here at home. Who knows…maybe we'll finally win the game!"

He tells us that every few days we'll move the goat pen to

42

a new spot, until the edges of the field are cleared. "Even after the game, the goats will stick around for the rest of the year," Mr. Farabi continues. "They offer a chance to learn not only about ecosystems and habitats, but also one of my favorite words: *responsibility*. Because you, as the oldest Mitchell students, are officially in charge of caring for these goats. We're going to supplement their diet with grain pellets, and you'll be the ones to feed them. Every weekday. All year long. You ready to learn how?"

As we move toward the goat pen, I learn something new: Goats stink. They smell like unwashed human hair, mixed with the scent of the soft white cheese my mom sometimes spreads on crackers.

Still, I have to admit, they're kind of cute. The babies are, anyway. The little ones play like puppies, leaping and jumping, ramming their heads together, and chasing one another. Most of the older goats just stand around, bleating and chewing.

At the far edge of the pen, there's one big, very grumpy-looking goat. His hair falls in long tangles, and he's got huge horns that spiral back on his head like snail shells. This big old goat stares right at me—like, right in my eyes—then utters one low bleat, his tongue sticking out. Like he's saying, *I want you out of here. Yes, you specifically.*

I stare right back at him, thinking, *Yeah, you and me both, big guy.*

Mr. Farabi lifts a bucket of pellets, steps into the goat

pen, and moves toward four empty bowls. Immediately, the animals swarm him. Wherever he turns, the goats go, too. They shove one another out of the way, each trying to get as close to the food as possible.

"See this?" he says, laughing. "You'll never get to their food bowls if they see you coming. That's why at each feeding, *most* of you are going to distract the goats, while one brave Original will sneak in to fill their bowls."

"Aw, Paulie would love this," says Diego.

"He'd do something ridiculous, too," says Yumi. "Like one day we'd show up to school and the goats would be missing from the pen…"

"…because he put them all in Ms. Glebus's office!" finishes Sam.

My mind wanders to the texts I'll send my friends back home about this. *I swear*, I'll tell them. *Actual goats.*

While I'm thinking about home, I fail to notice that one of the goats—the big ugly guy—is moving across the pen, toward us. The goat walks at first, then breaks into a jog.

Then he's running, his head lowered.

By the time I realize what's happening, it's too late. Through the fence, he rams his spiral-horned head into my legs. I stumble backward, lose my footing.

With everyone watching, I land squarely on my butt.

I Make a Decision

"Did you see that?" Fiona asks. "She flew back like ten whole feet!"

I keep my eyes on my sneakers. *Don't blink. Don't blink.*

I take one of those deep cleansing breaths, and I try to find the hard stone inside, the one that protects me. But my butt hurts where it hit the ground, and my eyes sting, and those awful goats are still bleating away, and it's hard to tell where the bleating of the goats meets the laughter of the other kids.

From inside the pen, Mr. Farabi calls, "Can somebody give Caitlyn a hand?"

Henry, the know-it-all glasses kid, comes over. He extends his arm, ready to help me up from the ground.

"I'm fine," I snap.

He lowers his arm, but he doesn't leave. "Did you know that goats have four stomachs?"

I stand, brush myself off, and smooth down my hair, trying to regain a little dignity. "Technically," Henry adds, "they have one stomach. But it has four separate chambers. Cows are the same way. And interestingly, giraffes, too."

"So?" I ask. My voice is hard, but it's better than crying. It's almost like mad beats sad, the way rock beats scissors, and paper beats rock.

Henry pushes his glasses up on his nose. "So that makes them all ruminants. Also, goats have 340-degree vision." He just stands there and blinks at me, as if he's helped somehow.

After science, as we head back inside, Henry keeps spouting new goat facts. This is the point where I start vaguely worrying about who I'm going to sit with at lunchtime. Will I have to sit with Henry and listen to him blab about goats or whatever? I know I shouldn't try to sit with the pom-pom kids—threesomes never, ever have room for a fourth. Yumi's a little too out there for me, and Fiona's too intense and confusing. And of course there's no way I'd ever try to sit with a boy. So that leaves pretty much one person: Gabby.

By lunchtime, no one has invited me to join them, and eating alone is the worst option of all. As I follow everyone toward the cafeteria, I turn to Gabby and ask, my words coming a little too fast, if I can sit with her.

"No," she says. *But you're the nice one*, I think. My look

must give me away, because Gabby smiles. "I mean, I'd sit with you if I could, Caitlyn. But I can't."

Sam, walking ahead of us, turns around. "It's because our Minis need us."

"Our...*what*?"

"The little kids!" says Gabby. "See, every table has at least one kid from every grade. The idea is that everyone gets to know each other. And since we're the oldest at the school, we're in charge of looking after the youngest kids. We're officially their *buddies*."

By now we've reached the cafeteria—which, naturally, isn't a cafeteria at all, it's more like an atrium, with more windows than walls.

"See, you check that list over there," Gabby says, pointing to a poster on the wall. "The list tells you your table for the next couple of months. Then you go up to Mr. Twilling, who's the kindergarten teacher, and you tell him your table number. He'll introduce you to the Mini who's assigned to that table. It's your job to sit with them, help them out."

"So we're like...free babysitters?" I ask.

Yumi rolls her eyes. "I guess that's one way to look at it."

"It's not a huge deal," says Fiona. "You just have to open their milk carton, remind them to take bites of their food."

"Occasionally pick tuna fish out of their hair or wipe their nose or whatever," Diego adds.

"The tuna fish and boogers are the worst parts," Lydia offers. "Otherwise, it's fine. Sometimes it's even fun."

No, I think. *Fun is talking with your friends at lunchtime. Fun is not feeding goats or forced babysitting, and I don't understand why none of you seem to understand the most basic things.*

"It's just...," I say, "at real schools, you get to sit wherever you want." But they're already wandering off to find their Minis.

I'm assigned to a kid named Kiera. She's wearing a poufy dress, and her hair is pulled back into two tight buns, like mouse ears. In one hand, she holds a lunch box. In the other, she clutches a stuffed bunny.

When Mr. Twilling introduces us, she just stands there staring at her feet.

"Uh...so...come with me?" I say, like it's a question.

At our table, kids of all ages are chattering away happily, like it's totally normal for kids of different grades to mix. I glance around. For some reason the other seventh graders all look perfectly happy with their buddies. Even Henry looks at ease, reading to his Mini from a fact book. My Mini just stares at her lap.

"You—uh—want help with your milk carton or whatever?" I ask Kiera. She doesn't answer, doesn't move at all. I'm not sure I've talked to a kindergartner since I was one.

I try again. "Um...I, um, like your stuffed bunny. Does he have a name?"

"His name is Rabbit," she says.

Then she whispers something I can't quite hear. I lean in. "What's that?"

She whispers again: "And he's real."

"Ohhh," I say. "Okay, yeah. Well…uh…real rabbits need to eat and drink, you know? And if you ask me, Real Rabbit looks a little thirsty."

I open up her milk carton, just like Fiona said. I bring it first to the rabbit's mouth, and I pretend he's taking a sip. Then I offer it to Kiera. She takes one tiny sip, then she whispers again: "I miss Mommy."

"Yeah." I swallow before saying, "I miss everything."

And I do. I miss knowing who to talk to, or what to talk to them about. Knowing where I'm going, instead of having to follow people around. At this moment, I even miss my mom, although I'm furious with her, since she's the whole reason I'm here in the first place.

Most of all, I miss not feeling like some sort of space alien trying to navigate an unfamiliar planet.

Ms. Glebus breezes into the cafeteria, still wearing those yellow boots. She bangs on a pot with a wooden spoon until everyone quiets down. "Welcome to a new school year," she says. "Welcome to our new goats. Welcome to our new students: Caitlyn Breen in seventh—can you wave to us, Caitlyn?—and Alonzo Ferroni in third, and of course a tremendous welcome to our kindergartners."

Then she starts telling the kindergartners about the

Good Day Bell in front of the school, the one I noticed when I arrived this morning. At the end of each afternoon, if you had a good day, you're supposed to ring it. "I hope I hear that bell ringing many times!"

Across the cafeteria, Fiona's Mini raises his hand. "But what if we *don't* have a good day?" he asks. Ms. Glebus smiles in that tight, forced way that adults do when a little kid asks a dumb question. She tells him that he doesn't *have* to ring the bell; it's up to him.

Then all these other Minis start asking questions: What if the day is sorta good and sorta bad? What if it's a good day but they don't feel like ringing the bell? What if it's a bad day, but they forget, and they accidentally ring the bell anyway? Finally Glebus calls on a little boy who holds up a plastic snack bag. "My daddy packed me Goldfish crackers in my lunch," he announces, totally out of the blue. Which makes a bunch of other little kids start showing Glebus what they have in their lunch boxes. By now, Ms. Glebus's smile is tight as a drum.

I glance at Kiera. She's still clutching her bunny to her chest, and now there's a trail of snot running from her nose, down her lip. I grimace, then grab a napkin and reach over to wipe her nose.

That's when I make a decision. My mom can make me move to Vermont. She can send me to this school where nothing is the way it's supposed to be and where the only semi-normal person is a kindergarten kid with boogers on her face who doesn't even want to look at me. And the teachers here can make me open milk cartons, and apparently they can even make me feed a goat.

But they cannot make me do everything.

"I'm never going to ring the Good Day Bell," I declare. And as soon as the words are out, I know they're true. I'm not going to ring it. Not today, not tomorrow, not ever.

My Mini nods. "Me neither," she says.

I'm so relieved to feel a little less alone, I hold out my little finger. "Pinkie promise?" She wraps her own finger around mine. I feel her pulse beneath her skin.

When lunch is over, I turn to her. What I want to say is, *Come on*, and *Don't forget your fuzzy little rabbit*. But what comes out instead is simply, "Come on, Fuzzy."

"Who's Fuzzy?" she asks.

"You are," I say. "You're Fuzzy."

"No, *you're* Fuzzy," she says. The edges of her mouth curl up into something that's not quite a smile, but maybe isn't so far from one.

"Sorry, kid," I say. "I am the *opposite* of Fuzzy."

"What's the opposite of Fuzzy?"

I don't answer her, but I think about that stone inside my chest, hard and cold.

Silence and More Silence

At the end of the day, I watch everyone line up at the Good Day Bell. First the Originals take their turns ringing the bell. Then they stand around high-fiving the younger kids as they do the same.

Me, I stand off to the side. I wait around just long enough to see Fuzzy get in line like all the others. When it's her turn, she shakes her head. She glances at me, and I hold one pinkie in the air. Pinkie promise kept.

Then I march to my mom's car.

"So how was it?" Mom asks. Her voice is eager, like she's expecting me to say, *Great, Mom, it was just a terrific day, thanks for uprooting me from everything I've ever known, it was totally worth it!*

I slam the door and turn away from her. I stare out the window and I don't say a word.

"I see," Mom says. She puts the car in drive.

On the way home, she tries a few more times. *Did you meet anyone nice? How were your teachers? Did you learn anything interesting?*

I don't answer, and I don't ask her about her first day at the clinic. Instead, I watch this depressing town roll past: the brick carcass that used to be Oxthorpe Textiles. An old shuttered movie theater. The Donut Lady bakery (IT'S ALWAYS DONUT TIME!!! says the sign in the window, although the place is closed for the day, so I guess it's not *always* donut time). Each storefront is sadder than the last: The Clothes Off Your Back Consignment Store. The Squeaky Clean Laundromat. Big Esther's Diner (SORRY WE'RE OPEN and LUKE-WARM COFFEE, LOUSY FOOD, BAD SERVICE, COME ON IN). When we arrive at the house that is not my house, I get out of the car and march straight to the room that is not my room. I close the door, pull out my phone, and check if I have any messages from my friends back home.

I don't, so I send a few to them:

You won't believe the day I had.

One word: goats.

And another: kindergartners.

How are things back home?

I wish I'd been w you today instead of here.

Hello?

Helloooooooooooo

No one replies. I don't know if that's because cell service in this town is so bad, or if it's because my friends are too busy to respond. Either way, it feels terrible.

When Mom calls me to the kitchen for dinner, I don't get up. Eventually, she taps on my door. She opens it a crack. "You ready to talk about it, kiddo?"

I turn away from her, toward the wall.

"Why are we even here?" I ask.

"You know why," she says, sitting down on the bed. "I got a new job."

"You *had* a job. It was fine."

"It was," she says. Then after a beat, she says, "But that's *all* it was: fine. I don't want my life to be *fine*. This move was my chance to do something different. To be in charge of something for a change. It feels like a window opening for me. Can you understand that?"

"Everyone in my class is weird. All they talk about is some stupid kid who's not here anymore. They kept chanting his name and everything. The whole day, like I wasn't even there."

She rubs my leg. "Give it time. Before you know it, they'll be chanting your name, too."

"Could you *please* stop talking to me like I'm a baby? You don't know how this stuff works!"

She gives my foot a quick squeeze, then stands. "There's pasta on the table when you're ready, Cait." She closes the door so quietly I have to check if she's really gone.

A few minutes later, my phone dings. It's my friend Ash:

OMG. I can't wait to hear.

Hi!!!!

Can't talk now though—my mom is screaming her head off, LOL

How was the first day?

This school has goats.

Did you know that goats have four stomachs?

Haha, I guess that's the sort of stuff I'm going to learn here.

But I guess she meant what she said, because she doesn't write again. I fall asleep with my phone cradled next to me. I never make it downstairs for dinner.

CAITLYN:

How did *you* think the first day of seventh grade went, Henry?

HENRY:

It was bad. Catastrophically horrible. Cataclysmically distressingly terrible. But then of course I have precisely zero chill.

CAITLYN:

Really? You seemed okay to me. Every time I looked at you, you were sitting there calmly reading your fact book.

HENRY:

I wasn't calm, actually. All day, my brain was whirring in circles like one of those spinning-teacup rides at a carnival— not that I like carnivals. They make my mouth turn dry, my palms sweaty. Other things that freak me out: ambulance sirens. TV shows about hospitals. Shows about police investigations. Shows about the news. Throwing up. The scale of the universe. Cat saliva. Ladybugs.

CAITLYN:

Okay, but we were talking about the first day of school.

HENRY:

That's what I'm saying. When my brain goes all spinny, facts calm me down. I like how steady facts are, you know? Every time you look at a fact, it'll always be exactly the same. It's very reassuring.

CAITLYN:
So...like the facts you told me about goats?

HENRY:
Exactly. More than a month later, they're all still true. And on the first day of school, I needed as many facts as I could get. Even before I learned Paulie was gone, I'd been freaking out. See, I had a secret that first day—one that was going to affect all of us. Even you, Caitlyn.

This wasn't just the beginning of a new school year. It was the beginning of the end. And I was the only one who knew it.

A WEEK
WITHOUT
PAULIE

Interview: Sam

The first day any of us ever met Paulie Fink? Sure, I remember that. It was the beginning of fourth grade, back when me and Lydia and Willow first started playing Creatures of the Underlair—

Wait, seriously? You've never played?

It's a role-playing game. You each pick a character, and then you go on campaigns all over the universe seeking treasure and stuff. You go through different battles by rolling dice and...oh, never mind. I'm just saying, the three of us were all checking out Paulie like he was a new character in our game, trying to figure out if he was friend or foe.

What did he look like? Ordinary, I guess. T-shirt, jeans, brown hair, sort of shaggy in his eyes. But that's the thing you learn from playing Underlair: You can never tell exactly who a creature is just by looking at them.

Anyway, Glebus came into our classroom on Paulie's first day. She was making the rounds, going on about rules and respect and responsibility or whatever. And as she talked, Paulie was just sitting there, very calmly, looking straight ahead as he stuck two pencils in his ears. They were pointy-side out, so they looked like crazy antennae.

Then, while we were watching him, he picked up two more pencils. And he stuck those in his nostrils.

Glebus stopped talking. Mid-sentence. Just closed her mouth and stood there staring at him. After a while, we started shifting in our seats. Uncomfortable, you know? I mean, any idiot, even a brand-new idiot, knows that something's wrong when a grown-up just plain stops talking.

After a while, Paulie started whistling. Like he was taking a stroll on a summer afternoon, not a care in the world.

Glebus cleared her throat. She was all, "Could you remind me where you are from, Mr. Fink?" We all knew that whatever he answered—Seattle or Chicago or Iowa—Glebus was going to say something like, *Well, I don't know how they do it in Seattle/Chicago/Iowa, but here at the Mitchell School we do not place our pencils in our orifices.*

But Paulie didn't give her that chance. Instead, he stood up, spread his arms out wide, all those pencils still sticking out of his head. And he said, all dramatic-like, "I come from the *stars*!"

He drew out the last word. *Staarrrrrrrrrrrrrrrssss.* Like he was an alien or something. Let me tell you: Things only got more interesting from there.

The Real Megastar

On the second day of school, I wake early, not quite dawn. Eerie gray light filters through my window. I'm still in my clothes from the day before, and my stomach feels empty and gnawing. Even though I fell asleep without dinner, my shoes are off, and there's a blanket over me. Mom must have come in to cover me up.

I get up and pad into the kitchen, but Mom's not awake yet. I pour myself some cereal and turn on the TV, looking for something to stream. All I want is to forget about the fact that I have to go back to that school again in a few hours.

I'm scrolling through different options when I see *The Search for the Next Great Megastar*. I find season two—the best season, Gabby says. I turn on the first episode, and I watch with the sound down low. By the time Mom comes into the kitchen, the episode is half over.

I expect Mom to be mad at me for watching television this early in the morning—especially reality TV, which she calls *unscripted garbage*. Mom doesn't scold me, though. She just sits down next to me on the sofa.

After a minute, she shifts a little. "C'mere," she says.

I decide to forget how furious I am with her. I curl up on the sofa, place my head in her lap, and let her wrap her arm over me. Like I'm a little kid or something.

And then I'm crying just like a little kid, too.

Mom doesn't ask me why or give me a pep talk or anything. She doesn't even mention that I'm making her pants all snotty. She just sits there. Holding me.

When I'm all cried out, she asks. "What are we watching?"

"*The Search for the Next Great Megastar.*" I sit up, wipe my nose against her arm, so now her shirt's snotty, too. "A girl in my class is obsessed with this show."

We watch as Jadelicious stands alone in a dressing room, talking to her own reflection. Most of the Megastars are hanging out together in a different room. They're all gossiping about Jadelicious, and you can tell she knows it. Her gray eyes are puffy and bloodshot, like she's been crying.

"I see that I'm going to need to learn a new set of rules." She leans into the mirror and begins applying fake eyelashes so big they look like spiders. "Well, okay. I'll do whatever it takes to keep playing the game. But I will not let anyone make me forget who I am."

We watch together as Jadelicious steps back from the mirror, blinks a couple of times. It's pretty amazing, because once the eyelashes are on, you can barely tell she's been crying. She eyes her makeup from one angle, then another. She places a lavender wig on her head, so gleaming and smooth it looks almost like a helmet. She slips on a pair of metallic-purple heels, tosses her hair behind her shoulders, and looks directly at the camera.

"Now," she says, "it's time to show the world who's the real Megastar."

Well, good for you, Jadelicious, I think. *While you're proving to the world that you're a Megastar, I'll be stuck here in the middle of nowhere, feeding goats.*

Interview: Gabby

When you watch enough seasons of *Megastar*, you begin to notice certain personality types emerge. Like, there's always a Fighter, someone who's ready to argue—that's sort of like Fiona, you know? And the Fighter needs an Archenemy, which I guess for Fiona would be Diego. Except that Diego's also her sidekick, so maybe that's not quite right. There's also some sort of Authority Figure—kind of what Ms. Glebus is to us. Usually they judge the whole competition, enforcing the rules, and they're always a little scary.

But there's another personality type, too: the Disruptor.

The Disruptors are the ones who refuse to follow the rules. Or, I don't know. It's not exactly that they don't *follow* rules, it's that they know something the others don't: Most rules aren't even actual rules. We like to *call* them rules, and most people *think* of them as rules, but it's not like they're written down anywhere. They're just the things people do to be polite, or because they want others to like them.

But that's the thing about Disruptors: They don't care about being polite, and they don't care whether you like them. So they're able to get away with all sorts of outrageous things.

Jadelicious was the best Disruptor of all time. Like, on the episode where all the Megastars were dropped off in Times Square and tasked with getting people to applaud. All the other contestants just stood around on the sidewalk, basically begging tourists to pay attention to them. Not Jadelicious. She marched right into a nearby Broadway theater and asked if she could join the cast onstage during the final curtain call. So without even trying, she got a standing ovation from a thousand people!

Here at Mitchell, we had our own Disruptor: Paulie Fink. And just like on reality television, nothing at Mitchell would have been the same without him.

Pick a Winner

"That's what I'm saying," insists Sam as I arrive in Mags's room. "It's like Paulie just vanished."

Most of the class is here already, clustered around the pom-pom kids. "We spent *hours* searching," says Willow. "Not only could we not figure out where he went, we couldn't find any record of *any* Finks living in Vermont. Anywhere."

"It's like he got beamed up somehow," says Timothy. "Like, maybe he really was an alien all this time."

"Come on, aliens aren't real," argues Yumi, and everyone turns to look at Henry, like they expect him to know.

"Statistically speaking, the probability of aliens existing is very high," Henry says.

"See?" says Timothy. "He totally was an alien."

Just then Diego arrives, posing dramatically in the doorway. He's showing off a neon-green T-shirt, a little too small, stretched over the top of his other clothes. On the front is a cartoon stick figure picking its nose. Underneath, in big block letters, it says PICK A WINNER.

Diego drops a gym bag at his feet, flexes his muscles, and holds the pose.

"Paulie's shirt!" Fiona shouts, and she leaps up. She's wearing another pantsuit today, turquoise and far too big.

Gabby leans over and explains. "Paulie wore that shirt in last year's soccer game against Devlinshire Hills," she says. "Our school can't afford uniforms, so we all just have to wear green T-shirts. Paulie always wore the ugliest ones he could find."

"Except Glebus made him wear that one inside out," Yumi adds. "She said it wasn't up to Mitchell's standards of self-respect."

"She was just embarrassed in front of all those rich Devlinshire parents," Fiona says.

"To be honest, I was a little embarrassed, too," admits Yumi.

Diego picks up the gym bag and takes his seat. "Check it out: I found Paulie's bag in the lost and found," he says. "Been sitting there all summer, I guess. This T-shirt was right at the top." Diego unzips the bag and pulls out an old sock, hard and crusty. He tosses it at one of the twins, who throws it at Lydia, who throws it to Fiona.

Fiona brings it to her nose, then hurls it at Yumi. "Do *not* smell that thing," says Fiona. "Do not do it." Yumi picks it up with a pencil and carries it to the trash.

Diego rummages through the bag. He pulls out a filthy baseball cap, a half-eaten granola bar, a plastic bag filled with crushed potato chips, an old binder jammed with notes and pages, and an origami frog. I try to imagine what kind of person could possibly get away with wearing that neon PICK A WINNER monstrosity. If I'd worn something like that last year, I'd have been shunned for all eternity.

"And check these out." Diego pulls several pieces of paper from the bag, each folded into thirds. "They're emails to his parents. From Glebus."

He puts Paulie's hat on his own head, clears his throat, and begins to read.

Dear Beatrice and Mark:

Thank you for sitting down with me yesterday to discuss my concerns about Paulie. In that meeting, I promised to keep you apprised of any new incidents as they unfolded.

Unfortunately, it didn't take long for more to unfold.

This morning, the class was ten minutes into a lesson on the Stamp Act of 1765 when Paulie reached into his backpack and pulled out a series of items wholly unrelated to the curriculum: three pieces of bread, turkey, cheese, sliced tomatoes, and a jar of Dijon mustard. Paulie spread these items across his desk, then proceeded to make himself a double-decker sandwich. When the teacher paused the lesson to ask what he was doing, Paulie took a bite, then held out his sandwich to his teacher. His cheeks now stuffed, he asked, "Oh, did you want a bite?"

While it's true there's nothing specifically in the handbook about sandwich-making during class, I'm sure I don't need to explain why we cannot allow our classrooms to become personal kitchens at students' whims.

    With all my best hopes that we can put this incident, and all the many others that we discussed, behind us.

    Alice Glebus

    P.S. Just in case, I've amended the handbook with a rule that prohibits the preparation of food during class.

———————————

Dear Beatrice and Mark:

    Perhaps I was too specific in my most recent email. My concern is not about sandwiches per se.

    Today a pizza delivery person appeared outside the window of the sixth-grade math class. Paulie walked over to the window, paid for the pizza, then proceeded to pass slices to his classmates.

    They were, as you can imagine, simply delighted.

    But classroom time is not mealtime, and I do hope you can make this clear to Paulie. Thank you for understanding.

    Alice Glebus

    P.S. I've updated the student handbook to indicate that no meals of any sort may be prepared during, delivered to, or consumed during class. I do hope this is clear enough.

———————————

Beatrice and Mark:

    Once again, I was apparently too specific.

    Today during class, Paulie opened up a jar of mayonnaise and began eating the contents in giant, glopping spoonfuls.

Well, that certainly got the other children's attention. Not in a good way. Several of them gagged, and one had to rush to the bathroom to dry heave into the sink.

How could a student possibly eat mayonnaise in heaping spoonfuls, you might ask? I asked the same question. Upon further investigation, it seems Paulie was eating vanilla pudding, which he'd carefully transferred to an empty mayonnaise jar.

Paulie is technically correct that pudding isn't a "meal" (nor, for that matter, is mayonnaise), so his actions today don't violate our new policy around meals in classrooms. That said, perhaps you can discuss with your son the difference between the *spirit of the law* and *the letter of the law*.

Your cooperation, as always, is appreciated.

AG

P.S. I have since updated the handbook for a third time. It now says, *Food products of any kind, including herbs, spices, condiments, or liquids other than water may be consumed only in the cafeteria, and only during a designated lunch period.* I believe, at last, that this finally covers it.

———————————

Beatrice and Mark:

If there's any good news in this letter, it's that we seem to have finally written the food-related rules in such a way that Paulie's moved on. The bad news, of course, is that one can never anticipate and write rules for every single scenario Paulie might be able to dream up.

I love shiny things as much as the next person, but I sincerely wish that Paulie had not placed piles of glitter on top of the ceiling fan in my office on a warm day.

Perhaps it's time to meet again.

Unintentionally bedazzled and not exactly thrilled about it,

A.

By the time Diego finishes reading the last email, he can hardly breathe, he's laughing so hard. Everyone's cracking up, even serious-looking Henry.

"I wonder what he was planning to do with those emails," he says.

"Maybe he was going to Scotch-tape them to her car, like that time he covered her windshield with images of his own face," says Yumi. "He always had some trick up his sleeve."

"Remember when Paulie spent the whole day calling Glebus 'Jan'?" Timothy laughs.

"Every time, she corrected him, and then he was like, *Okay, sorry, Jan*," Sam finishes. "She's not even named Jan. She's *Alice*."

"And remember the day he wore that chicken suit?" Lydia says.

"Stop!" Fiona laughs. "Stop! It hurts to laugh this much!" She sinks to the floor dramatically.

When Mags swishes in—"Good morning, Originals!" she says, her voice a little singsong—she looks around at everyone. "Oh, dear. Fiona, off the floor. Yumi, put the ukulele away. And Diego, you know the rule: no hats in the classroom."

Mags holds out her hand, and Diego reluctantly hands over Paulie's cap.

"Yesterday, we talked about myths," she begins, placing the hat on the fireplace mantel. "We talked about how people shared myths as a way of explaining the world, and trying to exert some control over it. But over time, this worldview was challenged by *philosophers*." She tells us that philosophers were people who sat around and tried to *think* their way into understanding the world.

"Ugh," says Fiona. "I wish Paulie were here right now. He's literally the only one I can think of who could find a way to turn ancient philosophy into something interesting."

But actually, what Mags tells us turns out to be kind of interesting all by itself.

Trapped in a Cave

Mags leans against the mantelpiece. "I want you to imagine," she begins, "that you are all prisoners."

"We *are*," says Fiona. "We're all prisoners of school." She sighs, then starts banging her forehead on the table. If Mags notices, she pretends not to.

"As prisoners," she continues, "you've lived your whole lives inside a cave, chained in such a way that all you can see is a single wall. That wall is all you've ever seen, all you've ever *known*. Occasionally, shadows from the outside world are cast on your wall. A dog passes by, and you see the shadow of a dog. A bird flies past, and you see the shadow of a bird. A chariot rumbles by, and you see the chariot's shadow. You learn the names of these things: dog, bird, chariot. But remember: You never see the objects themselves—only their shadows. As far as you know, a dog's shadow *is* the dog."

"So...," Diego says. He looks like he's really thinking about what she's saying, but it's hard to take him seriously because he's still wearing that awful PICK A WINNER shirt.

"You're saying we *think* we're seeing something, and we're even sure that we *know* what it is we're seeing, but we're wrong?"

"Yes, Diego. Excellent," Mags says. She glances around the room. "Now imagine this: One day, one of you prisoners is released. Which one of you wants to go free?"

Fiona's head is off the desk now. In a flash, she's on her feet, waving her hand wildly. "Me! I want to!"

But Mags points to Diego instead. "Diego, since you asked the first question, I choose you to leave the cave."

Fiona slumps down again, dejected. Gabby leans over and pats her arm in sympathy.

"So Diego steps out into the big wide world," Mags goes on. "But Diego, I'm sorry, the first thing that happens is this: You're nearly blinded by the sun."

"Been in a cave my whole life, Mags." He shrugs.

"Exactly. You can imagine how painful the sun might be at first, how frightening the world must seem. All those colors. All that motion and bright light. It takes quite a bit of time for your eyes to adjust. But with time, they do adjust. You begin to see the world outside the cave. You see an actual dog, an actual bird. You discover, oh *this* is a dog, *this* is a bird."

I look around the room and realize everyone's paying close attention. Maybe because the whole thing doesn't feel like she's lecturing or preparing us for a test or anything. She's just telling us a story.

"Ah, but Diego, you haven't forgotten about your old

friends," Mags continues, sweeping her arm toward us. "All those other prisoners, still trapped and staring at the wall. In fact, Diego, you're eager to share with them what you've learned about the world! So you rush back to the cave and explain to them that everything they know about the world is wrong. You try to explain to them that birds have color, and feathers, and three dimensions, and scaly legs, and that dogs have fur and eyes…"

Mags stops. She leans on the table and glances around. "And those of you who are still in the cave, remember, you've never seen anything but those shadows. Would you believe what he tells you?"

I think about that. I try to imagine someone insisting that all the things I know are just flickering shadows of something that's more real, more true. I mean, I think I'd believe the truth when I heard it… but would I?

"Maybe some people would?" says Lydia. But she doesn't look so sure.

"I think most people would think he's nuts," says Sam.

"I suspect you're right, Sam," says Mags. "How could you possibly believe him? You've seen those shadows with your own eyes. Besides, how could anyone accurately describe color, or three dimensions, to someone who's never seen these things? So here's a different question, the really big one: After Diego's visit, you're offered the chance to leave the cave yourself. Would you follow Diego?"

Fiona nods immediately. "Yes!" she says. "Definitely." She and Diego fist bump. Henry bites his lip, nods, but he doesn't look quite as sure.

I stare down at the dark wood of our shared table. I try to picture the whole thing—the dark walls, the dim shadows. I try to imagine stepping outside, seeing the real world for the first time. But all I can picture is squinting into white light.

"I'd be scared," Gabby finally says. "I might go, but I think I'd be really scared."

No one says anything else, and after a few beats, Mags says, "That, Originals, is the allegory of the cave. It's a brilliant, beautiful metaphor about unlearning assumptions. It was first described by a Greek philosopher named Plato around 380 BCE."

She starts passing out homework sheets. "Tonight I'd like you to spend a few minutes doing a little reflection on Plato's cave, and how this thought experiment might relate to your own life."

Out of the blue, Fiona bangs the table. "Hey!" She looks around the room. "Maybe *that's* what happened to Paulie Fink! Maybe we've all been trapped in a cave, and..."

"And Paulie got out!" Lydia shouts. Fiona practically throws herself across the table to give Lydia a high five.

"Nah," muses Timothy. "He came from the stars, and he finally figured out how to get back to his home planet."

Sam shouts, "Alien!" and Thomas hollers, "Cave," and

then all of a sudden, they're chanting again. Half of the class shouts, "*Cave!*" The other half shouts, "*Al-i-en!*"

And as Mags tries to get the class under control, I wonder how it's possible that Paulie's so-called friends didn't even know he was leaving Mitchell.

Interview: Sam, Willow, Lydia, Thomas, and Timothy

SAM:
Another funny thing about Paulie is the way he made stuff up.

WILLOW:
He once told us he was an exiled prince from the Republic of Endrisistan. He told us all about the history of the country, and about how it's the world's largest source of trinsulium...

LYDIA:
Then we looked it up, and there's no place called the Republic of Endrisistan *and* there's no such thing as trinsulium!

SAM:
Another time, he said his parents were undercover spies who'd been sent to investigate Glebus for running the world's only black market for scented candles.

THOMAS:
And he spent two weeks insisting to me and Timothy that he was actually our long-lost triplet. He said our mom had given him up at birth and never told us.

TIMOTHY:
He repeated it so often that he almost had us convinced. We actually asked our mom about it after a while.

SAM:

I mean, we're talking about a kid who once showed up to school in a chicken suit and spent the whole day insisting that he was wearing regular clothes, no matter how much we were like, "Paulie, we can see you. You look like a chicken." But he'd tell you things so often, and so convincingly, they almost started to seem real.

Trampled

Here, if you're interested, is how to feed a goat:

1. Everyone but one kid takes a fistful of grain pellets. Staying on the outside of the fence, the group walks together to the other end of the pen—as far from the gate as possible. The goats will follow along the inside of the fence, bleating and whining and jostling to get close to the food.

2. When you're far from the gate, toss a few pellets over the fence, like confetti. This isn't the goats' meal. This is just to keep the goats distracted.

3. Once the goats are focused on the kids throwing pellets, the person who remained behind slips into the pen, carrying a big bucket of feed. For that kid, the race is on. They must pour the food into the goats' bowls and get out of the pen before the animals realize they're in there.

And if the goats do figure it out? Good luck.

On the second day of school, Mr. Farabi asks Henry to carry the bucket into the pen. Henry blinks hard, swallows nervously. But he goes in.

We grab and throw the pellets, but we run out before Henry's done filling the first bowl. The goats notice him, and they charge at him. Panicking, Henry drops the bucket, sits down in it, and covers his head with his arms.

"Goats have no upper front teeth!" he shouts. "Goats are herbivores!" A second later, we can't see Henry, or hear him, because he's disappeared beneath a swirl of goat hair. By the time Mr. Farabi rescues Henry, his glasses are barely still on his face, and his hair is a mess.

As Henry stumbles out of the pen, Mr. Farabi lifts the bucket and asks, "Anyone else want to give it a try?"

Diego, still wearing that PICK A WINNER shirt, volunteers. The same thing happens: We run out of pellets, and the goats figure out that someone's standing inside their pen with a giant bucket of food. Again they charge. Diego responds by zigzagging all over the pen as fast as he can. The goats try to follow but wind up crashing into one another and getting all confused.

Diego slips out of the pen relatively unscathed. "Phew," he says, dropping the bucket. He looks down at the neon cartoon figure stretched across his chest. "Guess this is a lucky shirt!"

Mr. Farabi asks if anyone else wants to give it a try, and Fiona raises her hand.

We try to toss the pellets more slowly this time. Fiona manages to fill three bowls. But as she's moving toward the final bowl, she trips on one of her too-long pant legs. She stumbles and recovers, but by then it's too late. The goats see her.

Fiona doesn't run, and she doesn't try to protect herself. Instead she leaps up, plants her feet in the ground, and lifts the bucket high in the air, like it's a sword, or a shield. "Halt!" she hollers. "In the name of Paulie Fink, I command you to—"

Before she can finish, the big goat smashes into her. She flies backward and drops the bucket, sending food scattering everywhere. By the time she hits the ground, the rest of the animals have surrounded her, and they're slurping up all the pellets.

"Halt!" Fiona's voice rises from the ground. "In the name of Paulie Fink, I say halt!"

Next to me, the whole class whoops and cheers.

"You needed the shirt, Fiona!" shouts Diego. "I should have given you the lucky shirt!"

Mr. Farabi enters the pen and helps Fiona up. When she stands, her hair's a mess, there's a tear in one of the arms of her blazer, and her suit pants are muddy and rumpled. Food pellets are stuck to her neck. But she's not upset at all. She's actually laughing.

I remember that hot wave of humiliation that rose inside me when the big goat knocked me down yesterday. It's almost maddening, the way Fiona doesn't seem to feel that.

Whatever rules Fiona lives by, they're not the ones that the rest of the world knows.

In my head, I try writing out some new rules:

RULES OF LIFE AS LEARNED FROM WATCHING FIONA

1. Wear whatever you want even if it's ridiculous.
2. Be loud even when it's annoying.
3. Laugh when what you really should be is embarrassed.

RULES OF LIFE AS LEARNED FROM WATCHING DIEGO

1. Believe that an ugly shirt can bring good luck.
2. Fail anyway.
3. Fail to notice that you've failed.

RULES OF LIFE AS LEARNED FROM FEEDING GOATS

1. Create distractions so nobody sees what's really going on.
2. Do your best not to get trampled.

Zombies and Werewolves

I would've figured that everyone knows seventh graders are too old for recess, but I guess that news hasn't made it to this corner of the world. We get a long recess each day, just before lunch. Today, everyone sort of hangs out at the edge of the soccer field. Henry's got his nose in his fact book, and Yumi starts strumming away on her ukulele. Diego, still in Paulie's shirt, is trying to do tricks with a soccer ball, except Fiona keeps sneaking up on him to steal the ball. Every time she gets it, she sprints away cackling until he chases her and gets it back. Sam and Willow and Lydia bring out some cards and twenty-one-sided dice, while the twins start playing a game they call zombie vs. werewolf.

The game goes like this: (1) On the count of three, each of them shouts out some type of character—zombie, werewolf, cyborg, pirate, rabid megalodon that can molt like a python, whatever—for the other one to play. (2) They pretend-fight as those characters. (3) After a while, they wind up wrestling on the ground, which makes Yumi look up from her ukulele and shout that they're being annoying.

(4) When Yumi yells, they stand up and start the whole thing over.

I'm pretty sure that's the entire game, right there.

As they play, Gabby—whose name, I'm now realizing, is perfect for her—starts telling me everything she thinks I need to know about my new classmates. "Yumi's family are artists," she says. "They do these really crazy puppet shows."

Yumi turns around. "Excuse me, but we're a celebrated Shakespeare Festival that happens to use the puppetry arts as our preferred media," she corrects. "And for the record, we got a great review in the *New York Times* last summer."

"Exactly," says Gabby. "So Yumi spends her whole summer traveling around on a puppet bus. And Willow's mom knows about yoga. Also, she and Sam's mom have been together since we were in first grade. And let's see. If you want to know anything about bow-hunting, which I never do, the twins are the ones to talk to. Henry's dad is on the town council, so he can tell you everything that's happening in town. Diego's mom runs the Little Critters Day Care—he, Fiona, and I went there together when we were little—and as you can probably tell, he's obsessed with soccer. You do play soccer, don't you? Because we'll need you in the Devlinshire game."

Then everyone nearby starts talking at once, telling me about this ritzy town on the other side of the mountain. "Devlinshire's one of those touristy parts of Vermont," explains Yumi. "It's got one of the most expensive ski resorts on the east coast, so rich people come to ski but then decide they like the place, so they build mansions and stay."

"There's a retired rock star who lives there," says Gabby. "He's, like, *super*famous, and his kids play on the soccer team, so he's always at the game."

"Every house in Devlinshire has a swimming pool," says Diego, bouncing a ball from one knee to the other.

"An *indoor* swimming pool," adds Fiona. She reaches for the ball, but Diego turns away just in time.

Yumi frowns. "I don't know that they're all indoors."

"No, it's true," insists Fiona, and then she turns to me. "My mom cleans houses over there, so she *knows*."

"I heard all the kids inherit like a zillion dollars when they turn eighteen," says Sam.

"That's definitely true," says Lydia. "Although I think it happens when they turn twenty-one."

By this point, Timothy and Thomas are on the ground in some sort of alien vs. robot battle. Timothy is sitting on his brother's back, saying, "I. Have. Defeated. The. Alien."

"So annoying!" Yumi yells at them. I guess that's their cue, because the twins stand up, ready for a new match.

Henry glances up from his fact book. "You know, you two should try a Paulie vs. Glebus battle," he suggests. "In honor of our missing classmate."

"I call Paulie!" Thomas shouts.

They begin a new countdown, but Fiona shouts, "WAIT!" She tells Diego to give Thomas the shirt. "He'll need all the help he can get in the battle against the Gleeb," she says.

Thomas puts the T-shirt on—it's even smaller on him than it is on Diego—and then the battle begins. Timothy, as Glebus, shouts, "My office! Right now, Paulie Fink!"

Thomas shouts, "You can't get me, Glebus!" He tackles his brother at the waist, and within seconds, he's pinned Timothy to the ground. It's a clear victory for Paulie over Glebus.

"It works!" Fiona yells. "The Paulie shirt really works!" She and Diego turn to each other, wide-eyed.

RULES OF LIFE AS LEARNED FROM ZOMBIE VS. WEREWOLF

1. Attack the thing in front of you until someone knocks you down or yells.
2. Start over.

RULES OF LIFE AS LEARNED FROM THE MYSTERIOUS PAULIE FINK

1. Eat mayonnaise.
2. Wear ridiculous things.
3. Disappear without warning.
4. Become some sort of legend.

Interview: Sam, Timothy, Henry, Gabby, Yumi, Willow, Lydia, and Diego

SAM:

He was from San Fernando, I think. Or maybe San Jose. Wait, what's the difference between the two?

TIMOTHY:

Wasn't he from Massachusetts?

HENRY:

No, Timothy. I'm the one from Massachusetts. Remember, I moved here from Holyoke in third grade?

GABBY:

I think Paulie was from St. Louis. Maybe he went back there?

CAITLYN:

I don't understand why you can't text Paulie and find out where he went.

YUMI:

I don't think he had a phone. Most of us don't, which is totally Glebus's fault. A few years ago, she encouraged our parents to sign a pledge that they'd wait until we were in eighth grade before getting us phones. And most of them did. Can you believe that?

CAITLYN:

Well, his parents must have had jobs, right? Or friends in town who would know where they went?

GABBY:

His dad was...maybe a writer or something? I don't know, actually. We didn't see them much. My grandma says they were *away* people, not from here.

WILLOW:

Yeah, they weren't friendly. Like, at all. And it was weird, because we almost never saw them. Not at the grocery store or anything.

LYDIA:

I think he lived over by Sugarbush Lane, but I'm not sure. Timothy, you went to his house, right?

TIMOTHY:

Nah, we never went to Paulie's house, but Diego went there a bunch of times.

DIEGO:

Actually, no. I never did. He came to mine a few times. He never wanted to play sports, though.

CAITLYN:

Seriously? Paulie's, like, everybody's favorite person on earth, and none of you ever went to his house?

Once upon a Mini

At lunchtime, I plop down in the seat next to my Mini. "Hey, Fuzzy," I say. She looks up at me with those big eyes, like she's waiting for something. Like maybe I'm supposed to do something amazing now.

I reach over and open up her milk carton. It's hardly amazing, but it's all I've got.

At a nearby table, Fiona tosses a cracker in the air, tries to catch it with her mouth. She fails, tries again, and catches it. Then she laughs, spilling cracker crumbs down her chin and onto her shirt. Her Mini is beaming, like Fiona's the greatest thing on earth.

"Oh, hey!" I say to Fuzzy. "Nice job keeping our pinkie promise yesterday. With the Good Day Bell. I didn't ring it, either. A promise is a promise." I hold up my pinkie and wiggle it. She nods, her face serious.

Then there's this empty space where neither of us talks. I know that since I'm the older one, it's up to me to fill that space, so I just say whatever pops into my head. "Yup, I remember kindergarten. Nap time, snack time, all those hours on the playground…those were the good old days." I try to remember specific things about kindergarten, but all I really recall is how loud and scary everything seemed.

How small I felt.

I try to imagine that I'm seeing the cafeteria through Fuzzy's eyes. I can see how the room might seem huge to her, the way even this tiny school might seem crowded and chaotic. But the main thing I see is this: I'm big. All the kids at this table probably seem huge to her, but I'm the most grown-up of all of them.

The feeling only lasts for a second, and then I'm back in my own skin.

"Hey," I say, making my eyes level with Fuzzy's. "Do you think Real Rabbit wants to hear a story?"

She nods, so I begin. "Okay. So…once upon a time…"

I pause. I can't actually remember any great stories. I think about telling her the one Mags told us—the one about the cave and the person who gets out, but a story about prisoners locked in a cave is probably too scary for a nervous kindergartner. So I go for the opposite kind of story. Something stupid and silly, like that PICK A WINNER T-shirt that made everyone laugh.

"Once upon a time, there was a boy named Paulie." I start to tell her the story about Paulie getting pizza delivered to school, but she just looks confused, so I change it. I tell her that Paulie lived in a land that was ruled by an evil witch everyone called the Gleeb. Paulie wore a neon superhero cape, and he didn't just order pizza, he ordered a *magic* pizza, that made all the children of the land dance. They danced all over happily until the Gleeb released a pack of angry goats to chase them. That's when Paulie sprinkled the kids with enchanted mayonnaise, which gave them the ability to fly. So they flew away to safety and lived happily ever after, the end.

It's not a perfect story, but I use a dramatic voice, and I lean in like I'm letting her in on a giant secret. She gets this faraway look in her eyes, like she's watching a movie inside her head.

When lunch is over, she asks me if I'll tell Real Rabbit another story tomorrow.

"Uh...sure," I say. "I'll try to think of one."

She hands me Real Rabbit, then waits eagerly. I look at him, floppy and lifeless. I give him a tiny hug, and I guess that's what she wanted me to do, because then Fuzzy hugs me. Her hug isn't so little.

I feel something behind my ribs then. It's not a stone, but it doesn't feel swampy, either. It's like something is cracking deep inside me. It hurts a little, to be honest. But it also feels good. Like now there's a tiny bit more room for me to breathe.

Then Fuzzy runs off to Mr. Twilling. As I watch her go, I imagine a new list of rules:

RULES FOR DEALING WITH YOUR MINI

1. Open their milk carton.
2. Tell a story if you can think of one.
3. Remember you're bigger than they are.

These rules, at least, seem like things I can do.

I Figure Something Out

That night after dinner, Mom's on the sofa, doing a bunch of paperwork from the clinic. I'm staring at my own paper, the one with Mags's question:

> What do you think Plato's allegory of the cave is about? What might it mean in your own life? Please provide at least one example. Be specific.

I pick up my pen, set it down, and lift it again. I count the lines on the page. Twenty-seven. I hope Mags doesn't expect me to fill them all.

What would it be like to be stuck inside a cave? Boring, that's what. And also painful. Wouldn't you need to stretch, and how would you go to the bathroom, and also, isn't there some kind of sore you get if you don't change position frequently enough? I think I learned that from Mom.

In my head, I rewrite the assignment as multiple-choice questions:

There once was a Greek philosopher named:
   a. Jadelicious
   b. Glebus
   c. Plato
   d. Paulie Fink

Plato liked to talk about:
   a. an ugly T-shirt
   b. a jar of mayonnaise
   c. evil goats
   d. a cave

When the prisoner walks out of the cave he:
   a. rings the Good Day Bell
   b. orders pizza
   c. gets blinded by the sun
   d. plays zombie vs. werewolf

Why couldn't Mags have given us questions like that? I could just pick the right answer and be done, instead of having to make up some story about what Plato's cave means to me.

Probably the closest I ever came to discovering that the things I thought I knew were actually wrong was last year, when I started sixth grade. I'd been so excited to start middle school. But then when I got there, it's like I realized I didn't know how to do the most basic things. Like, what was

I supposed to do with my hands when I stood in the hallway laughing with friends? And how loudly should I be laughing, and did I look like an idiot when I smiled? It was like I suddenly needed an instruction manual that no one had ever bothered to give me.

But it's not like I'd ever admit *that* in a homework assignment.

I look back down at the empty page and sigh. Across the room, Mom looks up from her notes. "What are you working on?" she asks.

"Homework." I make a face. "I have to write an essay about some dumb philosopher named Plato."

"Plato, huh? That's fancy," Mom says.

"It's ancient, and I don't get the point."

Mom sits up a little straighter. "Tell me what you've got so far."

"It's fine, Mom," I snap. "I don't need any help with my homework." In my head, I add, *I really just need different homework. And while I'm at it, I could use a different school, and a different life.*

I close my eyes. I try to imagine being inside a cave, looking at flickering shadows. But I can't picture the cave, and I can't picture the shadows. All I see is the cafeteria—Fiona catching crackers in her mouth and not even caring about the crumbs.

I open my eyes and begin to write:

Plato's cave is a way of thinking about what it might feel
like to find out that the world is a lot more complicated
than you realized. It's also about how sometimes one person
might know things that they can't explain to anyone else.
One example of Plato's cave might be if you never left
elementary school, and so you stayed surrounded by little
kids even though you were way too big. You'd never know
what a real middle school is like. If you had to go to a
real school, you wouldn't even know what to do. You might
even totally freak out.

It's a pretty good answer, actually. And it's true. Fiona
and Lydia might have been joking about how the Originals
were stuck in a cave and Paulie got out. But they weren't
wrong.

The Mitchell School *is* a cave. And it's possible I'm the
only one in my class who's ever been outside of it.

Suit of Armor

That night, I keep thinking about the answer I didn't write down: how starting middle school last year really did feel like leaving a cave and entering the real world. There were so many new rules that nobody had ever bothered to teach me. Like about what you could wear. I'd show up to school in what I thought were normal clothes. Then someone would sneer, *Nice shirt*. Just like that, I'd see what they saw: My shirt was ugly. As soon as I got home, I'd shove it in the back of my closet.

In middle school, a person could do the wrong thing at any moment, anywhere, without even knowing. Even in gym class! One time, we were playing kickball and for some reason two of my friends barely tried to kick the ball. Easy outs. They'd both laughed, like the game was the stupidest thing in the world.

Then it was my turn. I knew I could get on base if I wanted. I had always been a strong kicker, one of the few kids able to hit the far wall. But suddenly I wasn't sure if I should. So when the pitcher rolled the ball toward me, I just...froze.

I felt everyone's eyes on me. I heard my friends laughing. Then I saw Anna Spang, standing alone in literal left field. She scratched her arm, all fidgety. The only thing I knew for sure was this: I didn't want to be *her*.

I let the ball roll past me. I laughed it off, like my friends. But that feeling—*I don't want to be Anna*—stayed.

I started watching her more closely. I noticed how tightly she pressed her books against her chest as she moved through the hallways, like she was protecting herself from some invisible harm. I watched the way she turned the locker dial slowly, hoping no one would notice that she didn't have anyone to talk to. Everything she did wrong reassured me. I mean, maybe I didn't know how to *be* ... but at least I knew more than Anna did.

I guess I wanted her to know that, too. Because I started doing things. Maybe I'd get my friends to stare at her. We'd watch from a distance—across the cafeteria, or in the library when we were supposed to be reading. We'd keep our eyes on her until she looked up. Then we'd laugh. Not because she was doing anything funny, but because we wanted her to know she was someone people laughed at.

Anna always tried to pretend she didn't see us, but we could tell she had by how quickly she looked in the opposite direction, like she'd been slapped. And when she did, I felt the swamp inside me hardening, turning into stone. Like I was building a suit of armor on my insides.

Challenge Accepted

Within a few days, I begin to figure out the routine here. I learn that Fiona really does wear a pantsuit every day. I know that Lydia and Willow and Sam will spend recess rolling dice for their weird role-playing game. I know that Fuzzy will ask for a story at lunch, and that the only time Henry doesn't look worried is when he's offering up some sort of random fact. I also know that the goats really do eat the heck out of shrubs; on Thursday, Mr. Farabi says it's already time to move the goat pen to the next spot.

I'm starting to figure out other things, too: like how much harder it is to feel connected to my old friends than I ever expected. Every night I text them, and sometimes they text back. Even when they do, they seem a million miles away.

On Friday morning, the last day of the first week of school, Mags writes on the board: DEMOKRATIA: RULE BY THE PEOPLE.

"Okay, Originals," she says. "We've talked a bit about mythology and philosophy in ancient Greece. Today I want to talk about the rise of democracy in the city of Athens."

On one side of me, Fiona moans like she's in pain. She's

wearing Paulie's neon T-shirt under her electric-purple blazer. After the Paulie vs. Glebus match, everyone actually started sharing that dumb shirt for good luck.

Diego leans back in his chair. "Come on, Mags, why do we have to learn about all this ancient junk?" he asks.

Mags lifts one eyebrow. "Is there something you'd prefer to discuss, Diego?" Mags asks.

"Well, sure," he says. "Lots of things."

"What sorts of things?" She waits, like she's really expecting an answer.

"I don't know," Diego says. "Stuff that's…you know… related to our lives."

Mags taps her chin and looks up at the ceiling for a moment. "Okay," she says. "How about we put this to a vote. We can either spend the day discussing political systems and the rise of democracy, *or* we can do what Diego suggests, and discuss things you consider more relevant to your daily lives. Quick show of hands: Who wants to talk about democracy?"

Everyone glances at each other. No one's hand goes up.

Mags looks around the room. "So that would be, let's see, zero votes for democracy. And who would like to discuss a topic that's more relevant to your lives?"

Nearly everyone's hand shoots up. Only Henry doesn't raise his hand. He's watching Mags with this funny look, like he's both amused and impressed.

As soon as I see him, I realize exactly what's going on.

"Okay, so *stuff that's relevant to your lives* wins in a land-slide vote," Mags says.

The class cheers, and Mags walks over to the board. She circles the word DEMOKRATIA, then she turns around and grins. "For the record," she says, "you just participated in something called *direct democracy*. So I'd say it is pretty relevant to your lives, no?"

Now everyone understands what she's done. The room fills with groans. "You tricked us!" shouts Fiona.

"Only to prove a point," says Mags. "But I am a teacher of my word. So here's what we're going to do." She pulls a stack of index cards from her desk drawer and passes a handful to each of us. "I want you to write down topics you think are more relevant to your lives than the study of humanities," she says. "Write down one topic per card—anything you'd prefer to discuss during class time. Fold up the cards and place them in this hat."

She picks up Paulie's hat, the one she took from Diego on Tuesday. "Starting on Monday I'll pull one card from this hat every day. If I'm unable to connect what's written on the card with the ancient world, then I will agree to spend the whole class discussing what you've written. But if I *can* connect the topics, then you'll agree to trust me that the ancient world does, indeed, have relevance to your lives today. Do we have a deal?"

"Wait, you're serious?" asks Yumi. "We can write down anything we want?"

"Anything. I'll connect it to the ancient world in some meaningful way, or you kids can lead the discussion."

Everyone picks up their pen and starts scribbling. I glance over at Diego. He scrawls *The annual soccer game against Devlinshire*, then folds up the index card and immediately grabs another one. *Why Devlinshire is the worst.* Then another: *Why Mitchell rules and Devlinshire drools.*

I turn to peek at Fiona's card. Already, she's got three cards folded, and her pen is flying across a fourth. *Our favorite Paulie Fink memories*, she writes, then adds the card to her pile. She keeps going: *Powerful women. Strong women. Women who aren't well-behaved. Recess. Goats. Are birds just modern dinosaurs and if so, will they ever grow fangs and devour us?*

When Fiona runs out of cards, she asks if she can use one of mine. I nod. I'm still staring at my first card, wondering what to write. It's only when Mags begins walking around the room, picking up cards, that I write anything. I cover the words as I write them, so no one can see:

How to be brave when everything changes too fast.

It's stupid, I know, but it's the only thing I could think of. I fold the card in two, and Mags takes it from me before I can change my mind.

Mags smiles, satisfied. "Challenge accepted, Originals. Let's see how this goes."

Raising the Scarecrow

"Ugh!" Fiona declares dramatically at recess that day. Nearly the whole class is sprawled out on the grass. Only Diego and the twins aren't with us. They're off in the distance, wandering around at the edge of the soccer field.

Henry looks up from his book. "What's wrong, Fiona?"

"Everything," says Fiona. Diego's drawn two big smiley faces on her cheeks, so it looks like she's got face tattoos. "Summer's over. The first week of school is always sort of exciting, but now that's almost over, too. All we have left is boring old school."

"Paulie would know how to liven things up." Sam sighs.

"Well," says Gabby, a little too hopefully, "at least Caitlyn's here."

Fiona eyes me skeptically, then frowns. "Caitlyn would *never* wear a chicken suit to school."

"That's true," I agree. "I wouldn't."

"See?" Fiona continues. She throws herself backward onto the grass and directs her complaints toward the sky. "There's no more fun. Decades from now historians will point to this moment in history—this very week, even—and they'll say, *That's it. That's when the fun died forever. That's when we entered the Land of Blah.*"

She sits up again, flings her arms out to the side. "Welcome to the Land of Blah!" she bellows to no one in particular. "Welcome to the boring-est school that ever existed!"

Yumi plucks out a little tune on her ukulele. "The boring-est school...that ever exiiiisted..."

"I dunno," I say. "Mitchell might be all kinds of weird, but it's not exactly *boring*."

Gabby looks confused. "What's weird about Mitchell?"

I want to say, *Everything. Everything here is weird. Isn't that obvious?* But the way everyone's looking at me, I guess it's not obvious. Not to them.

"Well, for one thing, look around." I sweep my arm toward the mansion, the broken statues, the long fields. "Literally, this is the only school on the planet that looks like this. And...you know...*goats*?"

"Well, sure, *those* things," says Fiona. She waves her hand dismissively. "But those are exceptions."

"Plus, other schools have rules," I add.

"We have rules," says Willow. She throws out two dice. "There's a whole student handbook. It's filled with rules."

Fiona starts listing them off on her fingers. "No cheating on tests... No throwing balls inside the classroom... No sledding down the back hill on a cafeteria tray." She glances up at me. "That's a real one, by the way. It's written down."

"Yeah." Yumi laughs. "Thanks to *you*."

"I don't mean those kinds of rules," I say. "I mean the rules that people never bother to write down, because they're already obvious."

"If it's not written down, it's not a rule." Fiona shrugs, like it's that simple.

Yumi stops strumming. She squints out at the field. "What in the world are they doing?"

At the edge of the woods, Diego picks up a long, thin tree branch with several broken limbs. He and Thomas start dragging the branch across the grass toward a spot just behind the far soccer goal. As they do, Timothy runs to the far edge of the playground. He examines the bottom half of a broken basketball hoop—just a plastic base and a hollow pole—and drags that toward the goal. I notice Diego's got Paulie's good-luck shirt hanging out of his back pocket.

Fiona scrambles to her feet. "Whatever they're doing," she says, "I want in." She sprints across the field, her blazer flapping behind her like a cape.

Diego slides the PICK A WINNER shirt over one end of the branch. Then Fiona and the twins help him lift the branch so it's vertical. They slide the bottom of the branch into the basketball hoop base. The shirt dangles from those broken limbs.

Just like that, the whole thing is a scarecrow. An odd, headless scarecrow wearing the world's ugliest shirt.

They secure the contraption by setting some rocks on the

base. Fiona sprints back to us. "Hey!" she shouts. "We're building a whole new Paulie! Good luck for all of us! Come see!"

Everyone starts running toward the weird scarecrow, or statue, or whatever it is they just made. A few steps in, Henry stops and turns around. "You coming, Caitlyn?"

I want to ask Henry what makes this Paulie Fink kid so unforgettable. I mean, I left a school, and do I think for a minute that anyone back home is making a monument in honor of me? That they're fighting over a T-shirt of mine, or chanting my name?

They're not. Already, it feels like my friends barely remember who I am.

I shrug. "I never even met Paulie."

Henry eyes me carefully. "I'm not an Original, either. I didn't come here until third grade. So you and me, we're sort of in the same situation."

Huh. So Henry has been out of the cave, too.

"And Paulie," he adds. "He came in fourth grade."

"Well," I say. "I guess that makes us the Unoriginals."

"Unoriginals," he says. He smiles. "Yeah, that's good. The Unoriginals. It's like we're our own little club."

"We should get uniforms or something," I say.

In the distance, the Originals have formed a train, each person's hand on the shoulder of the person in front of them, and they're dancing around the field.

"You were right, you know," he says. He looks away from me, toward the other kids. "What you said before. About

109

how the kids here don't seem to know the same rules as in other places. In my old school kids used to steal my backpack. They'd play keep away with it, and if I hadn't zipped it up, all my stuff wound up all over the floor. Sometimes even my closest friends did it. Then they'd tell me they were just kidding." He says this all very matter-of-factly, like he's not even embarrassed to admit it.

In the distance, they're chanting again. *"Paul-ie! Paul-ie!"*

"Anyway," Henry says, and now he's looking right at me, "all I'm saying is that different doesn't have to mean bad. And as long as it's here, maybe we should try to have fun."

"As long as what's here?" I ask.

"Huh?"

"As long as *what's* here? That Paulie scarecrow?"

He looks confused for a second, then he pushes his glasses up on his nose. "Yup," he says. "That's what I mean. Anyway, I think we're all Originals now. So let's go check out our new Paulie."

I shake my head no, and he jogs away.

I try to picture my friends back home chanting my name: *Cait-lyn! Cait-lyn! Cait-lyn!* For a second, I can even see it, too: a train of kids dancing their way down my old hallway, past my old locker. But it's just a quick flash, and then it disappears.

Nope, you're right, Caitlyn. I wasn't talking about that scarecrow-statue thing when I said that as long as it's here, we might as well try to have some fun.

No, I guess I wasn't talking about the Paulie statue at all.

I meant everything. The school. This whole hidden world up here, like our secret fort in the woods.

Miss U

I wish Henry telling me to have fun was enough to make me enjoy being here, but it's not. Every day I just keep sending texts to my friends back home, wishing I was there. Sometimes they respond, sometimes they don't. Here's what it looks like when they don't respond:

> Hey, how are you

> This place is still super weird

> I have one friend though!

> Unfortunately she happens to be in kindergarten, LOL

> I liked that photo you sent of everybody all together

I WISH I COULD BE THERE

I miss u

Write back, okay?

Please

Mom says she'll bring me back
home to see you guys

Tell me when is good for you

Mom needs a couple of weeks to plan
the trip, she works a lot of weekends

She says her job is tiring

I'm like, Mom, you had a job that
was tiring before you moved.

Could have just stayed, LOL

> Do you ever watch Next Great
> Megastar

> A girl here is obsessed

> But she also likes goats

> you got my message about me coming down?

> miss you

Then out of the blue my friend Mira writes to tell me
that she's planning a huge sleepover, and that I *have* to be
there. I write back immediately:

> Yessssssss!

> Tell me when it's happening!!!!!!

> My mom says she needs a little notice is all

> omg, I can't even describe what it's like here

114

One kid is really into puppets

And the boys keep playing these
dumb wrestling games

And everyone is obsessed
with an ugly neon shirt

For a while they took turns wearing it

The same filthy shirt

Now it's hanging on a
branch like a scarecrow

They say it's good luck

Maybe I'll steal it and wear it to the party LOL

seriously

can

not

wait

It takes some back-and-forth to find a date for the party that I can actually make. When we do figure it out, I'm so excited, I can barely contain it.

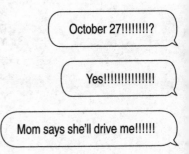

October 27!!!!!!!!!?

Yes!!!!!!!!!!!!!!!!

Mom says she'll drive me!!!!!!

Oh wait.

We have a soccer game that day.

And since I'm the 11th person in the class, they need me on the team.

No, actually never mind. I don't care.

Just don't tell my mom about it haha

She'd just tell me I have to play.

I WILL BE THERE!!!!!!!!!!!!!!!!!!!!!

Anna Spang will be there too right?

Ha—that's a joke

I really really really really really really really really really really really can't wait to come home.

A MONTH WITHOUT PAULIE

The Land of Blah

I'll say this for television: You never have to slog through any boring parts. Take *Megastar*, for example: The show jumps from one dramatic moment to the next. If that requires skipping ahead in time, the editors have all these little tricks to show time passing. Need to jump forward a few hours? They might show clouds passing overhead at high speed. An entire day? They'll show a time lapse of the sun setting, then rising again. They even have tricks for showing longer periods of time: a hand crossing off red *X*s on a calendar, or pages from a daily calendar fluttering away into some mysterious wind.

In real life, you just have to suffer through every excruciating moment.

Two more weeks pass. All I want is to fast-forward to Mira's sleepover on October 27. I wish I could edit down the endless hours between now and then, compress them all into a single, fast-paced thirty-second montage:

Clip 1: The sun falls on that bizarre statue of Paulie Fink. By the time it rises again, the green leaves in the woods behind the statue have given way to shocks of rust and crimson, the start of a Vermont autumn.

Clip 2: a high-speed of the class moving the portable-goat-pen fence. We do it again, then again... a few feet every few days, the soccer field growing a little bigger each time.

Clip 3: Mr. Farabi cheers from the sidelines of the soccer field as we practice for the big Devlinshire game. Then the camera might pan to me, barely trying. What's the point, when I won't even be there for the game?

Not that I've told anyone that yet.

Other clips might show my mom and me watching *Megastar* as we eat dinner. Me marching past the Good Day Bell, refusing again and again to ring it. The class listening to Mr. Farabi rattle on about ecosystems. Mags reaching into Paulie's hat, pulling out an index card, then connecting whatever's written to the ancient world.

Mags keeps her promise about that. By mid-September, Diego's card about the Devlinshire rivalry has inspired a discussion of the first-ever Olympic games. Fiona's cards about *strong women* and *powerful women* have led to lessons about Athena, the Greek goddess of wisdom; Artemis, the goddess of the hunt; and the Amazons, a mythical tribe of women warriors. Cards like *zombie vs. werewolf* and *Creatures of the Underlair* have prompted lectures about gorgons (who have snakes instead of hair), three-headed dogs, and lots of other mythical creatures that people used to fear.

When Mags pulls out Fiona's card about favorite Paulie

memories, she starts talking about some guy named Herodotus, who is one of the first true historians. She tells us that Herodotus traveled all over the ancient world, collecting stories from different people about their lives and about their understanding of what led up to a war. He wove all these tales into a book called *The Histories*.

"Herodotus showed that our understanding of history is never objective truth," Mags explains. "It always depends on who does the telling. To get the fullest understanding of history, you need to listen to as many different voices as possible." She tells us that we'll talk more about Herodotus soon, because we're going to have to do some sort of oral-history project using his techniques. Naturally, that makes everyone groan.

Mags's stories might not make Mira's party get here any faster, but they do give me something to talk about with Fuzzy. Actually, I guess that should be a part of my time-passing montage, too: me opening up milk carton after milk carton, a new one each day, and leaning in to tell Fuzzy a story.

"What happens next?" Fuzzy's whisper is so soft I can barely hear her over the cafeteria noise. It's been nearly three weeks since I told her the first story of Paulie vs. the Gleeb. She's wanted one every day since.

"Take a bite of your sandwich first," I tell her. Then I

continue my story. "And when the wooden horse was safely inside the Land of Blah, Paulie leaped out of the horse. 'Surprise!' he shouted at the Gleeb. Wow, was she shocked!"

This is a kindergarten-friendly version of a story that Mags told this morning.

Today's index card said *Paulie's desk drawer prank*. Mags said that Paulie's best pranks demonstrated the power of surprise. "But one of history's most famous examples of the element of surprise was something called the Trojan horse." The Greeks, she explained, wanted to invade an enemy city surrounded by a high wall. So they built a giant statue of a horse out of wood, then hid a bunch of soldiers inside. They presented the statue as a gift to their enemy, and as soon as it was behind the city walls, the soldiers jumped out, destroying everything in sight.

But I can't tell war stories to a kindergartner, so I modify it. "Paulie wasn't the only one who had been hiding in the statue," I say. "His entire army of naughty, chaotic chickens leaped out, too. Those birds went squawking all over the Land of Blah. They scared the goats, and they knocked things over, and they...pooped everywhere! All the Gleeb could do was shake her bony fist, shouting, 'I'll get you, Paulie Fink, you and all your feathered friends!'"

Fuzzy covers her mouth and looks at me like I'm naughty and amazing. But really I'm just passing along a story that someone else told me, changing it a little as I go.

"Last bite," I say when I'm done. "Hurry, lunch is almost over."

As Fuzzy finishes her sandwich, Glebus walks into the cafeteria. She steps up onto a chair and calls out, "Excuse me! Students of the Mitchell School! I have an announcement! It's my pleasure…to hereby declare that on this day, September 18…"

The room gets very quiet, and I glance over toward Gabby. She's crossing her fingers, eyes closed. She's mouthing, *Please please please.*

Glebus continues, "…all usual afternoon activities are canceled. Because today is…Zucchini Day!"

The place goes crazy.

The Opposite of Zukeball

"Let the sorting begin!" Mr. Farabi shouts.

There's a pickup truck parked behind the school, near the statues. It's filled with piles and piles of zucchini. Some are pretty crazy-looking: They're twisted into curlicues, or squat and fat like tomatoes. Others are as long as my whole arm and nearly as thick as a loaf of bread.

"Grab yourself an armful of vegetables and sort them into piles!" Mr. Farabi directs us. "Place the zucchini for cooking over by the statue of Zeus. See this ugly one right here? All gnarled? A little bruised? This is what we call a launcher. Launch pile's over there next to Athena, she's the one with the shield. Whoa, Timothy, look at the size of that one; that's a zukeballer for sure! Put it next to that headless statue, the dude with the harp. Mags, who is that? That's right, Apollo! Zukeballers near Apollo!"

As Ms. Glebus fills my arms with vegetables, Gabby tells me that Zucchini Day is an annual tradition. "There are always a couple of weeks in September when all the farmers have way more zucchini than anyone knows what to do with," she says. "Plus, nobody wants to buy ugly zucchini, or bruised ones, and the overgrown ones never taste very good. So Glebus drives around to all the local farms to collect surplus zucchini."

I drop a monster zucchini into the zukeballer pile, whatever that is. "Yeah, but why? What are we supposed to do with them?"

"Well, if they're good for eating, kids can take them home to their families. But the rest of them . . . well, you'll see."

Once we get the zucchini sorted, the younger grades head off to make zucchini muffins with their teachers. My class follows Mags and Mr. Farabi out to the soccer field. There are some handmade catapults set up, miniature versions of weapons the ancients used.

For the next half hour, we use the catapults to fling zucchini across the soccer field. As Mags talks about ancient battles, Mr. Farabi asks us to predict where each might land depending on its size and shape.

I add this to the list of things I'll tell my friends when I see them. *Yes, we launched zucchini with a catapult.* I imagine them gathered around me, rapt as I describe life here. *I keep telling you*, I'll say. *It's, like, so bizarre.*

Diego places a gnarled zucchini in the catapult. Before releasing it, he looks over at the Paulie statue. "Come on, Paulie," he murmurs. "Make this one fly."

It sails clear across the field in a perfect arc.

After that, everyone else starts talking to the Paulie statue before launching their own. They all want theirs to go the farthest, or the fastest.

"In the name of Paulie Fink!" shouts Fiona, just before lobbing hers. It releases too early and lands with a splat, but I guess it doesn't matter, because everyone just keeps calling on that headless statue for help.

"Come on, Paulie. Send this baby toward the trees."

"Gimme some distance, Paulie!"

Even Henry does it. After one especially nice launch, he gives the statue a little salute. "Thank you, Paulie," he says.

When the "launcher" pile is empty, we play zukeball. It turns out to be just like baseball, except we use oversize zucchini as bats, and the smallest, most misshapen ones as balls.

When it's my turn at bat, I thwack a zucchini so hard that it explodes in midair, splattering green chunks all over my face.

At the end of the day, the field is covered with smashed vegetables. Naturally, it's our job to clean them up and feed them to the goats.

"See, this is what I mean," I say to Gabby. "Real schools don't drop everything to play zukeball." I've been trying to explain that Mitchell's just different from other places. I've tried to explain that most seventh graders aren't in the same

128

building as kindergartners, and even if they are, they definitely don't sit with them at lunch. Most schools don't have
fireplaces in their classrooms, or statues on the lawn. Heck,
lots of schools don't even have *trees*.

Ahead of me, Fiona, arms loaded with zucchini, spins
around. "You know what, Caitlyn? I'm getting pretty sick
and tired of you complaining about everything here."

"Fiona." Diego shakes his head. "Come on, it's not
worth it."

Fiona throws her zucchini onto the grass and places her
hands on her hips. "No, I'm serious." Then she imitates me,
the same voice I've heard her use to imitate Glebus. "*Real*
schools don't have goats. *Real* schools have desks and lockers, *real* schools are *blah blah blah*."

"I never said other schools were *better*," I say.

"You might not have said it out loud," says Yumi quietly.
"But you said it."

"You talk about *real* schools as if Mitchell isn't one,"
says Fiona. "But *hello*: You're at school, and this is real life.
So apparently this *is* what a real school looks like. And if you
don't like it, go home. Or better yet, go to *Devlinshire*! You'll
fit right in there."

Everyone's eyes get really wide.

"Okay, Fiona," says Diego. "Shut it."

"It's rude!" Fiona shouts. "*She's* rude!"

Stare at something, I tell myself.

Take a breath.

Turn to stone.

I do the first two, but for the life of me, I can't find that stone behind my ribs.

"How about instead of talking about what's wrong with Mitchell," Gabby suggests, like she's the peacemaker, "you tell us about some of the things you liked most at your old school."

I liked that the rules told me how to fit in. I liked that as long as I followed the rules, I knew I'd always have a cluster.

"I liked that it was *normal*," I say. "We did normal things."

Fiona looks like she's about to start swinging at me, but Diego puts his hand on her shoulder.

"*Normal . . . ,*" says Diego. Like he's trying to figure out what I mean.

"Normal, like . . . whatever the opposite of zukeball is!"

"What's the opposite of zukeball?" Timothy asks Thomas, who only shrugs.

Everyone's watching me now. I remember standing in gym class last year, freezing up as that red ball rolled toward me.

"Kickball!" I finally shout. "We played *kickball*, okay?"

For a few seconds, no one says anything. Then, in an instant, they burst out laughing.

"Oh, you played *kickball*," says Fiona. Just like that, she doesn't seem mad anymore. "Of course. Kickball."

"Because here in Vermont, we've never even *heard* of kickball," adds Diego.

As they head toward the goat pen, still laughing,

Timothy starts shouting, *"Caitlyn likes kickball! Caitlyn likes kickball!"*

Next thing I know, they're all chanting it. They chant it while they toss zucchini to the goats. They chant it at the Paulie statue, a few of them stopping to pretend to give the branch a high five, like that stupid T-shirt-on-a-branch is actually the great and powerful Paulie Fink. Then they chant it all the way to the school building.

I walk to the goat pen only when the others have left. Then I hurl my zucchini in as hard as I can.

Mean Old Goat watches me, and I swear I see a smirk on his face. Like he knows I'm a coin without a cluster. Like he knows that I'll never find my place.

Some Grand Drama

"In an ecosystem, everything is connected," Mr. Farabi declares the next morning. For today's science class, he's taken us into the woods, not far from where they found the branch for that stupid Paulie statue. He's spent the last ten minutes explaining how trees and moss and bugs and birds are all connected. "Each species fits into its habitat like a piece in an elaborate jigsaw puzzle," he tells us. "Disrupt one part, you ruin the whole picture."

He starts telling us about things that are happening all around us, things we can't see. He says that beneath our feet, the roots of some trees are tangled up into a web, and they're sharing water and nutrients back and forth. Other plants aren't cooperating with one another, they're competing, even going so far as to release poisons into the soil.

As he talks, I look at the other kids. After yesterday's fight, I was certain I'd walk into Mags's classroom this morning and find them all glaring at me … or worse, *laughing* at me. But instead, everything was just like it was the day before, and the day before that. Almost as if someone had pushed a reset button—like the way Yumi yelling at Timothy and Thomas gets them to restart their dumb zombie-werewolf game.

Maybe that's how it works in a school this small. Maybe when there aren't enough people to sort into clusters, you have to just keep starting over.

Gabby leans toward me. "It's just like *Megastar*," she whispers. It takes me a second to realize she's referring to what Mr. Farabi is talking about—the way different parts of an ecosystem cooperate or compete. "There are heroes and villains and competitions and alliances."

I smile, partly because she's right, and partly because her whispering to me is proof: I did get some sort of do-over.

As I stand there watching the sunlight filter through the leaves, I can almost feel what Mr. Farabi is describing. It's like I'm surrounded by some grand drama, something that's bigger than me, but also invisible. Something most people never even imagine is going on.

Mr. Farabi is so obsessed with ecosystems, he even finds a way to work them into soccer practice. "A great team is like the ultimate ecosystem," he tells us that afternoon. "Everyone matters! Everyone contributes to something bigger than themselves! If we're going to beat Devlinshire, we're going to need each of you!"

But as far as I can tell, there's no delicate balance with this team, no working together. Which I guess is why it only takes a few minutes before Mr. Farabi's pep talk about ecosystems gets replaced by more frustrated shouts:

"Stop hogging the ball, Diego! Pass to some others, will you?"

"Timothy! Thomas! What are you doing, some kind of robot battle on the field? Get your heads in the game!"

"Fiona, you cannot pick up the ball and hurl it at your teammates every time you feel frustrated!"

Not exactly the ultimate ecosystem. I guess it's a good thing they've got that dumb Paulie statue for good luck. No matter where this game gets played, Mitchell's going to need all the help it can get.

During the third week of September, we come outside at recess and see Mr. Farabi with an unfamiliar woman. She's got bleached hair slicked back in a tight ponytail, and she's wearing a bright blue tracksuit embroidered with a large *D*. Everyone stops dead in their tracks.

Gabby sucks in her breath. "The Devlinshire coach," she murmurs.

Sam nods. "They're deciding where the game will be played."

Fiona makes a low noise, like a growl. Then everyone's

silent for a few minutes, watching as the two coaches pace out distances, pull out a tape measure, discuss their measurements.

"Come on, Paulie...," Diego urges. "Work that magic. I don't want to play on that stupid rich-kid field again this year."

"In the name of Paulie Fink," says Timothy.

"In the name of Paulie Fink," Thomas agrees.

The coaches shake hands. As they walk toward the school building, I hear the Devlinshire coach say, "...regulation... non-standard...my players have been training hard..."

Mr. Farabi's face is dead serious. He doesn't so much as glance our way.

It's only when the coaches are a few yards beyond us that Mr. Farabi turns around. Without saying a word, he flashes us two huge thumbs-up. I've never seen him grin this big. Almost immediately, he turns back around, and he continues nodding along seriously with whatever the Devlinshire coach is saying, as if he hasn't revealed a thing.

But by now the Originals are cheering and pumping their fists in the air. Timothy and Thomas chest bump so hard they both stumble backward, then move straight into a wrestling match.

This doesn't affect me, I think. *I won't even be here. While they're playing Devlinshire on this field, I'll be back home at Mira's party instead.*

Behind Gabby, Diego hollers, "Victory lap!" He starts zooming all over the field, arms high over his head.

"No!" shouts Fiona. She points at the Paulie statue. "Take your lap around Paulie!" Diego nods, then sprints toward it.

Next thing I know, they're all on their way over, hollering things like *Vic-tor-y! See, I told you he's good luck!*

As they begin chanting his name again, Paulie stands mute, that PICK A WINNER shirt flapping in the breeze like the flag of some ridiculous new nation.

FIFTEEN THINGS I WOULD RATHER DO
THAN SET FOOT IN DEVLINSHIRE
A List by Diego Silva

1. Scrub my eyeballs with sand.
2. Get sealed into a giant vat of lime Jell-O for precisely three years.
3. Get bitten by a scorpion.
4. Get bitten by ten thousand scorpions each with the face of Ms. Glebus and the voice of Mickey Mouse.
5. Accidentally call Ms. Glebus "Mom."
6. Walk barefoot on a path sprinkled with Legos.
7. Get tied to a chair and listen to Yumi play the same song on her ukulele for nine years straight.
8. Have arms that are made of spaghetti.
9. Have T. rex arms.
10. Have T. rex arms and a nose that never stops itching.
11. Lick a skunk.
12. Actually eat an entire jar of mayonnaise like I thought Paulie did that day.
13. Admit to Gabby that I've secretly watched every single season of Megastar. Twice.
14. Set fire to my eyeballs.
15. Literally anything, because Devlinshire is the actual worst.

Listen, I'm not gonna lie. It's tough having Devlinshire as a rival. Those Devlinshire kids show up to the game with the best of everything. Professional-quality cleats. Actual coaches, instead of well-intentioned science teachers. Those fancy dry-wick sweatpants with their school logo emblazoned on them. Here at Mitchell, we still don't even have uniforms. We make do with any old green T-shirts.

We've got some decent players, and they've gotten better and better through the years. But something happens to Mitchell kids when they see Devlinshire. They get all psyched out, like they're defeated even before the whistle blows.

And until now, we always had Paulie to deal with, too.

How to describe Paulie's soccer skills, exactly? Paulie would go to kick the ball, and he wouldn't just fail to make contact, he'd kick the air so hard his feet flew out from underneath him. Next thing you knew, he'd be lying on his back like Charlie Brown. Two years ago, I kid you not, Paulie picked up the soccer ball halfway through the game and started dribbling it like a basketball down the middle of the field. Do you know how *hard* it is to bounce a soccer ball across a grass field?

Sometimes I wondered if he was doing it on purpose, like some sort of performance artist. Like instead of actually playing, he was making some commentary about the whole game.

Either way, there were times Paulie seemed like an *unlucky* charm.

So if the Originals wanted to believe that their unlucky charm had been replaced by a lucky one? In the form of that statue they'd built for themselves? I wasn't going to argue, and I sure as heck wasn't going to make them take it down.

Who knows. Between Paulie being gone, and the kids believing in their own good-luck charm, maybe this year we finally had a shot at beating Devlinshire.

Glory and Renown

On the Monday of the final week of September, Mags pulls another index card from Paulie's hat. She holds it up and reads: "*The Search for the Next Great Megastar.*" She thinks for a minute, then heads to the board and writes:

kleos

Then beneath that:

κλέος

And beneath that:

Renown. Glory.
Being remembered.

She turns around. "Greeks believed that immortality was strictly for the gods. So their best hope for any sort of immortality was to accomplish something in this life that would keep people talking after they were gone. *Kleos* is a word that represented their hope that they might be remembered. It's related to the word *kluein*, which means *to hear*. So *kleos* means, quite literally, *what people say about you.*"

She tells us that the opposite of *kleos* is the English word *oblivion*. "That's what happened to most people. For every Plato whom we remember today, there are countless others who lived and died and were forgotten entirely."

Forgotten entirely. The words give me a heavy sort of feeling. Almost like instead of a stone *inside* my chest, there's one sitting on *top* of my chest, so massive it's hard to catch my breath. I guess maybe that's because I've texted Mira about a million times about her sleepover: I asked what time I should get to her house on the twenty-seventh, and if I should plan to eat dinner first since it's a five-hour drive, and my mom needs to know if she has to cancel all her afternoon appointments. I offered to bring donuts from the Donut Lady and if so how many I should bring. I guess maybe my questions are annoying, because Mira didn't reply to any of them.

I raise my hand. "Mags?"

She looks surprised, and I realize this is the first time I've raised my hand at Mitchell. Part of me wants to sit on my hands and shut up, but Mags flashes me the tiniest smile.

"Well, so let's say you're one of those lucky ones who happens to get remembered," I say. "The thing is, it's not even *you* that people are remembering. Not really."

Mags looks like she's trying hard to understand, but even

141

I'm not entirely sure what I want to say. "Like that guy who talked about the cave," I continue. "That Plato guy. I mean, you said he achieved—what do you call it—*kleos*, right?"

She nods. "He sure did."

"And how much do we even know about *him*?"

"Well, considering that he lived two thousand years ago, I'd say we know quite a bit. But keep going."

"I mean...do we know the stuff that made him *real*? Like, I don't know, was he—"

I break off. Something's been nagging at me ever since Henry told me about the kids in his old school, the ones who played keep away with his stuff. Those kids were jerks. I mean, that's obvious. But if Anna Spang were to tell stories about me, I'd probably sound like a jerk, too.

The person she'd describe wouldn't be *me*. Anna never even knew me. She knew only a few random moments out of my whole life. Yet for the rest of her life, she gets to tell whatever stories she wants about me? How is *that* fair?

"It just seems like even when we do remember people, the things we remember aren't enough," I say. "They're... incomplete."

I see Mags watching me carefully, deciding what to say.

"Unless of course you're Paulie Fink," I add. I'm trying to make a joke, but it's possible that something else, some hard edge, comes through. "Then, of course, people remember *everything*."

Yumi nods. "Paulie did have *kleos*," she says.

"Paulie had *major kleos*," says Diego.

Mags smiles. "Actually, he did."

"I wish we could just *hire* a new Paulie, you know?" says Diego. "Just get ourselves a new Paulie who can show up in a chicken suit now and then."

"It could be like Shakespeare," Yumi says. "Some of his plays were about real people, like Julius Caesar and those kings, Henry whatever and Richard whatever. Now those roles get played by different actors, over and over again. Everyone has their own interpretation of the role, but it's always that character they're playing."

Mags starts to say that these characters are great examples of *kleos*, but Gabby interrupts.

"That's what *Megastar* does, too!"

Yumi rolls her eyes. "That's not exactly the same thing, Gabby."

"It's similar, though," Gabby says. "It's different people trying to capture the essence of a Megastar."

"You know, that is sort of what we need," says Fiona. "Like if we can't have the real Paulie, then we'll have to do the next best thing, which is find someone to play the *role* of Paulie. Someone whose official job it is to make school... *memorable*."

"That was my idea," Diego insists. "That's literally what I just said."

Mags tries to steer the conversation back to *kleos*, but she's only a few words in when Gabby leaps out of her seat.

"*OhmahgahIhavethebestideaintheworld!* We *should* have a competition! Just like *Megastar*!"

Everyone looks at her, confused. Gabby fixes her eyes in the distance, moving her hands like she's reading the words off a giant screen. "The Search for the Next Great Paulie Fink!"

Diego repeats after her, thinking it over. "The Next Great Paulie Fink."

"Gabby," says Sam. "That's maybe the best idea anyone's ever had."

"It is." Henry nods. "It's actually a very, very good idea."

"It was my idea," Diego repeats.

"Actually, Diego, it was *my* idea," says Fiona.

"Well, I'm the one who talked about actors playing Shakespeare roles," argues Yumi, "so it was kind of my—"

"It was Gabby's idea!" I yell.

Henry leans forward. He blinks hard. "But Gabby," he says, "how would it work?"

Plot Twist

At recess, we sit beneath the Paulie statue. Gabby explains the basic premise behind all reality shows, as if we don't already know: Regular people compete for some title by participating in challenges. After each challenge, one person gets eliminated. Eventually, there is only one person left, and that person is declared the winner.

"Gabby, we *know* how reality shows work," says Diego. "The question is how is *this* one going to work? Like, what are we going to do for the challenges?"

"Okay, let me think for a minute," says Gabby. "So, *Megastar* challenges test for the things that celebrities and performers have to do well. Singing. Dancing. Connecting with an audience. Getting people to talk about them."

Next to her, Fiona scribbles notes on a scrap of paper. "*Test for specific traits,*" she murmurs as her pen flies across the page.

"But in this case," Gabby continues, "we'd be testing for *Paulie's* characteristics, so that means we need to..." She frowns.

145

I'd like to hear what she comes up with, actually. Even with all those stories they tell about him, Paulie still doesn't seem like a real person to me. In my mind, he's part scarecrow and part fictional superhero who fights the Gleeb while wearing a chicken suit, like in those stories I tell Fuzzy.

Besides, how would a competition like this even work? You can't replace *an entire human being*.

"Well." Gabby waves her hand. "We can figure out the challenges later. Let's talk about prizes. There's usually a big prize at the end, like a recording contract."

Big prize, Fiona writes. Then she looks up. "Maybe we could get that old rock star from Devlinshire to hook up the winner with a recording contract?"

"No way," says Diego. "We're not asking anyone from Devlinshire for anything."

"Besides," says Yumi, "even if that weren't absurd, we need a prize that fits *Paulie*."

Everyone's quiet for a few seconds.

"*Kleos*," suggests Henry. "I mean, the winner will get *kleos*, right?"

"Not enough," says Fiona. "If we're going to pick a winner, we need to give them—"

"That's it!" says Diego. He looks around at us. "*Pick a winner*? Get it?"

"The T-shirt!" shouts Timothy.

"Good," says Fiona. She writes down: *Winner gets the good-luck T-shirt. And also kleos.*

"Also, there needs to be at least one judge," Gabby says. "Someone who makes the final decision about who gets eliminated after every challenge. It's usually best if the judge is strict. Maybe even a little *mean*."

"Glebus!" exclaims Lydia, but Willow shakes her head.

"No way," she says. "Glebus won't do it."

"Glebus will shut down the competition in a heartbeat if she finds out about it," Sam agrees.

"Gabby, I still don't get it," Yumi says. "Why do you keep watching? Episode after episode, season after season? It's all the same thing: challenges, elimination, ceremony, end. Repeat. How is it not totally boring?"

"Well…" Gabby thinks for a minute. "It's about the people, you know? The participants are all different, and they're together *all the time*, so they start getting on each other's nerves. After a while, they start fighting with each other, and—"

"Then this place is *already* a reality show," I joke.

Fiona leaps up. "You!" She points at me. At first I think she's yelling at me, the way she did on Zucchini Day. But instead of looking angry, she's smiling. "*You* have to do it!"

Wait. What?

"*You* have to be the judge!" she insists.

I stare at her. She's standing there in a red pantsuit, her too-long pants caked with mud. Her nostrils are flaring and her face is flushed. She looks like some tiny-but-fierce colorful bird, ready to move in for a kill.

147

"Yeah!" Diego nods. "You should be in charge, Caitlyn."

No. No way.

"It's perfect!" Fiona says again. "You're always cranky, and you keep talking about how we don't know some stupid rules. Now you can write rules for us. Like, officially."

"Actually, this makes a lot of sense," Gabby says.

"But I never met Paulie," I say.

"Doesn't matter!" says Fiona, at the same time that Diego says, "Who cares?"

Henry's watching me carefully. "It's true you haven't met him," he says. "But that means you can be impartial. You should do it."

So then I turn to Yumi, but she's nodding, too. "I think you have to," she says.

I try to protest. I do. But then everyone starts chanting my name, and well...I guess you already know how that turns out.

Interview: Henry

CAITLYN:

I was surprised that you wanted to do the competition, Henry. It seemed like a silly thing, and you're always so serious. Like all those fact books you're so obsessed with.

HENRY:

When we first moved here, I was obsessed with this one book: *The Facts You Need to Survive in the Wild*. It was filled with information like *Don't go into the woods in hunting season without wearing orange. If you meet a black bear in the woods, never run; bears run faster than you can. Raccoons are nocturnal, so if you see one during daylight hours, stay away; chances are good it's rabid*. Most of this stuff you wind up learning just by living here for a while.

But there was one fact this book didn't mention: *Never stand too close to a river after a storm*. Turns out, soggy riverbanks sometimes give way. I learned that the hard way. About six months after I got here, I was standing at the side of Miller's Creek after it rained, and the ground beneath my feet just...gave way. I slipped into the water, washed up about a hundred yards downstream. I had nightmares for the next year, but even so, I was lucky. Some people don't make it out of the river at all.

CAITLYN:

Yikes!

HENRY:

Yeah. Well, that's how it felt to me when Paulie didn't come back. Like he'd slipped away without us even realizing it... and maybe all of us were on shakier ground than we'd realized. This competition felt like a chance to, I don't know, pull Paulie back to us. And even if it couldn't do that, at least we'd all be together if we fell in after him.

THE SEARCH FOR
THE NEXT GREAT
PAULIE FINK

Boxed into a Corner

I tell my classmates that I need a little time to think about the competition. I don't really have any idea who Paulie is, let alone how to create challenges that will test for his traits. I ask if he ever had an online account where he would have posted photos.

They just look at one another and laugh. Yumi explains that the only profile they ever saw him create was for something called BoxMan. They try to describe it to me, but they keep bursting into hysterics.

"You had to be there, I guess," Fiona says.

At home that night, I search online for BoxMan. I find it, but...I don't *get* it. It's just a bunch of pictures of a kid with a cardboard box on his head. I click on a photo of Box-Man holding up some matches. The caption: *Boxing match*.

I click on the next one. BoxMan sitting under a tree, resting his box-chin against his human hands. The caption: *Thinking outside the box*.

I click again. There's BoxMan leaning against a brick

wall, exactly at the point where it meets another brick wall: *Boxed into a corner*.

There's even one of him sitting in Glebus's office. He must have snuck in to take it, because she's nowhere to be seen. But he's standing next to her desk, box-head hanging low like he's getting scolded. *Penalty box*, it says.

Seriously? *This* is what made them laugh so hard?

No, I definitely don't get it: Why they're chanting *In the name of Paulie Fink*, or why they built a statue in his honor, or why they feel they need another Paulie. I mean, if I'd met this kid at my old school, we'd probably all have treated him the way we treated Anna Spang.

How am I supposed to run this thing? I kind of feel like BoxMan myself: I've boxed myself into a corner.

Then I ask them to tell me all the stories they remember.

Interview: Diego

I'll tell you something I'll bet you didn't know about Paulie:
The dude was amazing with Minis. He had, like, a cult
following with little kids.

Like, there was this one time, last spring, when Mr. Farabi
announced that the sixth grade was going to be leading a
game of team tag, which is basically a giant game of hide-and-
seek, with kindergarten, first, and second grades. Now, let's
face it: Minis are terrible at team tag. They're so short they
can barely run, which makes them ridiculously easy to tag.

But Paulie raised his hand and said, "I'll be on a team
with the Minis."

"That's what I'm saying," Mr. Farabi said. "You all will.
Each of you will take two or three Minis, and—"

And Paulie was like, "No, Mr. Farabi. I'll take them all."

We were like, *Wha—?* Because Paulie was lousy when it
came to sports. This wasn't even going to be a contest.

Mr. Farabi shrugged, and Paulie called the Minis in for
a huddle. Then they all ran off to hide while the rest of us
counted.

Let me tell you: Minis are officially the worst hiders on
earth. Some were peeking out from behind trees whose trunks
were narrower than they were. Others were just curled up
on the ground covering their eyes. A few Minis were hiding
behind *those* Minis. These kids were never going to make it
to base.

We Originals had only taken a few steps when we heard something strange. Almost like a siren: *"Whoop-whoop-whoop-WEEE! Whoop-whoop-whoop-WEEE!"* Paulie was standing there with his hands cupped around his mouth. The second he made the noise, they all came running. Tons of Minis. They ran toward base at exactly the same time, far too many for us to catch.

I remember Yumi was like, "What's happening?" as eight gajillion Minis barreled past her, each of them touching base safely.

Meanwhile Fiona was laughing her head off, shouting, "This is a complete and total Mini-geddon!"

And like pretty much everything interesting that happened here, it was all because of Paulie Fink. Like the banana-peel fiasco...Ask Mr. Farabi to tell you about *that*!

Interview: Mr. Farabi

Okay, I fully admit that Paulie's banana-peel fiasco was my fault.

Last year, the sixth-grade students had to do a research project. They got to pick whatever topic they wanted, as long as they showed an understanding of how scientific research works.

For the most part, they came up with good proposals. Diego did a report on the giant squid, and Gabby did a project on flesh-eating bacteria. Yumi decided to study the effect that different types of music have on her classmates' ability to play a memory game.

But Paulie? He had trouble coming up with a project. He had no trouble brainstorming, mind you—that kid was an idea machine. They just weren't exactly what you'd call practical.

Paulie's first idea was clever, but also incredibly creepy and quite literally impossible. Apparently there's a jar in a museum holding three of Galileo's fingers and one of his teeth. And Einstein's eyes are sitting in a safety deposit box in New York City. And it's possible Mozart's skull is held by a foundation in Austria. Paulie proposed collecting all these body parts and then inventing a supergenius.

Terrific idea for a story. But not the greatest science project. First of all, even if he *could* build a genius Franken-monster from scraps of dead guys all over the world, it was highly unlikely he could get it done in four weeks.

"Just give me an idea you can execute, okay?" I said. "Something simple."

A week later, Paulie handed me a piece of paper with a new project idea. Hold on, I've got it around here somewhere...

...Okay, here it is: *The effect of decomposition on the exocarp of* Musa acuminata, *a tropical herbaceous flowering plant, and the implications for human peregrination.*

Listen to this summary he wrote for me:

Musa acuminata is a tropical herbaceous flowering plant which has a long history of uses in human societies. It's been cultivated since at least 5000 BCE. Today, many societies derive nutrition from it, and its outer casing, which is usually discarded, can be used to feed livestock and aid in composting efforts. My project will involve observing the decomposition of these casings and how easily the casings can be integrated into the human environment at different points in the decomposition process.

I'll be honest, Caitlyn: I was kind of skimming. Half the kids in school were planning projects, and I was also doing my regular teaching, and coaching. So when I read Paulie's abstract, I assumed Paulie's parents had a dead houseplant or something, and he was trying to figure out how to turn it into an experiment.

Listen, if I could go back in time, I'd do it differently.

I'd look up *Musa acuminata*. And I'd discover that this happens to be the Latin name for banana. Then I'd pay more attention to that word *exocarp*, which means the outer layer of a plant's fruit. Another way of saying this: peel.

And *peregrination*: walking.

Which means you can interpret his proposal like this:

The effect of rotting on the peel of the banana…on humans walking.

Or, put even more simply:

I'm going to put rotting banana peel on the floor, and see if I can make people slip.

Did Paulie put one over on me? Yeah. He sure did. Like I say, the kid was an evil genius.

Interview: Diego and Fiona

DIEGO:

Paulie ate bananas every day for weeks. Before long, he had dozens of peels, each individually sealed in a plastic bag. And let me tell you something, Caitlyn: Banana peels get nasty after a few weeks.

FIONA:

They turn black, and then get liquidy, and then they start to bubble.

DIEGO:

He hid the banana bags in various spots all over school. It didn't take long before the fruit flies showed up. At first there were just a few. Annoying, you know? But within a week, it was an infestation.

FIONA:

Fruit flies were everywhere. All over the hallways, in every classroom...Teachers had to keep interrupting their lessons to swat at them.

DIEGO:

You'd step in the building and you'd just be swarmed.

FIONA:

And no one knew why! No one but Paulie!

DIEGO:

Finally Glebus made us clean everything out. Closets. Gym bags. The whole school. That's when she figured out what was going on.

FIONA:

They had to— [*Cannot continue, because she's laughing so hard*]

DIEGO:

They had to— [*Also cannot continue, also because he's laughing so hard*]

FIONA:

Fumigate! They had to *fumigate* the whole school!

[*Indistinct laughter, goes on for about three full minutes before recording ends*]

Interview: Gabby and Yumi

GABBY:

Oh boy, was Glebus ever furious about the fruit flies. Mags, on the other hand, just laughed. She told Paulie that he was a Shakespearean Fool.

YUMI:

Actually, Gabby, I believe what she said was, "You are a character out of literature, Paulie Fink. You are an archetype. You are a Shakespearean Fool."

GABBY:

Right, but most of us only cared about the fool part. Because it's not every day that you hear a teacher call a kid a fool.

YUMI:

Then she explained to everyone—everyone *else*, that is, because I already knew it—that Shakespearean Fools aren't fools at all: They're actually some of the wisest people around. They misbehave as a way of poking fun at powerful people. I remember Mags said, "To mock the arrogant, to outwit the vain." I remember her exact phrasing, because I wrote a song by this title. I could play it now if you want to hear—

GABBY:

And I was like, "Oooh, a Shakespearean Fool is just another way of saying Disruptor!" I was thinking about what Shakespeare would have thought about Jadelicious, but Mags started talking all about how Shakespearean Fools are really there to drop truth bombs about society. She started getting really excited about the fact that she was connecting him with this long tradition, and after she'd gone on forever, Paulie looked up at her. I remember he blinked a couple of times, and was like, "Wait. Are you talking to me?"

YUMI:

None of us could tell if he was playing the fool in the middle of the conversation about playing the fool, or if he just honestly wasn't paying any attention.

GABBY:

The next week? Paulie showed up and spent the whole day talking like a character from Shakespeare. I swear, he must have spent the whole weekend reading Shakespeare, because he was all, "Good greetings, my lady, pray tell how dost thou fare on this glorious morn!" And, "How, now, good sir! Methinks 'tis a morning of good cheer." Which were both just fancy ways of saying hello.

YUMI:

I remember him saying to one teacher something like, "I do beseech that thou wilt forgo the accursed work of the pencil to be done by the hearth," which was his way of asking for us not to get any homework.

GABBY:
And then when Glebus yelled at him for running too fast in the hallway, he turned around, lifted one finger in the air, and declared, "I desire that we be better strangers."

And she was all, "Huh?"

YUMI:
The next morning Paulie was back to his normal self, talking like any other kid, like the whole Shakespeare episode never even happened.

Say It Like You Mean It

I spend the final week of September collecting Paulie stories. Each recess, I interview someone about Paulie and record their answers for the official record. I tell the Originals that interviews will help me design the right challenges. But it doesn't take long to discover that I actually kind of like interviewing. As soon as I press record, I'm in charge. I get to ask the questions, steer the conversation however I want. Whatever I ask, they answer. The stories are funny, too...and they're great material for entertaining Fuzzy. Best of all, the interviewing has distracted me from obsessing about Mira's sleepover.

What the interviews don't do, though, is give me any clear ideas for the competition.

At night, I double up on *Megastar* episodes, but Gabby's right: All those challenges are about performing. They don't relate at all to the legend of Paulie Fink.

After a few days, the Originals grow impatient with me.

"We could do a giant game of zombie vs. werewolf," suggests Timothy as we head down to feed the goats.

"Or you could make us run around or something," Diego offers. "Like the Olympics."

Fiona throws up her hands, exasperated. "What do zombies or running around have to do with *Paulie*, you blockheads?"

"Just think about the Paulie stories you've heard," Gabby whispers to me.

"Don't worry," I tell them, hoping I'll sound in control. "We'll start the competition soon enough. Just a few more interviews, okay?"

"But *when*?" asks Fiona. "When can we start? I want to start now!"

"Friday," I finally snap. "I'll announce your first challenge on Friday afternoon, okay? September 29. Soccer practice."

But by soccer practice on Friday afternoon, I still don't have any great ideas. I mean, it's not like there's some manual I can get: *The Beginners' Guide to Running Your Own Reality Show in Order to Replace a Middle School Kid You've Never Met!*

They surround me after practice, waiting to hear their challenge. I stare out toward the mountains, now blazing with autumn colors, my mind racing. I could make it a sandwich-eating competition, I guess, but that seems dumb. Didn't Paulie do something with glitter? But what's a competition I could do with glitter? There was that whole "I come from the stars" thing… and the chicken suit, and that time he talked like…

166

"Shakespeare!" I burst out. "Your first challenge is a Shakespearean one."

"*What* is this challenge?" asks Diego. "We have to read Shakespeare?"

"I declare Monday Talk Like Shakespeare Day," I say.

The twins shake their heads, kick at the dirt. Fiona wrinkles her nose like she smells something terrible.

Yumi clears her throat. "Caitlyn," she says. "I know *all* about Shakespeare. But I'm not sure everyone here is…uh, quite so familiar with the work of the Bard."

Fiona makes a face and imitates Yumi. "I'm not sure everyone's quite so *familiar* with the work of *the Bard*."

"What Yumi's trying to say," says Diego, "is that we thought we were going to do real challenges. Like running and stuff. Like in the Olympics or whatever."

"That's *not* actually what I was trying to say, Diego," Yumi says.

"This challenge stinks!" shouts Timothy, and then they all join in.

"*This challenge stinks! This challenge stinks! This challenge stinks!*"

Look, it's not like I think it's a *good* idea. It just happens to be my only idea.

"Shakespeare," I say, like I mean it.

Swallowed by the Night

That night, Mom and I are watching *Megastar* when my phone buzzes. It's a video call from Mira. "She probably wants me to help her plan the sleepover," I say. I rush into my bedroom and close the door.

When I answer, I'm surprised to see not just Mira's face, but a whole bunch of my old friends, too. "Hey!" they all say at the same time.

"Oh...hi!" I hate how eager I sound.

All my friends from last year are there. There are also a couple of girls I recognize but haven't really hung out with. "Wow," I say. "What's going on?"

Mira draws the screen closer. "It's my party," she says. "We had to move the date forward because Gigi's going to be out of town on the twenty-seventh. If we didn't do it this weekend, we weren't going to get another chance until almost Thanksgiving!"

Wait. This can't be the party. I'm supposed to be at the party.

It's happening without me, because somebody named Gigi's going to be out of town.

"But who's Gigi?"

"She's new this year, from Ohio," Mira says. "I can't believe you don't know each other. That's so weird." She moves the camera, so now I see an unfamiliar dark-haired girl. She waves, so I do, too.

Then Mira's back, but only for a moment. "Hold on," Mira says, turning away. Now I'm looking at a close-up of her hairline and ear. "You told Jeremy we'd be here?" she asks someone.

Then to me: "OMG, Jeremy Newby and his buddies want to crash the party."

I laugh, but nothing feels funny.

"Here, say hi to everyone," says Mira. The screen moves from one kid to another. Mostly what I see is a fuzzy swirl of movement. I can make out familiar details—a pair of denim-covered knees, Mira's family portrait, framed and matted in white, on the wall. A different friend's eyebrows. Another's lips, half-open in laughter. The images are pixelated. They freeze and unfreeze.

Everyone says pretty much the same thing. *How are you? How's Vermont? Is it pretty there?* Between questions, they turn to each other and say things like, *No, not that one. I hate that movie. Wait, pause that!* Then they return to me. *Wait, so how's school? My mom says Vermont is really pretty. You meet any cute lumberjacks yet?*

I don't know how to describe how I am, or how Vermont is. I don't know how to describe what it feels like to look up and be surrounded by mountains that don't seem

169

to offer you any way out, or in. Or how those first days at school made me feel like I'd dived all the way to the bottom of a swimming pool: panicky and squeezed too tight. And I definitely wouldn't be able to describe how much I've been thinking about Anna lately, let alone why.

I smile and say things like, *I think this state has more cows than people.* I'm pretty sure that's not true—it's one of those things that people treat like a fact, but it isn't.

Yeah, it's gorgeous here. The views are, like, incredible.

There's a rock star who lives near me. I'm blanking on his name but he's, like, really famous.

I got picked to run a competition. It's hard to describe, but the other kids voted for me, so that's cool.

But nobody seems especially impressed or interested, and before long, Mira's back. "Hey, again," she says.

"So…uh…oh, how's Anna Spang?" I ask. I'm trying to make my voice sound casual, the way it always did when we talked about her.

"Wait, don't text him yet!" Mira says, not to me. Then she turns back to me. "Who? Oh, Anna? Pathetic, as usual, I guess. I don't really see her this year." Then there's another blurry swirl, as she shouts, "What did he write? Hold on, I'm coming!"

When I say I have to go, she doesn't object. I end the call while she's still waving good-bye, mostly because I want to be the one to hang up first.

Then I'm alone, and everything seems even quieter than it did before.

When I walk out to the kitchen, Mom smiles. "How's Mira? Getting excited?"

I tell my mom that the party had to be moved up, that it's happening now. I say it like it's no big deal, but Mom winces.

"It's fine," I say. "Turns out there's a soccer game I'm supposed to play in that day anyway, so I probably wouldn't have been able to go."

I walk outside, onto the tiny porch that overlooks our backyard. It's a moonless night, and the dark is so thick it's almost like a monster that could swallow you. *Maybe that's what happened to Paulie Fink,* I think. *Maybe he just got swallowed up by the night.*

After a while, Mom comes out. She wraps a blanket around me and rubs my shoulders. When I look up, the sky is filled with a million or so stars.

Until now, I've been telling myself that Vermont's just the place where I'm living. For now. I've believed that my home, my real one, was somewhere else.

But now I know for sure: The place I'd been thinking of as home isn't. Not anymore.

When I show up to school on Monday, the twins are standing outside Mags's classroom, with big dopey grins on their faces. They look like they're up to something.

"Uh . . . hey guys," I say.

Both open their sweatshirts at the same time. Beneath, they've got matching green T-shirts, with letters drawn on them in thick black marker.

I look a little closer. Thomas's says, NOT 2B. Timothy's says 2B. I can tell they're waiting for a reaction.

I don't get it, though. NOT 2B? 2B? What does that even...?

"Wait," says Timothy. Then they switch places. Now 2B comes first.

"To be or not to be," I say, finally understanding. That's one of William Shakespeare's most famous lines of all time—*To be or not to be. That is the question.*

The Shakespeare challenge. After that call from Mira, I'd forgotten all about the Paulie competition, actually.

But when I step into the classroom, it's clear that I'm the only one who forgot.

No, I had not been psyched about the whole Shakespeare challenge. But it wasn't like I was going to let someone else win.

So here's what I did: I went home and searched online for *How to talk like Shakespeare*. I figured I'd find a few suggestions—change *you* to *thou*, add *eth* after every verb, which would make ordinary sentences come out sounding like *I brusheth mine teeth*, or *Some days, I wisheth to smacketh thou in the back of thine head, Sir Diego*.

Instead, my search turned up something else entirely.

I always thought Shakespeare was stuffy—the sort of thing that was only for, like, that old Oxthorpe guy who glares at us from that portrait in the humanities classroom. But it turns out Shakespeare is all about insults! There are, like, so many put-downs in his plays! There are even a bunch of websites entirely dedicated to his best burns. Some were so great I can't believe I never thought of them myself. Like:

I am sick when I do look on thee. That's Shakespeare for *Dude, you make me want to throw up.*

Would thou wouldst burst! That means, *If I could, I would make you explode into eight jillion pieces.*

The rankest compound of villainous smell that ever offended nostril! Just a fancy way of saying *You stink.*

There were so many great ones: *I scorn you, scurvy companion! He hath not so much brain as earwax. You viperous worm that gnaws the bowels!* And my favorite, because it's so simple: *You ruinous butt.* I imagined myself glaring at Diego and saying that: *Diego, you ruinous butt.*

I tried to memorize them, but there were too many, plus most of them fell out of my brain as soon as I read them. So I wrote a few down on my arm. Then I added a few more. By the time I fell asleep, I was covered with marker right up to my shoulders, and my head was swimming with phrases like *shard-borne beetle*, and *bolting hutch of beastliness*, and *prince of fiends*, and *plague-sore*, and *puke-stocking*, and I didn't know what half those words meant, but I didn't even care, because, hello, who ever thought to call someone a *puke-stocking*?!

I was totally going to win this competition. I just knew it.

As it turned out, though, I wasn't the only one who discovered that site.

The Shakespeare Challenge

Fiona springs out of her seat as soon as I walk into Mags's class. "Good dawning to you!" she shouts, way too loudly. I notice her arms are covered in scribbles.

Diego has markings all over his arm, too. He steps directly in front of Fiona. "How fares Caitlyn?" he asks.

I glance around the room. Yumi's wearing a velvet cap with a giant feather sticking out of it, like something that Shakespeare himself might have worn back in the day. Her T-shirt says KEEP CALM AND READ THE BARD. Sam and Willow and Lydia are wearing their usual pom-pom headbands, but they're also wearing white T-shirts with different phrases all over them:

IN A PICKLE

DEAD AS A DOORNAIL

BREAK THE ICE

CHARMED LIFE

ALL THAT GLISTERS ISN'T GOLD

"What's all this?" I ask them.

"Cheat sheets, kind of." Willow grins, pointing to the words. "Shakespeare invented these. Inventeth them. Hast inventeth them?"

Sam nods, and adds, "Isn't that so cool? I mean, 'tisn't it?"

Everyone's pretty quiet at first, barely speaking at all—like they know they're being judged and are afraid of getting the words wrong. But as we walk down the path toward the goats, Diego and Fiona start trading insults.

"You crusty botch of nature," Fiona reads from her elbow.

Diego checks his wrist. "You…Banbury cheese!" he replies.

"Heedless jolthead!"

"Thorny hedgehog!"

"Dull and muddy-mottled rascal!"

"Minion of the moon!"

"I don't even know what that means, you…you…popinjay!"

Yumi turns to me. "This is *so* Shakespeare," she says. I have no idea if she's being sarcastic, but then she tells me that back in Shakespeare's time, audiences always got really rowdy. "They'd cheer for the insults, boo the villains, throw rotten fruit at the actors onstage. Sometimes fights broke out in the middle of the performance. It was chaos!"

By the time they reach the goat pen, Fiona and Diego are ready to fight about anything. "'Tis my turn," Diego tells Fiona, grabbing the feed bucket.

"'Twas yours most recently," she says. She's smiling, but

her teeth are gritted. She yanks the bucket toward herself. "'Tis *mine*."

"You're a fusty nut with no kernel!"

"No, you're the fusty nut!" Fiona screams. She puts both hands on the bucket and pulls as hard as she can. Diego lets go, which sends her flying backward. Goat feed spills everywhere. She scrambles to her feet, picks up a handful of food, and hurls it at him. He grabs his own handful and tosses it at her. "You're a bladder!" Fiona shouts.

Timothy and Thomas get in on the action. "'Tis a food fight!" They scoop up pellets and run around throwing them at everyone.

"Yumi's a fusty nut!" Timothy shouts, tossing pellets at her. "Sam's a fusty nut! Gabby's a fusty nut!" They each respond by grabbing and throwing pellets of their own.

The twins start flicking their sweatshirts at each other like wet towels. "Hellhound!" Timothy taunts his brother. "Mildewed ear! Quintessence of dust!"

Thomas lashes back. "Quintessence of dust, my butt! Shakespeare vs. Shakespeare is on!"

As they begin wrestling, I look around. Sam's chasing Lydia, who's chasing Willow. Yumi's leaping all over, sprinkling pellets like they're flower petals. That feathered cap on her head keeps slipping down over her eyes, but it barely seems to bother her. By now, Fiona's snapped off a honeysuckle branch and is twirling it above her head in circles. "I'll

177

whip thee with a rod!" she's shouting at anyone who comes near her. Meanwhile, Gabby's just smiling through the whole scene, sometimes applauding like she's an audience member appreciating one of Shakespeare's plays.

Only Henry's not fighting. He steps into place next to me and surveys the scene. "Some are born great," he says very seriously. "Some achieve greatness, and some have greatness thrust upon them. And some..." He waves his arm toward the chaos, and doesn't finish.

It's all so unexpected. Flying goat feed. Shakespeare's words mixing with the bleating of the goats. Timothy and Thomas in the middle of their Shakespeare vs. Shakespeare brawl. Fiona in her suit, wielding a honeysuckle branch like a lasso. And Henry acting like a wise old man.

I burst out laughing, and that's the thing that surprises me most of all. The sound of my own laughter. I can't remember the last time I laughed.

But then I stop, just as fast as I started. Because Mr. Farabi is striding toward us, and he's not alone. Glebus is right behind him, and she arrives just as Yumi—eyes covered by that feathered cap—releases another sprinkle of pellets.

They catch Glebus right in the eye.

Interview: Gabby

GABBY:

Of course Glebus screamed at us, but what I remember most about the Shakespeare challenge is how in just over a month, you'd gone from not wanting to speak to any of us to running an entire competition.

You reminded me of a *Megastar* contestant from season four, Maryellen Papademiera, from Indiana. She was pretty quiet, so everybody assumed that Maryellen would be on the first bus back to the Midwest. Except guess what? It turns out that quiet little Maryellen had ambition. Before long, she'd renamed herself Spicy G and was hanging out with Jadelicious at the poshest nightclubs.

I'd planned to spend my weekend learning to speak Shakespeare, but I started the weekend by watching just a few minutes of the one where Maryellen becomes Spicy G. Then a few minutes led to a few more minutes, and I sort of lost track of time.

Before I knew it, it was Sunday night, and my grandma was hollering at me that it was time to "turn off *Megastar* and go to bed, right this very second." I never even looked up any Shakespeare words.

So my plan for that first competition was to be like Maryellen before she became Spicy G: I'd stay quiet, slip through to the next round.

CAITLYN:

But I noticed how quiet you were. And as we walked out of Glebus's office after all her yelling, I told you to say something Shakespearean, and you were all, "Mmm?"

GABBY:

I guess I'm not so great at being put on the spot, because my mind just sort of went blank. I tried to remember what Diego and Fiona had shouted, or what the twins had called each other, or *anything* Paulie had said on the day he talked like Shakespeare, but I just froze. You were looking at me like you hoped I *could* say something that sounded like Macbeth or whatever. But all I could think of was Maryellen and something she'd said: "People assume they know everything there is to know about me. But when they look at me, all they're seeing is their own darn selves."

I don't know. That seemed sort of profound, and Shakespeare's supposed to be profound, so I said to you, "All people see is their own darneth selves."

You shook your head sort of sadly. That's how I knew it was over for me.

Victory Lap

By the time we leave Glebus's office after the Shakespeare fiasco, it's already recess. Diego bursts out of the building and shouts, "That was awesome!"

No one seems upset at all that we just got hollered at. In Glebus's office, they looked at the floor, all shame-faced. But now that we're outside, they're laughing and high-fiving.

"Caitlyn!" shouts Sam. "You just started the Mitchell School's first-ever food fight!"

"It wasn't just any food fight, it was a goat-food fight," adds Willow. "Which is like eight thousand times better than a regular-food fight!"

Even Henry is looking happier than I've ever seen him. "That was pretty cool, Caitlyn," he says.

Diego nods. "It was classic Paulie Fink."

"While also being classic Shakespeare," Yumi agrees.

"Yeah," says Gabby, "take a bow, Caitlyn!"

Timothy and Thomas start chanting, "*Take a bow!*"

But Diego shakes his head. "Don't just take a *bow*," he says. "Take a victory lap! Once around the playground!"

The twins switch their chanting from *"Take a bow!"* to *"Vic-tory-lap! Vic-tory lap! Vic-tory lap!"*

"I didn't do anything," I say. "I just—"

"Take the lap," Diego insists. *"Always* take the victory lap."

I take a few tentative steps, and everyone explodes into cheers. A few steps in, Fiona leaps in front of me. "Hold up! Stop!"

She peels off her blazer. "Here. Take this."

It's the one she wore on the second day of school: turquoise, and missing some buttons. The collar is ringed with dirt. "Come on, Caitlyn," she says. "You deserve the power of the blazer."

"Uh...thanks, but...," I begin, trying to figure a way out of this, but everyone's watching, and Fiona looks like she's handing me the greatest gift on the planet. "Oh, okay." I slip my arms through the jacket. The arms are too short. I feel ridiculous, but everyone's applauding, so I just start running. The others jog alongside me, chanting my name for the second time in two days.

"Cait-lyn! Cait-lyn! Cait-lyn!"

Gabby dashes onto the playground and finds Fuzzy at the swings. The two of them run toward me, and a bunch of other Minis follow. Fuzzy and I take the rest of the lap together, hand in hand, and she beams at me like I'm some sort of superhero. A mass of other kids, from lots of different grades, trail behind. Most of them don't know why they're chanting my name, but they also don't seem to care. They chant anyway.

When the lap is over, Gabby looks at me seriously. "Caitlyn," she says. "Can you come to my house after school tomorrow? You and I have some serious work to do."

The Megastar Creed, aka All the Things I Know
About Life from Watching Reality Television
A List by Gabby

1. You can never predict how contestants will turn out.
Very few people will be the same in the final episode as they
were in the first. If they stick around long enough, they'll
change.

2. Every show has heroes and villains. At the start of
the season, it's hard to tell the difference. Sometimes it
takes you all the way to the end of the season to know
for sure.

3. Know who you are. The audience can *always* tell the
difference between an authentic Megastar and an imitation.

4. Go for it! Throw yourself in headfirst. Be fearless. Most
of all, make sure *you're* having fun. What's the point of being
there if you're not?

5. The honor matters more than any prize. You won't
believe the things people do when their pride is at stake.
Everybody wants *kleos*.

6. There's no guarantee you'll win. Do your best, but know
this: Sometimes the good guys lose.

Interview: Henry

CAITLYN:

Tell me about how you first got the bad news.

HENRY:

It took me longer to figure out than it probably should have. My dad's on the town council, and I saw the way he came home from his meetings, with stacks of papers. They were spreadsheets, some sort of budgets, but to me they were nothing but pages with numbers. After a while I noticed that lots of the numbers were red. Red is bad on budgets, but I still didn't understand.

Even when I saw the articles lying around the house— they had headlines like RURAL SCHOOLS CAUGHT IN DEATH SPIRAL or CLASS DISMISSED FOREVER: RURAL SCHOOLS FACE CLOSURES—I still didn't get it. I mean, I saw those words: *Death Spiral. Forever.* But I didn't know I should be concerned.

Then early in the summer Dad drove home from a meeting and sat in the driveway for a long time. When he finally came through the door, the rims of his eyes were all red. And the next day, he left an email open. It said: *It's time we face the facts; without something drastic, Mitchell cannot afford to keep its school open.*

My dad walked in at that point, saw me looking. "You weren't supposed to see that," was all he said.

And that's when the ground beneath my feet gave way.

What Would Jadelicious Do?

Gabby's house smells of soup, wet dog, and medicine, but Gabby's grandmother looks so happy to see us I barely get a chance to notice. She hugs me like I've known her forever.

Next to us, Gabby scoops up a tiny wire-haired dog. "C'mere, Buster," she says. She kisses him as he wriggles in her arms. "You mean old beast, you. You fierce and terrible creature."

"You look just like your mama," Gabby's grandmother tells me. I wonder how she knows that. But before I have a chance to ask, Gabby's pulling me down the hallway to plan.

Everything in Gabby's room is some shade of purple: carpet, pillows, walls. And Jadelicious's face is everywhere— pages ripped from magazines, then taped to walls.

Gabby jams something into my hands: THE MEGASTAR CREED. "Memorize this, okay?" Then she hops up onto her bed and sits cross-legged on a rumpled lavender comforter. "Also, you're going to need a speech."

"A speech?"

"Yeah. A great one. Technically, you should have done

this *before* announcing the first competition. But you hadn't really found your footing yet."

"I've never made a speech."

"This one's easy. You just have to lay down the rules of the competition. Tell them what you're looking for. Remind them that you're in charge. You need to scare the contestants, you know? Let 'em know who's boss."

I guess she sees me looking doubtful, because she says, "Oh, come on, you can do it. You're tough! You're from *New York City*."

For a second, I'm confused. Then I remember: That's the white lie I told her on the first day of school. Already, that feels like a hundred years ago.

"And if you get stuck," Gabby continues, "just ask yourself one question: *What would Jadelicious do?*"

I peer at one of the images on the wall. Jadelicious is hip-jutting on a red carpet in front of a sea of photographers. She looks like she's daring them to get a bad photo. In another, fans are pressed up against the front of a stage, with rays of purple and magenta lights beaming down on Jadelicious from every direction.

"She looks like she doesn't care what anybody thinks," I say. "I wish I knew how to do that."

"To not care, or to *look* like you don't care?"

Again, I get a flash of that old kickball game, the one where I panicked. "Both," I say.

"Hold on," she says. "I know what you need." She jumps

up, opens her desk drawer, and rummages through a million pieces of paper: old drawings, greeting cards, math homework, crumpled essays.

"Aha!" She pulls out a magazine article. "Read from here," she says, pointing to a paragraph about halfway down the page. I read aloud:

> *Jadelicious, who has legally changed her name to erase any distinction between her stage persona and her former self, admits that she didn't always feel so confident being in the public eye.*
>
> *"What I realized early on," says the Megastar, whose most recent music video has already been viewed nearly three million times, "is that you can't wait for others to see you as a star. You have to believe you're a Megastar, no matter what others think. That goes for everything in life: What do you want? Who do you hope to be? Nobody's going to give you a permission slip. So just strike your pose and hold it."*

Gabby nods. "I think what she's saying is *Fake it till you make it*, don't you?" Gabby steps into a diva pose, like the one from Jadelicious's red-carpet picture. "See? I feel more powerful already. You wanna try?"

Above Gabby's desk there's another photo. A crowded room—a party or something. Jadelicious is the center of a swirl of activity, everyone around her a blur. She's wearing a purple sparkly bodysuit, purple cape. She doesn't look like she's posing, exactly. She just looks strong, like a super-woman: Her feet are planted firmly. Her hands are on her hips, her chin high.

I study it, then move into that position.

"Oh, that's a good one," Gabby says. "How do you feel?"

"Exactly the same."

"Well," she says. "I guess you're going to have to *fake it till you make it*, then."

At recess the next day, I lead the class to the Paulie statue, and that's what I do.

My First-Ever Speech

Greetings, fellow seventh graders. You've successfully completed the first challenge in the reality-style competition that will determine the Next Great Paulie Fink of the Mitchell School.

The winner of this competition will be the student who best embodies the spirit of Paulie. By now, I've listened to endless stories of your Great Paulie Fink. I've learned that he was a fearless prankster, a mischievous troublemaker who turned the world upside down and left chaos in his wake.

He also sometimes wore a chicken suit and a cardboard box on his head.

He may not have been an Original, but he sure seems to have been original.

Every reality competition has rules. So here are the rules of this competition:

1. I, Caitlyn Breen, will design all challenges.

2. You, Originals, are to participate in every challenge as directed.

3. If you refuse to participate in a challenge, you will be eliminated.

4. If you rat me out to Glebus, you will be eliminated.

5. Hereafter, if you are sent to Glebus's office as a result of this competition, you have failed your challenge, which means you will be eliminated.

6. My word is final. I am the judge and jury. Don't like it? Tough.

It is important that I clarify at the outset that this is not remotely a real competition, which is why the official prize you are competing for is, perhaps, the world's ugliest T-shirt, which may or may not be good luck.

Ah, but there's a prize that's even greater than that. It's the same prize that humans have sought throughout history, ancient Greeks and Megastars alike.

You will have kleos. You will never be forgotten.

Citizens of Mitchell, we have one challenge down, many more to go. Are you ready to hear the next one?

When I finish, there's a beat where no one speaks. Then Fiona jams her fist in the air. "Yes!" Several of them start applauding.

Behind them, the PICK A WINNER shirt billows a little in the breeze.

Gabby raises her hand. "Um, excuse me, Caitlyn?"

She glances at the others, then steps over and whispers in my ear, loud enough for everyone to hear. "Before you tell us the next challenge, we need to have a formal elimination ceremony. Where you officially kick me out of the competition."

"Oh, right." I hadn't planned on that.

She steps back into place solemnly, her hands straight down at her sides.

"Gabby," I say, trying to sound stern, like the mean judge they expect me to be. "You...are not the Next Great Paulie Fink."

She looks at me. "Good," she says. "Now tell me why."

"Because...," I guess, "you didn't talk like Shakespeare?"

She shakes her head. "No. It's because Paulie Fink was a kid of many personas. He was like those gods of Mount Olympus who could take endless forms. I failed to demonstrate that particular aspect of his personality."

"Ohhh," I say. "Yeah, that. So is everyone ready to hear what the next—"

"Now I'm ready to make the first sacrifice," Gabby interrupts. She reminds everyone that each time a *Megastar* contestant is eliminated they have to leave something behind—"some personal object that represents their dashed dreams."

She digs in her backpack and pulls out a box of thumbtacks and that photo of Jadelicious in her purple bodysuit—the one where she's standing like a superhero. Gabby holds the photo high. "I sacrifice this photo of the world's greatest reality-television star," she says. "Because Jadelicious inspired this whole competition, and also because I think she and Paulie have a lot in common."

She sticks the photo to the Paulie statue, then sets the box of tacks on the ground for future eliminations.

"In the name of Paulie Fink," she says. When no one replies, Gabby whispers to the group, "You're supposed to say it, too."

She tries again. "In the name of Paulie Fink!"

This time, in unison, they all follow, like it's a call-and-response: "In the name of Paulie Fink!"

"Okay." Gabby turns to me. "Now you can tell them about the next challenge."

In Charge

"Your second challenge is inspired by the story about Paulie and his Mini-geddon," I tell them. "As you know, he proved that he could get the attention of younger children. He could see their strengths. He also managed to use those strengths in surprising ways. The question is...can you?"

The challenge, I explain, is a simple one: Tomorrow at recess, they need to engage with Minis. "Find an activity and lead a group of Minis through it. The goal is to get them interested, and to *keep* them interested. Whichever of you appeals to the fewest Minis will be eliminated."

"Unless you get sent to Glebus's office, right?" adds Gabby.

"If you're sent to Glebus's office, you're automatically eliminated."

Diego sighs. "I want a *running* challenge," he says.

I glance at Gabby. She flicks her eyes to the photo of Jadelicious. Reminding me, I guess, that I need to *fake it till I make it.*

I swallow. "Diego, are you telling me you want a running challenge?"

"Yup."

"Okay, then. As head of the Search for the Next Great Paulie Fink, I hereby issue a running challenge. Diego, you're going to run around this field ten times."

"Wait, what?"

"You heard me."

"But you mean . . . just me?"

I nod.

"But that's not fair!"

I look down at my speech. I ask him to read rules one through three:

1. I, Caitlyn Breen, will design all challenges.
2. You, Originals, are to participate in every challenge as directed.
3. If you refuse to participate in a challenge, you will be eliminated.

When he finishes, I plant my feet a little wider apart, move my hands to my hips. "Ten laps," I repeat. "Unless you want to skip to the next elimination ceremony right now."

Fiona points at Diego. "You got in trouble," she sing-songs. I turn to her, lift my eyebrows. She immediately stands up a little straighter and stares ahead innocently.

Diego kicks the grass. "Fine," he mutters. He starts off running.

I have this strange feeling then, the same one I had during the Shakespeare challenge: *I did this*.

I don't just have to follow rules. I can *write* rules for other people to follow.

I tear the list of rules from my speech. Using one of Gabby's thumbtacks, I post the list to the Paulie statue, above that image of Jadelicious.

Just so they don't forget. Or maybe so *I* don't.

The Mini Challenge

I feel a little like Glebus as I walk around at recess, monitoring what everyone's doing in the Mini challenge.

Yumi, standing near the sandbox, starts playing her ukulele. That gets kids' attention right away. A bunch of them run toward her.

"Can you play that princess song?" asks one of the Minis, a girl with a tutu over her jeans. "From the movie where it's winter?"

Yumi shakes her head. "Sorry, but that song was only written so a multinational corporation could make a lot of money. It's just not part of my artistic vision."

"'Wheels on the Bus'?" asks a little boy with a buzz cut.

"Ugh." Yumi rolls her eyes. "'Wheels on the Bus' is *so* overrated."

Another kid suggests "Ring Around the Rosie," and Yumi raises an eyebrow. "Don't you guys know that song is about the plague?"

"What's the plague?" asks the "Wheels on the Bus" kid.

"It's a disease," Yumi says. "An awful one. It begins with painful sores all over your body. Then your organs rot from the inside, and—"

"Yumi," I warn.

"It's a death song," she finishes with a wave of her hand. "I don't think children should sing about death."

"How about the gummy bear song?" a Mini asks.

"Well, I don't actually *know* that song, but I'm also not sure that I want to sing about sugar. It's addictive."

"What's *addictive*?" asks the "Wheels on the Bus" kid.

"Okay, Yumi," I say. "Maybe you should just play them *your* favorite song." But Yumi's favorite song sounds sort of like a ukulele version of a funeral dirge: depressing and oddly cheerful at the same time. One by one, the Minis grow bored and return to their games.

I spot Lydia and Willow leading some Minis toward the soccer field, but Fiona's closest to me, standing at the bottom of a slide, shouting to Minis as they come down.

"What I'm saying is that the world will ask you to sit still, be quiet, follow their rules. But you don't have to!"

If the Minis are listening, they don't show it. They go down the slide a couple of times, then dash off toward the swings, like Fiona's not even speaking.

Fiona follows them. "Have you noticed that it's *girls* who are expected to be neat and organized? *Girls* who are expected to resolve conflict peacefully? How is this in your interest?"

The Minis pause to listen only for a second. Then one of them says, "Wanna see how high I can swing?"

Fiona keeps trying, following groups of kids who basically ignore her. "You are our future Eleanor Roosevelts! Our future Malalas!"

Finally, Fiona flings her arms wide and shouts up to the sky. "What is the *matter* with everyone? Don't people know that they should listen to strong and powerful women every chance they get?!"

But apparently they don't.

Gabby comes running over. "Okay, so Henry is building a really great fort with some Minis," she says. "He's got six Minis gathering sticks, and he's explaining about building structures as they go, so he's doing great. And Diego's showing four Minis how to do soccer tricks, and Timothy and Thomas…" She points to a part of the playground where a crowd of Minis are cheering. "You've got to see them."

The twins are doing their zombie-werewolf game, but they're letting the Minis call out the characters. Thing is, the Minis don't seem to understand the game at all.

"Puppy!" one of the Minis shouts. Timothy starts romping toward his brother on all fours with his tongue out.

"My mommy!" shouts another.

Thomas tries to make himself look taller and glides around, wagging his finger. "Did you do your homework?" he says in a high voice, while the puppy, his brother, bounds into his shins. "Clean your room!"

The Minis seem to love it.

Gabby tells me that the pom-poms have gotten permission to take some Minis over to see the goats. But when I walk over to check out what they're doing, I realize...they're not just *at* the goat pen. They're actually *inside*.

Willow leads everyone into a yoga pose. She balances her left foot against her right thigh. Presses her hands together at her chest, almost like she's praying. Sam and Lydia and the Minis—at least ten of them, maybe more—wobble as they move their bodies into the same position.

Even Fuzzy's there, eyes closed. She loses her balance, then stands again.

"What is this?" I ask.

"Goat yoga," Sam answers.

"Goat yoga? That can't possibly be a thing," I say.

Inside the pen, Willow smiles, her eyes still closed. "It's a thing. My mom teaches a goat-yoga class over at Morning Glory Farm in Devlinshire on Saturday mornings," she says. "Tons of people come."

"To do yoga with goats?" I scratch my head. "Because these two things go together...how?"

Sam shrugs. "Oh, who knows with rich people. They love that sort of stuff."

Willow moves into a different pose. She bends down, places her hands on the grass in front of her, and then walks her legs backward until her whole body forms an upside-down V. "This is usually called downward-facing dog. Today, we call it *ground-facing goat*."

Fuzzy follows, bending her little body into an inverted V.

The whole thing is absurd, but the Minis are happy. Actually, even the goats seem to like it. They're calmer than I've ever seen them. A couple of the little goats wander among the Minis, stopping to sniff them curiously, but for the most part, they're still.

Huh. Apparently Willow's the Pied Piper of both Minis and goats.

"Take a moment to feel your breath," she says. "In. Out."

She lowers herself into something she calls child's pose: on the ground, legs folded beneath her. She stretches her fingers out in front of her and presses her forehead to her knees.

"Really feel the stretch in those arms," Willow is saying. "That's right. Don't forget to breathe. *In. Out.*"

The grumpy old goat moves toward them slowly. *They've even tamed my archenemy*, I think. When he reaches Willow, he bends his back legs, lowering his backside toward the ground, almost as if he's moving into the pose, too.

Instead, the goat sends a long stream of pee right onto Willow's outstretched hand.

Her eyes pop open. As soon as she understands what's happening, she shrieks and scrambles to her feet.

Startled, the big goat jumps backward. This rattles

every other goat. They bleat and dash all over the pen, which freaks the Minis out completely. A couple of Minis scream.

Teachers look up and start sprinting toward the pen.

Amid all the commotion, Fuzzy is still. She's gone rigid, her eyes huge and wild, like Henry's were on the day he got trampled.

I'm through the gate before I even realize what I'm doing. I scoop her up. She's lighter than I expect, and her skinny little limbs curl around me like she can't cling tightly enough.

"You're okay," I tell her. She buries her face in my neck, and I smell coconut in her hair. "I've got you."

Fuzzy doesn't let go. Not once we're out of the goat pen, not as we cross the soccer field, not when we reach the sandbox. Not even as Mr. Farabi marches the pom-poms toward the building, where Glebus waits, frowning. I let Fuzzy cling to me, and I sway her back and forth.

After a while, I feel her limbs start to relax. She lifts her face from my neck, and she sniffles and wipes her nose. There's a wet spot on my neck, and my arms are heavy from holding her. But even then, I don't put her down. I can feel her heart thumping away behind her ribs. I picture it there: tiny and strong, just inches from my own.

Bad Luck

In the morning, everyone's still laughing about the goat-pee disaster—*goat-geddon*, everyone's calling it—when Mags arrives. She picks up Paulie's hat filled with index cards. "Good morning, Originals! Take your seats, because today we're going to talk about…" Next to me, Diego does a drum-roll on the table.

"Well, isn't this quite the coincidence," Mags says. She looks at Lydia, Sam, and Willow and holds up the card. It says in big, block letters: GOATS.

It turns out goats were pretty important in the life of the ancient Greeks.

Mags explains that goats were a huge source of food for the Greeks, which is probably why they're all over Greek mythology. Zeus, the king of the gods, was raised on goat's milk, Athena carried a goat's hide, and there was even a god, Pan, who was half-goat/half-human. "Pan was the god of wild things," Mags tells us. "Of untamed creatures and mountains and such. I suspect he'd fit right in here." Then she tells us that goats were also commonly used in ritual sacrifices.

"*Sacrifices*?" asks Gabby.

Mags nods. "Yup. To some degree all of us are affected by circumstances outside of our control. That was especially true in the ancient world. Back then, a single drought could destroy an entire community. Famine was common. The ancients lacked the medicines we now have, so epidemics were rampant."

She turns then, and writes on the board:

pharmakos

And beneath that:

φαρμακός

"So during especially hard times," Mags continues, "they'd select someone from the community to be what's called a *pharmakos*. They'd parade that individual through town. Community members were encouraged to beat the person with twigs and branches. Finally, they'd chase them out of the village and demand that they never return."

"But...why?" asks Fiona.

"The idea was to transfer all the bad luck onto a single person. So when that individual left, all the misfortune would disappear with them."

Mags writes on the board:

katharsis

κάθαρσις

"The process was called *katharsis*, which is the Greek root of the modern word *catharsis*, with a *c*. When we use the word now, it means a great release of powerful negative feelings, the kind that ends with a sense of relief—like a good cry, or a primal scream. Chasing out the *pharmakos* was a way of trying to find relief."

"What's that got to do with goats?" asks Gabby.

"Later, the humans were replaced by animals, usually goats."

"So...," says Yumi, "like, actual scapegoats."

Mags smiles. "Exactly," she says. "The word *scapegoat* doesn't show up until much later, but that's what we're talking about here. Scapegoats."

Scapegoat. I knew the word well, actually. Teachers used the word *scapegoat* in my old school. Always in a lecture. Usually, that lecture was about Anna Spang. *Why are you scapegoating her? Can you imagine how it feels to be the scapegoat?*

I always felt like those lectures missed the point. I mean, it wasn't as if we didn't know we weren't being nice. You don't pick on someone because nobody's ever taught you about kindness or whatever. Like, all those things we did to Anna—laughing at her, or sniffing the air when she walked by, like there was suddenly a bad smell—those things weren't about chasing away misfortune. When we did them, we were...

We were...

Well, to be honest, I have no idea why, exactly, we were doing those things.

"Caitlyn," Mags says. "You look like you're thinking hard about something."

"Huh?"

"There is little that brings me more joy than seeing a student concentrate with furrowed brow during a class discussion. So if you're willing to share, I'd love to know what you think."

"Oh," I begin. "I just...I think the Greeks got it wrong, is all."

"Tell me why."

Obviously, I can't talk about Anna, so I simply say, "It just seems like sort of a stupid thing to believe. I assume their lives didn't miraculously improve as soon as the goat was gone, so why would they keep doing it?"

From across the room, Henry says, "I think I understand why they did it." We all look at him in surprise. "I'll bet it did work, in its own way."

How could Henry, the kid who's obsessed with facts—believe in something like *pharmakos*?

Interview: Henry

I have a lot of books about the ancient world. So I already knew a bunch of what Mags was teaching us. I knew about Plato's cave, and I knew about Greek democracy, and I knew about all those gods and goddesses. I knew that Paulie had been kind of like Hermes, who was a trickster god, and that Fiona was kind of like Artemis, a goddess who protected girls and also had a hot temper and once got so mad she turned a guy into a deer, then watched as the guy's dogs chased him down and ate him.

I knew other things, too—things Mags wasn't telling us. I knew that the Greeks weren't always so great. In some places, they abandoned weak-looking babies outside to be eaten by wolves. And often kids were told it was okay to attack each other in school, because people thought that this would make them strong.

But the thing Mags told us about the scapegoats? That whole *pharmakos* thing? I hadn't known about that.

Did I believe it? Not literally. But I know this: A person's brain can get stuck. It can cycle over the same old problems, or the same old fears, until there's no room to think about anything else.

Maybe believing you can send your problem away is just a way of getting yourself unstuck.

You do it because you've run out of other ideas.

You do it because you see bad luck hurtling toward you fast, and your only other option is to stand there and wait.

Every reality show has a scapegoat. The scapegoat is the person you love to hate.

Most of the time, the scapegoat is just someone who can't sing, and they play the footage of the person's worst performance over and over again, until the whole world has seen it and eventually that person gets to go on talk shows. But sometimes the scapegoat is a villain. Like, maybe they sabotage the other contestants, or they tell other people's secrets, or they try to weasel out of doing work that everyone else is doing. And the thing is, the scapegoats just keep winning, as all these other contestants—better ones—get kicked out of the competition. And the longer it goes on, and the closer they come to winning, the more you can't stand them.

Like Rexx Rowdy, who battled Jadelicious all through season two. The only talent he had was picking on Megastars he didn't like. And for some reason, lots of people just ate that up. Audiences even started holding up signs that said THE REXX EFFECT and REXX WRECKS!

There's no one Rexx hated more than Jadelicious. I don't know why, but it's like her very existence made him furious. So he'd get crowds to boo her and throw things when she was onstage. Everywhere she went, there were people in REXX WRECKS! T-shirts flashing a thumbs-down.

At a certain point, rooting *for* Rexx Rowdy was the same thing as rooting *against* Jadelicious. That became his whole *thing*. At first, I was pretty sure he wouldn't win. But as the season went on, I started getting really worried. Because he was getting a lot farther than a villainous scapegoat ever should.

When he was finally eliminated in the second-to-last episode, I jumped up and danced around the living room. Even my grandma, who has such a hard time moving around, stood up and danced.

We had...what did Mags call it? *Katharsis*, that's right.

Point is, I'm pretty sure that's how it's *supposed* to work. The scapegoats should never, ever win.

The Banana Challenge

We hold the second elimination ceremony on a Monday morning, just before feeding the goats.

I had only planned to eliminate Willow, but Lydia and Sam said that they were one for all, all for one. "Our campaigns begin together, and they end together," Lydia told me.

"But if it's okay, we'd like a few days to prepare our sacrifice," Sam added.

At the time, I was relieved. I didn't have a clue what the next challenge would be. Now, even as we gather at the Paulie statue, I still don't know.

"Lydia. Willow. Sam," I begin. I look at them holding hands, three in a row in matching pom-pom headbands. Their grips get a little tighter, even though they know exactly what I'm about to say. "I'm sorry, but none of you are the Next Great Paulie Fink."

"We wanted to make some pom-pom ears for Paulie," Sam says. "We thought they could be antennae, since he comes from the stars. But the Paulie statue doesn't even have a head, so we have nowhere to put them."

Lydia reaches into a paper bag. "So we made these instead." She pulls out three long garlands of pom-poms, in every color under the sun.

They take a turn decorating the Paulie statue. Lydia wraps one garland around the branch, then Sam does the same. Willow drapes the final garland around the neck of the T-shirt, like a scarf, or a many-layered necklace.

The three of them step back to survey their work.

"He looks friendlier," says Willow.

Lydia nods. "More festive somehow."

"Also, you can't see the PICK A WINNER part as much now," Yumi remarks. "That seems like an improvement."

I squint at the Paulie statue. By now, early October, most of the leaves have changed color. The neon T-shirt and rainbow pom-poms seem out of place against all those autumn colors.

"So, Caitlyn..." Gabby rubs her hands together in anticipation. "What's the next challenge?"

I squeeze my eyes shut and try to think. I know that the challenges are supposed to get more interesting as the show goes on. And the most popular challenge so far was the one that descended into chaos. So how do you plan for chaos?

I run through every Paulie story I've heard. *Chicken suit turkey sandwich desk drawers pizza glitter BoxMan fruit flies banana p—*

That's it.

Banana peels are funny. Everyone knows that, even me.

They're like the oldest joke in the world or something. I take a deep breath. "Aspiring Paulies," I say. I've got my Speech Voice on, my *fake it till you make it* one, as if I hadn't just come up with this challenge on the spot.

"Your departed classmate left one very crucial project unfulfilled," I say. They stare at me blankly, so I add, "Think science projects."

When they still don't get it, I add, "And fruit flies."

"Banana peels!" Thomas shouts.

I nod. "For this competition, I want you to finish the thing Paulie never could."

"Are we going to try to make a teacher fall?" asks Fiona. "'Cause if so, I call Glebus!"

"You have to make *someone* fall," I say. "Someone other than me, that is. Over the next few lunch periods, I want you to collect banana peels. When we have enough, you'll lay them down in strategic places. The last one to make someone fall—"

"No," Henry interrupts. "This isn't a good challenge. Paulie never would have done this."

"But he *did* try to do it, Henry," says Lydia.

"He wrote that report," Diego adds. "Remember?"

Henry turns to Diego. "But he never *did* it. The point of that project wasn't making someone fall. It was trying to see if he could put one over on Mr. Farabi."

"But he had the peels," said Diego. "He was just getting ready."

212

Yumi shakes her head. "Actually, I think Henry's right. He had those peels for weeks. He had plenty of chances to use them, but he never did."

"Exactly," Henry says. "Because making someone fall would have been mean. And Paulie knew that funny and mean were two different things."

I glance at the image of Jadelicious, still visible behind the pom-pom garland. I plant my feet a little farther apart, pull my shoulders back, and look straight at Henry. I give him my best *I'm in charge* look. If he notices, he doesn't show it.

"But wait, Henry," Fiona says. "Weren't we sort of mean to one another in that Shakespeare challenge? All we did was insult each other. Why is this any different?"

"In the Shakespeare challenge, everyone was equal," Henry explains. He's like a little teacher right now, and for some reason that makes me feel furious. In the back of my mind, I get an ugly thought: *You were the scapegoat, Henry. You were the one who had your backpack stolen for games of keep away. Not me. You.*

"Each of us knew what all the others were up to in the Shakespeare challenge," Henry continues. "With this challenge, you're trying to trick someone who's unaware, and you're doing it in a way that could hurt them. You can't see how this is different?"

Timothy shrugs. "I think it's funny."

"Maybe," says his brother, "but Henry is usually right about stuff."

"Besides," adds Henry, "it's dangerous. People have gotten skull fractures from slipping on banana peels. Some have actually died."

"So hold on, Henry," I say. I place my hands on my hips. "You think someone's going to get a *skull fracture* if we do this? You think someone will *die* if we do this?"

"It's statistically highly unlikely that someone will die," he says. "But there's a hundred percent chance that it's mean."

Well, that shuts everyone up.

Then they turn to me, waiting to see what I'm going to do. I want to reverse time right now. Go back to yesterday when I rescued Fuzzy from the pen. Or to the Shakespeare challenge, when I realized I could be in charge of something. No, as long as I'm going back in time, I'll go back even further than that. I should have just said no when they asked me to run this competition.

Why did I ever think I could do this?

"Well, *Henry*," I say. There it is, behind my ribs: that thing that makes me stronger than other people. "Since you're so smart, why don't you remind everyone of rules two and three?"

He doesn't shift his gaze to the rules at all, just pushes up his glasses and keeps his eyes on me. The stone inside me hardens a little more.

"Gabby," I say, my eyes still on Henry. "Can *you* read them, please?"

"Uh…okay." She steps forward. Her voice shakes a little

as she reads, "*You, Originals, are to participate in every challenge as directed. If you refuse to participate in a challenge, you will be eliminated.*"

"Do you want to be eliminated, Henry?" I ask. When he doesn't answer, I turn to the others. "The competition's on," I say. "And apparently we have one less contestant."

Henry gazes at me for a second. Then he puts his hands in his pockets and walks away without a word. He heads over to the goat pen. He picks up the feed bucket and opens the gate. Somehow, he manages to feed the animals without anyone there to distract them, before Mr. Farabi even arrives. And this fact alone—that he can do this without anyone's help—is probably the most maddening part of all.

I stare past him, out toward the trees, and I remember the one time when Anna refused to play the part I'd written for her. She'd been standing at her locker, minding her own business, when I walked over. I didn't have a plan; it was the act of saying something that mattered more than the words themselves.

"Hi, Anna," I said. She'd been reaching for a book from the top of her locker, and her hand froze there, in midair. I heard muffled snorts of laughter from my friends behind me.

"I *said*, hi, Anna."

"Hey," she finally said. She kept her eyes on her locker. Pulled her book out slowly.

"*Soooo,*" I drawled, "did anyone ever tell you that you're . . . a giant . . . *dork*?"

I expected she'd just look down. Say nothing. Take it. But that's not how it went.

"Yes," Anna said. She turned around, and she met my eyes. "*You've* told me that. About a million times already."

"Oh. Well...good. Because you are."

As I walked away, I glanced at my friends and rolled my eyes. I'd had the last word. But the whole thing left me feeling unsteady. Like somehow, by suggesting that I was repeating myself, she was saying there was something wrong with me.

When really, the whole conversation was supposed to be about her.

A Meeting of the Unoriginals

The worst part of what Henry said is the way I can't get it out of my head all morning: *There's a hundred percent chance that it's mean.* Maybe that's why I shift in my seat when Mags starts talking to us about honor and virtue.

She tells us that the Greeks had this concept called *arete*, which she pronounces like ah-REE-tay.

"*Arete* has no exact translation," she explains. "But in English, honor and virtue come close. Most references to *arete* you find in literature involve soldiers in battle—so *arete* meant fighting wars bravely. But it was also about being your best self—bringing the bravest, fullest version of you into a situation, no matter what was happening around you."

The whole lecture makes me feel squirmy and small, which is annoying.

I mean, it's not like banana peels are *that* big a deal.

At lunch, Fuzzy asks me for a Paulie vs. the Gleeb story, just like she always does.

"Once upon a time...," I start. And then I pause. I don't want to think about Paulie Fink right now. Henry's words tumble around inside my head: *Paulie knew that funny and mean were two different things*.

"You know what?" I say to Fuzzy. "My throat hurts. I think I need to take a break from telling stories today."

When her lower lip sticks out, I hold up my pinkie, like I did on that first day. And just like on that first day, she wraps her finger around mine. I'm not sure what we're promising this time. Maybe that she's still my Mini, and I'm still looking out for her, even if I'm not in a storytelling mood.

I'm relieved to see that the kids who are still in the competition—the twins, Yumi, Fiona, and Diego—each have at least one banana peel next to them.

See, Henry? I won, I think. Which should make me feel good, but it just makes my food taste sour.

After lunch, Timothy and Thomas start picking through the garbage, searching for more banana peels. Fiona weasels her way between them. Then Diego joins them, and even Yumi. They're fighting their way through the trash bin, all diving at the same time for any yellow peel they can find.

"Well," says Sam drily. "This competition has reached a new low."

None of us see Glebus coming.

"Excuse me," she bellows across the cafeteria.

Instantly, everyone stands up straight with fistfuls of fruit scraps. Fiona and Timothy each grip a single peel by different ends.

"Can you explain to me," Glebus says, drawing out her words, "why, precisely, you are removing food waste from the garbage?"

There's a pause. Yumi and the twins look down at their feet. Fiona stares up at the ceiling and says, "Hmmmm…" like she's thinking hard.

"First I discover your class throwing goat food at each other. Then I learn that some of you were doing yoga with younger children inside the goat pen. Now I find you rummaging through garbage in search of—" Glebus looks at the banana peel that Fiona and Timothy are both holding. Instantly, they both let go, and it falls, splat, on top of Fiona's sneaker.

"—banana peels," Glebus finishes. "So now I'm asking… *why?*"

"Um…," begins Timothy.

"We're…uhhh," says Thomas.

They glance at each other, then Timothy bursts out, "It's Caitlyn's fault!"

Thomas nods. "Caitlyn made us!"

They go back and forth:

"We told her not to."

"*Everyone* told her not to."

"Well. Some people told her not to."

"You didn't."

"Shut up."

"*You* shut up."

"Shut up, fusty nut."

"You're the fusty nut, idiot."

Ms. Glebus holds up one hand. "Excuse me, gentlemen. What is it exactly"—she eyes me for a quick second, then turns back to the twins—"that Caitlyn *made* you do?"

"Caitlyn had *such* a good idea, Ms. Glebus!" Fiona starts rambling. "It's so great. She thought we should...um...Well, I mean, you know Caitlyn *always* has good ideas, do you know that about her? She's, like, an idea factory, it's actually very impressive..."

"Goats!" exclaims Henry, taking a step forward. "Caitlyn thought it was silly to just throw out all these scraps when there are goats living here who might like them." Henry pushes his glasses up on his nose, keeps his focus on Glebus. "It's a very good idea."

"I see," Glebus says. But she's eyeing everyone carefully, like she doesn't know what to believe. "Well, it is true that the goats might like them..."

"Of course it's true," says Fiona. "Why would we lie? There'd be no reason to lie about this, not today, not tomorrow, not ever." Diego gives her a tiny kick, like he's telling her to shut up.

"Caitlyn," Glebus says, "if that is, in fact, what's going on here, then I suppose that's quite thoughtful. There's no harm in bringing those peels to the goats, but the experiment ends today. I can't have students rummaging through the trash every day. Go ahead. You may bring these down to the pen."

Everyone breaks for the door at once, but Glebus shakes her head. "Not all of you. Caitlyn, you may go, and…Henry, you can help her, since you were so enthusiastic about the idea. The rest of you: to class, now."

It's a pretty awkward walk down to the goats. Henry and I are silent until we pass the fort he built during the Mini challenge. "It's still standing," I say.

"Yeah," he responds. And then I don't know what else to say.

When we arrive at the pen, we begin to pull the peels into thin strips, tossing them in one at a time. It turns out goats do like banana peels. A couple of them eat them, but others seem to enjoy playing with them—tossing the peels up in the air, or nudging them around in the dirt with their noses.

I keep my eyes on the goats. "Well, I guess this is the second meeting of the Unoriginals," I finally say. "Is every member present?"

"Not quite," Henry says. "Remember, Paulie was an Unoriginal, too."

"He's over there," I say, and I gesture toward the Paulie statue. Then, after a beat, I add, "I'm glad we're getting rid of the peels. It was a dumb idea."

"It wasn't dumb," Henry says. He doesn't add, *It was just mean*, but I assume that's what he's thinking.

"Anyway, you kind of saved my butt back there," I say.

He peels a long thin strip and tosses it to one of the baby goats. Almost immediately, the big mean goat steals it from the baby.

"Why'd you do it?" I ask.

"Do what?" he asks.

"Save me. From Glebus."

He tries again, sending another strip to the baby goat. This time the little goat gets it, and runs away before anyone can take it. "I guess I don't think you're a mean person."

And that makes my throat tighten a little.

"I am, though," I confess. "At least I was."

"Nah." He shrugs. "I shouldn't have argued with you in front of everyone."

"I don't mean I was mean to *you*," I say. "Or at least not *just* to you. I mean…before. In my old school. I was…kind of a jerk, actually."

The words hang there in the air. And…that's it. The world doesn't end or anything.

"It was only to this one girl," I continue. "I was so mean. I teased her all the time. And it's so weird, because now,

I look back, and I don't really know *why*. I keep thinking about it, but I just…"

I trail off. Then I shake my head. "Anyway, you're still in the competition, okay?" I say. "I mean, I *have* to eliminate the twins for how quickly they threw me under the bus, right? So that's two eliminations right there."

The big goat steals another peel from a smaller goat. I watch as he chews on it, then gulps it down. *Stupid goat*, I think. *Don't you know the difference between funny and mean?*

Henry finally turns to me. "Caitlyn, I have no idea if Paulie would have used those peels if Glebus hadn't found them. That's just the thing I wanted to be true."

Huh. It's like Henry wanted the competition to capture the best version of Paulie—his *arete*, Mags called it—even if it wasn't necessarily the *whole* Paulie.

Henry tosses the final peel into the pen, then wipes his hands on his jeans. "The thing is, I don't actually *want* to be the Next Great Paulie Fink."

"You don't?"

He shrugs. "Not really. I just liked the idea of the competition. I liked that it was something we could do together. Give us some memory we'd all share, no matter what happens."

It makes me sad that Henry doesn't want to be in the competition anymore, but I get it. I mean, figuring out how to be one person is confusing enough. Who wants to try to be two?

We do a quick elimination ceremony at the end of gym. Still sweaty from class, Timothy and Thomas stand in front of me, pencils in their ears. When I announce that neither of them will be the Next Great Paulie Fink, they shout, in unison, "We come from the *stars*!" Then they jam the pencils into the soil.

"I'm out, too," Henry says. He places, carefully, his nature-facts book at the base of the statue. "Only three competitors left," he says.

"Me, Diego, and Yumi," says Fiona. "The Final Three!"

This means there are only two more challenges. I don't want to mess this up again.

Interview: Henry

HENRY:
Remember what I told you? About the time I fell into the river?

CAITLYN:
After the rainstorm. Yeah.

HENRY:
I've been thinking about it a lot lately. Remembering exactly how it felt when the ground beneath me was just... gone. There was only a split second between the ground disappearing and my being in the water, getting carried by the current, but it was long enough to understand that it was too late, that I was falling, that I didn't have any control over what happened next. And you know what I wished for in that moment?

CAITLYN:
I don't know. A life vest?

HENRY:
It wasn't some fact, that's for sure. I wished that I didn't feel so totally alone. I think that's why I ended up telling you my secret.

The Transcript

At the end of the day, I'm walking toward the parking lot when Henry catches up with me. "Hold up," he says. "I have something to show you."

He hands me a piece of paper, folded in half. When I try to take it, he doesn't let go. "Swear," he says. "Swear on the Unoriginals that you won't tell anyone."

I nod. "Okay. I swear on the Unoriginals."

He lets go. I unfold the paper and begin to read.

www.VT/gov/towns/Mitchell/Council/Mtgs/
Trscrpt/0827
TRANSCRIPT: Mitchell TOWN COUNCIL
Meeting: August 27
Page 7 of 12

_____

Councilperson Cardinali: How can we possibly
    be talking about this? These are our
    children.

Councilperson Gloster: We're talking about this because we have a $387,000 structural deficit in our budget. We're in a financial death spiral here. Do you remember what happened over in Marshall Falls? Their deficit wasn't much bigger than ours is now. Within three years, it ballooned to more than $2 million.

Councilperson Miller: Cripes. Somebody please tell me how we got into this situation.

Councilperson Gloster: The usual way, Angie. Higher costs than we bring in from taxes.

Councilperson Cardinali: We can't balance the budget on the backs of our kids.

Councilperson Gloster: The school was an experiment. We gave it our best shot. It's just too expensive.

Councilperson Cardinali: What is a community without a school?

Councilperson Gloster: Plenty of towns don't have their own school.

Councilperson Cardinali: No family will move to a town without a school. And some that are already here will move away. We'll be like a ghost town if we allow—

Councilperson Miller: We're a ghost town already, Hector.

Councilperson Cardinali: How long before we have to vote?

Councilperson Gloster: We're committed to funding the school through the end of this year. But if there's not going to be a school next year, families are going to need time to prepare. I say vote as soon as possible.

Secrets and Broken Promises

Standing there with Henry, I read it over three times, just trying to figure it out.

By the time I finish the third read, my heart is pounding. Ahead of us, kids start to line up at the Good Day Bell. *Clang.* One kid rings it, then another. *Clang. Clang.*

"They're...talking about *here*? About Mitchell?" I ask Henry.

He nods.

"It's going to...?" I don't finish the sentence, but I'm thinking, *Close. It's going to close.*

He nods again.

"And your dad's the one who..."

"Is trying to keep that from happening, yeah. He's trying, but he's not succeeding."

I look down at the paper again. I feel like there's something I must be missing, some solution that I could find if I read this right. *Balance the budget on the backs of our kids... Financial death spiral...Gave it our best shot...* "But...what happens to—?"

"Us?" he asks. I nod. And I realize that *is* what I was going to say. *Us.* Not *you.* Not *Mitchell.*

Us.

"Tons of schools close," he says. "Happens all over, all the time. Happened to Mitchell once already. Kids go somewhere else. We will, too, I guess. Anyway, I think you should make the last few challenges really fun. For everyone's sake. Kind of a last hurrah, you know?"

Ahead of me, the kindergarten class takes its turn at the Good Day Bell. Mr. Twilling hands the bell's rope to a girl whose backpack is almost as big as she is. "Serena," he says, "did you have a good day?" *Clang.* Another kindergartner. "Max, how 'bout you?" *Clang.*

And then it's Fuzzy's turn. Mr. Twilling offers her the rope. "You read three different words today," he says. "Sounds like a good day to me!"

She shakes her head. *No.* Mr. Twilling smiles at her. "Maybe tomorrow," he says.

That pinkie promise. It seems so stupid now. Why would I ask a five-year-old not to ring a bell? What did I think I was accomplishing? For her, or for me, or for anyone?

I don't know what to do about what's on the paper I'm holding. I don't know what to do about the next couple of challenges. But I do know what to do about the kid in front of me holding a stuffed bunny.

I hand the paper back to Henry, then jog over toward

the Good Day Bell. "Hey," I say to Fuzzy, squatting down. "Did you really read three words today?" She nods.

"Do you know how many words I could read when I was just one month into kindergarten? Zero, that's how many. Sounds to me like you did have a pretty good day. I'm thinking maybe you *should* ring that bell."

She looks down at her feet. "I promised."

"Huh. Well…then…what if we both break the promise? Both of us? At the exact same time?"

She considers this.

"With Real Rabbit, of course," I add. "Because I'm pretty sure he's really, really been wanting to ring that bell."

Mr. Twilling mouths the words *thank you* to me as he hands us the rope. Fuzzy positions Real Rabbit, and I count to three, and then we ring the bell together. It makes a loud, satisfying *clang*.

Fuzzy skips down the path and she doesn't look back.

I'm not ready for this to be over, I think as I watch her go. *Not yet. Not when I'm just getting started.*

Gone Is Gone

"I'm just getting started, Jadelicious!" Rexx Rowdy shouts through the dressing room door. He's locked her in there even though she's supposed to take the stage in mere minutes. It's a dirty trick, as dirty as they come.

Next to me on the sofa, Gabby's jaw hardens. "Rexx Rowdy is the worst."

Her grandmother, on the other side of Gabby, nods. "He's a bully, that's for sure."

It's two days after Henry told me about the school. Gabby and I are at her house watching *Megastar* for inspiration, because I don't have a clue what I should do for the last couple of challenges. All I know is that Henry was right when he said *I think you should make the last few challenges really fun*.

I've kept my promise to Henry, by the way. I haven't told anyone about the school closing. I haven't mentioned it to my mom, or to any of the kids, or anyone else. But I think about it all the time. I wonder what Gabby would say, or her grandmother, if I just blurted it out: *The school is broke. It might close.*

I look around Gabby's living room. There are a million pictures of Gabby on the wall, so I walk over to take a closer look, quickly scanning the chubby-baby and toddler shots and locking my eyes on a group shot. My class, Mini-sized, lined up in front of THE MITCHELL SCHOOL sign. There's a tiny Diego. There's a young Yumi, not a speck of pink in her dark hair. There's little Fiona. She'd be almost unrecognizable in that pink dress if it weren't for her wild hair and glinting eyes. They're all standing with a happier-looking Glebus, holding a banner: OPENING DAY: HISTORY IN THE MAKING!

"Oh wow." I peer at it. "Is this kindergarten?"

"Yup," Gabby says. "First day."

Her grandmother smiles. "Now, that was an exciting day. Finally something opening for a change. Breath of fresh air after everything closing—the mill, then the hospital, then all those shops..."

"There used to be a hospital around here?" I hadn't known that.

"Used to be a lot of things around here," she says. Buster runs into the room and starts barking for attention. "Okay, okay. Come on, Buster." She lifts herself off the sofa and takes Buster outside.

I turn back to the photos and peer at a picture of baby Gabby seated on some concrete stairs with a man and a woman. The man's skin is much darker than Gabby's, but his eyes are the same: brown and warm and wide and earnest.

"Is that your dad?"

"Yeah," she says. "He died—you heard that, right?"

I shake my head.

"He was a refugee. From Kinshasa. Came here when he was six. He had the best laugh out of anyone in the whole world; just hearing it was enough to make you laugh, too. But he got stomach cancer. I was in fifth grade when he died."

The woman in the photo has long hair and very dark eyeliner. Her face is frozen mid-laugh. She's thinner than Gabby, and very pale, but the smile is unmistakably Gabby's. And her grandmother's, too. "That's..."

"My mom, yeah." Gabby keeps her eyes on the screen. "She's gone, too. Longer than my dad."

I don't know if *she's gone, too* means gone away, or gone the way her dad is gone. Maybe it means something else altogether. After a beat, Gabby adds, "A different sort of sickness, I guess."

She doesn't say anything more, and I don't ask. Maybe it doesn't matter what kind of gone it is. Gone is gone.

On the television, Rexx Rowdy takes the stage. The audience has been expecting Jadelicious, and you can see this ripple of shock go through them. As soon as they realize what's happening, half of them cheer like crazy, while the other half boo and flash thumbs-downs.

Gabby shakes her head. "I wish I could beat that guy with a stick and chase him away forever."

"Like that thing that Mags talked about," I say.

"Yeah," Gabby says. "*Pharmakos.* If only." When Rexx

Rowdy starts to sing, she makes a face and hits mute. "So what about you? How come you live only with your mom?"

"It's always been just the two of us."

"You never had another parent?"

"Nope. Mom decided that she wanted a kid even if she didn't have a partner. So when she turned thirty-five and she was still single, she did."

"Huh," Gabby says. "Don't you ever wish you had more people in your family?"

I shake my head. The truth is, I can't really imagine anything else. It's not like Gabby, who had a dad she adored, and then lost him. It's always been just me and Mom. I guess you can't miss something you never had. It's like everyone just assumes that their own life is the normal one.

"Gabby, I have to tell you something," I say. She waits.

"I'm not really from New York City," I admit. It's not the biggest secret I've been keeping from her, but it's the one I can confess without breaking a promise to someone else. "I *am* from New York, but not anywhere near the city. I don't know why I lied on the first day. I guess it's because nobody was all that interested in me. I made something up to make myself feel special. It was dumb."

"Nobody was *interested* in you? Are you crazy? People were so excited when you got here."

I shake my head. "No, remember? Everybody kept talking about Paulie all morning. And then you were dancing, and then you were chanting about the goats..."

She waves her hand sort of dismissively. "Well, sure, we *were* shocked that Paulie wasn't coming back. But people were totally showing off for you. That whole morning. You couldn't tell? Like when Fiona and Diego kept leaning over you to fight? And then Yumi started playing her music in the middle of class? Everyone was, like, *freaking out* that you were there. Wait, hold on, I love this part."

Gabby unmutes the TV as Jadelicious, freed now from the dressing room, steps onto the stage. Her eyes are glinting, and her gown falls in layers. Something about the way she's standing—the lift of her chin, maybe—makes her seem almost like one of those ancient gods from humanities. She begins to sing, and Rexx Rowdy's eyes go dark with rage. She's not only turning Rexx Rowdy's solo into a duet, she's making it seem like his whole song was just a warm-up for her all along. The audience roars.

"Anyway, I already knew you weren't from New York City," Gabby says. "My grandma told me after she saw your mom at the clinic last week. It doesn't make any difference to me."

I sit back against the sofa, wondering if anything is ever really how it seems.

The Fable of the Elephant

"How was the playdate?" Mom asks on the drive home from Gabby's.

"*Mom*," I say. "It wasn't a playdate. It's not like we're *four*, you know."

Mom doesn't respond, so I glance over at her. Her eyes look really tired. I remember how she looked on our first drive into Mitchell, the way she kept cranking up songs that I didn't even know. How once we got to Vermont, she wanted to roll down the windows to breathe the fresh air, and I was so mad. Not just because the wind made my hair fly all over, either. I was mad because she was so *happy*.

"Mom, are you glad we moved here?" I ask.

She thinks for a minute. "Mostly," she says. She smiles. "You seem to be settling in, so that helps. It helps a lot."

"Is it what you expected? Living here?"

"Well, I guess nothing's ever *exactly* what you expect, is it? The job's harder than I expected, that's for sure."

"But you're good at it," I say. "You know what you're doing."

"Oh, honey, I don't think anyone ever *really* knows what they're doing. Everyone's just winging it. But people are counting on me, so I do my best, and most nights when I put my head on my pillow, I feel good that I did what I could. That's worth a lot."

She drives for a while, then she adds, "Tell you what, though. It'd be nice to make a friend or two around here."

I didn't realize grown-ups even thought about that stuff. I thought it was only kids who worried about having friends.

"What if we had to move again sometime?" I ask. "Like what if the clinic closed down tomorrow and you had to go back to your old job?"

"I don't know that I'd go back to my old job. But if I *had* to? Yeah, I'd still be glad I did this. Because now I know that I *can*. I can move, I can run an organization, I can have hard days, and then I can get up the next morning and have a better one. So yeah. Even if I did have to go back to my old job tomorrow, it actually *wouldn't* be the same job. Because I wouldn't be the same person that I was before."

Ahead of us, there's a line of cars, all stuck behind a slow-moving tractor. This is one of those things that happen here: You get stuck behind a tractor, or a flock of ducks cross the road from one field to another, or a deer leaps out in front of you and you have to stop short. At first these sorts of things were annoying. Now it's just the way things are.

In the distance, I see the old Oxthorpe factory, looming and massive. As we roll toward it, I try to get a good look.

There are huge silvery windows, each divided up into tiny panes. Some of the panes are broken, dark spots that look like missing teeth.

"What do you think is inside that place, anyway?" I ask.

"Memories, mostly," she says. "Most of the town worked there once upon a time."

I try to imagine the building filled with machines whirring and people chattering. And now it's all rust and broken glass and crumbling bricks.

As we get closer, Mom sighs. "Just look at it, though."

"I know, right?" I say. "The place is so creepy."

"Hm?" For a second she looks confused. "No, I mean the flowers. Look at the way they catch the light."

As soon as Mom says that, I see what she's seeing: wildflowers, a riot of them, rising through the cracks in the abandoned lot, like they're determined to reclaim the place. They're purple and golden, almost electric in color, glowing in the late-afternoon sun.

It reminds me of a story Mom used to tell me, from a book of fables. In the story, a bunch of people who couldn't see were asked to describe an elephant based only on touch. One felt the trunk and said that an elephant is like a snake. Another felt the leg and said that an elephant is like a great tree trunk. A third felt the tail and said an elephant is like a rope. All of them were right, and at the same time all of them were wrong. Or rather, they were all wrong, until you added all of their impressions together.

I think about asking Mom if she remembers that story, but her fingers are tap-tapping on the steering wheel, some tune that's playing inside her head, and she looks sort of content.

Ahead of us, the tractor turns onto a dirt road, and Mom speeds up the car, and we head for home.

Among the Statues

The next morning, Mom drops me off at school extra early so she can get to some appointments. The door to the humanities room is still closed, so I go outside to visit the goats.

I'm halfway through the statue garden when I see Mags's legs jutting out into the path. She's sitting on the ground, wrapped in a chunky sweater, her back resting against the statue of Athena. Mags's eyes are closed, her fingers curled around a travel mug.

"Mags? What are you doing?"

"Oh, Caitlyn!" She sits up. "You're here early! I'm enjoying my morning coffee before heading in to start the day. I find that my friends here"—she gestures vaguely at the statues—"are pretty good company when you've got something on your mind."

I do have something on my mind. Lots of somethings.

"Mags." I hesitate. "Do you remember when we were talking about *kleos*?"

She nods.

"Remember when I said that when people have *kleos*, it's not really them we're remembering, not exactly?"

"As I recall, Caitlyn, you said that what we remember about others is always *incomplete*. I thought that was a very good way of describing it actually."

"Well, what if everything we know about *everyone* is incomplete? Not just people from a long time ago, but even the people we supposedly know right now?"

In a way, I'm asking about Paulie. It's like there are all these different versions of him, and I can't figure out which version is right. But I'm not *just* asking about Paulie. I'm also thinking about my mom's wish that she had a friend, and about Gabby missing her dad, and about her dad moving here from so far away, and about gone being gone. I'm also thinking about Henry holding on to his secret, and all the other stuff that might be happening around me—things that I don't even know to wonder about, let alone ask about.

"Everything we know is always incomplete," Mags says. "In the end, we get to fully know exactly one person only: ourselves. And that's only if we work hard at it."

After a minute, I ask, "Was Paulie Fink really as great as everyone says?"

Mags smiles. "Paulie was pretty special. But then, so are all my students."

"But all those stories people tell about him. Did they really happen?"

"Sort of. But has anyone told you about how furious they used to get at him?"

"They did?"

"Sure. Sometimes Paulie got the whole class in trouble. I can remember more than a few missed recesses for them. That never went over well."

That's not something they've mentioned. Not once, in all these stories.

"When people tell stories," she says, "they make choices. They emphasize some parts. Leave out others. Otherwise, it wouldn't be a story. It would just be a collection of facts. For example, do you remember when I talked about Greek democracy?" she asks.

"Yeah."

"Well, here's a different way of telling that story: Even as the Greeks advanced the notion of democracy, they deliberately denied at least three-quarters of the population— maybe even more—the right to vote. As a woman, I wouldn't have been able to vote. Nor would I have been able to teach, or have any sort of a public voice. Neither would most of the people you know. There are other stories we could tell about the Greeks, too: They were fiercely opposed to outsiders. They fought many, many wars—brutal ones. They enslaved fellow human beings."

"Wait," I say. "So why does everyone talk about them like they're so great? They sound like a bunch of hypocrites."

"*Hypocrites*." Mags says the word like she's turning it over, examining it closely. "Yes, you could say that. You could also say that the story many people have chosen to tell about the Greeks through the centuries is itself a kind of myth."

"So why are we learning about them?"

"Well, the easy answer is this: For the rest of your life, you'll come across things—laws, literature, art, sciences— that were born in the days of Plato. Even the word *hypocrite*, Caitlyn, comes from a Greek word that means actor. But like I say, that's just one answer, and it's the easy one."

"What's the harder one?"

"Caitlyn, there is not a single thing that the Greeks did wrong that humans aren't still wrestling with today. Not one."

Huh. So thousands of years have gone by since Plato talked about walking into the light, and people still keep getting stuff wrong.

"The thing is," Mags adds, "we get a choice. We can choose which aspects of our world we want to keep, and which to leave in the dustbin of history."

Mags takes another sip of her coffee. We sit like this for a few minutes—quiet and surrounded by gods who were never real in the first place. I wonder if she knows about the school closing. I want to ask her, but I'm pretty sure she wouldn't be able to tell me even if she did.

Then it's time to go in. As we walk toward the building, Mags says, "You know, sometimes I wonder what Julius Oxthorpe would think about us being here. Sitting in his old rooms, talking about myths and legends in his sculpture garden."

"I guess he'd think it's kinda cool?"

"Maybe," says Mags. "But I'm not so sure. Look around. This place is like a shrine to the ancients. But it's so secluded, it feels like old Mr. Oxthorpe built it entirely for himself. I suspect he'd hate our being here. So being here makes me feel like a rebel. Like I'm claiming something that was never intended for me in the first place. Actually, it's the same thing that makes me enjoy studying the classics."

"Mags the rebel." I laugh.

It occurs to me that she might be a Disruptor in her own way.

The Office Challenge

Later that morning, as we head toward the goats, I stop the class in the statue garden, near where Mags sat earlier. "Paulie Fink earned a reputation for bringing people and things into places you'd never expect," I say. "He brought pizza into classrooms, placed glitter on ceiling fans, introduced fruit flies...well...everywhere. And of course, there's the famous example of him hiding in Glebus's office."

I pause. I look at all those statues, then at the mansion where Mr. Oxthorpe probably never imagined us, wouldn't want us. Yet here we are.

"So the challenge for our final three contestants"—I glance at Yumi, Diego, and Fiona—"involves going somewhere they don't belong, and where they're definitely not wanted."

"Yessss...!" Fiona hisses. She turns to Diego and gives him a fist bump.

"Where?" asks Yumi. "Where do you want us to go?"

I lean in and whisper, as if those stone gods might be listening, "Glebus's office."

Diego and Fiona and Yumi exchange looks.

"We're going to get caught," whispers Fiona.

"Yeah," Diego says. "We'll all be eliminated by the time this is done."

"If you get caught, that's okay. This one is a timed competition. Only the length of time matters. Whoever gets kicked out first gets eliminated."

"That's it?" Yumi asks. "That's the whole challenge? It seems sort of... straightforward."

"That's true," says Gabby. "But on *Megastar*, the most straightforward challenges are usually the ones that get the most interesting."

In the distance, I hear Mr. Farabi calling us. "Yoo-hoo! Originals, we've got some hungry goats down here waiting for you!"

"Challenge begins at recess," I tell them.

Interview: Yumi

There's plenty of sneaking around in Shakespeare's plays, did you know that, Caitlyn? That's how I felt at recess, as Diego, Fiona, and I stood outside Glebus's office: like we were three heroic Shakespearean characters nearing the end of a great drama.

Hopefully not a tragedy, though!

We tapped lightly on Glebus's door. When she didn't answer, we scurried in. We knew we probably didn't have much time—Glebus usually walks around at the start of recess, but she returns to her office pretty quickly.

Once we were inside, Fiona and Diego both moved at once toward the closet. Diego's quick, but Fiona's small and sneaky, like a fierce little jackrabbit. She darted in front of Diego, reached the closet first, jumped in, and slammed the door behind her.

I ran to Glebus's desk, figuring I'd hide behind it just like Paulie had. I climbed over the top, then lowered myself into the space behind.

But I could only crouch down a few inches before my knees banged the wall. I shifted position, tried again. No go! Paulie was always smaller than I was, and, I suddenly realized, he'd been a year younger, too. So it made sense that he could fit there and I couldn't. No matter which way I moved, I stuck out like a jack-in-the-box.

Meanwhile, Diego zipped around the room looking for a place to hide. He tried squatting behind Glebus's rolling desk chair, but he just looked like a Mini during team tag. He slipped behind the blinds, but his jeans and sneakers were still totally visible.

The whole situation was so absurd: my top half sticking up behind the back of Glebus's desk, and Diego's bottom half sticking out from under her blinds. So I started cracking up.

That's when I heard a *click-click-click*. Glebus's footsteps.

As Glebus approached, Diego stepped out from behind the blinds. He wasn't laughing, like I was. His jaw was tense, and his eyes were hard, and I could tell: He was determined not to lose.

That's what makes Diego such a great competitor, see.

He leaped toward the closet where Fiona was already hiding, yanked the door open, and jumped in there with her.

He pulled the closet door closed just as Glebus pushed the door to her office open.

And there I was, all alone and totally exposed.

I had exactly one option left: try to will myself into invisibility. I pressed myself flat against the wall and did my best to blend in with Glebus's floral-patterned wallpaper.

It didn't work.

"Yumi!" Glebus sputtered. "What... what in the world do you think you're doing?"

I guess, for me, it turned out to be a tragedy after all.

Well. As you can imagine, when Diego jumped into the closet with me, I was all, *What the—?*

And then I was like, *No. Not fair. This is my hiding spot.* I told him that, too. I said, "This is my hiding spot, so you get your ruinous butt right out of here, Diego Silva." At least I tried to say that, but with Glebus on the other side of the door, my only means of communication was smacking him on the arm. Through the crack in the door, I saw him point to where Yumi had been hiding. He shook his head and made a *you're out* motion, like an umpire might in a baseball game.

On the other side of the door, Glebus started barking at Yumi. She was caught. Out. *Eliminated.* That meant Diego and I were the last two remaining. One of us was going to be the Next Great Paulie Fink.

I realized that this meant Diego, in addition to being my best friend, was now officially my mortal enemy.

My *nemesis*.

Inside the closet, I glared at him. It was the sort of death stare that I hoped said, *I will destroy you, Diego Silva.* And you know what he did in response? He glared right back.

We sat like that for a while, each of us death-staring at the other as Glebus lectured Yumi. We death-stared during Yumi's apology, and we death-stared as Glebus barked, "I don't even have time to figure out what made you crawl back there, young lady, because I'm now late for a very, very important phone call. Yes, shut the door behind you, I will find you later, and we will most definitely deal with this situation."

We death-stared as Glebus shut the door and punched numbers into her phone, and we were still death-staring as we heard her say, "Northland Free Press? Yes, this is Alice Glebus at the Mitchell School. I'm returning a call from one of your reporters."

And then I realized we were going to have to settle in for a bit. That's about the point where all that death-staring started to feel awkward. I turned my face away from him dramatically.

In the name of Paulie Fink, I will fight you, Diego Silva. Only one of us will get kleos, I said to myself.

Paulie would have loved this if he could have seen it.

Something Is Very Wrong

By the time the bell rings for lunch, Fiona and Diego are nowhere to be seen. On our way to the cafeteria, we walk past Glebus's office. "Are they still in there?" wonders Henry.

"They can't possibly be," says Yumi. Earlier, as she described her failed attempt at invisibility, she was laughing. Now she just looks worried.

Gabby tiptoes up, presses her ear to the door. "Glebus is talking," she whispers. She listens for a minute. "She's saying *distressing . . . Like I said earlier, nothing is final . . . No . . . no . . .*"

"Is she talking to Fiona and Diego?" asks Sam.

"I can't tell," Gabby whispers.

After lunch, the door's still shut. Which means either Diego and Fiona are in huge trouble, or they're as good at hiding as Paulie Fink ever was.

We head up to math class. Mr. Farabi asks where Fiona and Diego are. Timothy coughs, looks down at his desk. "Glebus's office," he says.

"Uh-oh, that doesn't sound good," says Mr. Farabi, and he begins the lesson without them.

We're almost twenty minutes into class when the door finally opens. Everyone looks up eagerly. I expect Diego and Fiona to be cracking up. Or at least trying not to smile. But something's odd. They don't look at any of us, or at each other. They quietly slip into their seats and stare at their desks. Then they stay like that. Silent, and perfectly still.

Which means something is very, very wrong.

It's all fun and games until you sit in a closet in your school principal's office listening to her talking to a reporter saying stuff you were never meant to hear. Stuff like "Those budget numbers are correct....No, they're not sustainable."

At first, I wasn't even listening. But then Glebus started saying other things, like, "Laying off teachers wouldn't solve the problem. We barely have any teachers already...Yes, we did have some high-level donors until this year...I'm sure you know that the town of Mitchell doesn't have a lot of high-net-worth donors...Yes, I voluntarily reduced my own salary. Yes, I realize that a school faced with closure is news, but I'm asking you to hold the story until we're certain...This isn't how I want our families to find out. These are children, after all, this the only school they've ever known..."

Somewhere in there I was like, *Hold on. Wait. No.*

I turned and looked at Fiona then. I wanted to ask, *Are you hearing what I'm hearing?*

Because what I was hearing couldn't be real. No way could it be real.

But I saw the look on her face. And I knew that she was hearing it, too. And that meant it was real after all.

I mean, it didn't take a brain surgeon or a rocket scientist or even a half-sentient robot to understand what was happening. Somebody was trying to close the school. And Glebus was trying to keep us from finding out.

To the Mitchell School Community,

This afternoon, I learned that a story will soon appear in local news outlets. The story is about the town of Mitchell's budget crisis and the undeniable difficulty this crisis poses for our community's only school.

I'll be honest: The news is not good. Rising costs and falling tax revenues have placed such a strain on the local budget that the town council may soon vote to cease funding our school altogether.

The situation with which we are faced is not uncommon— either across our state, or across the nation. Nearly 70 percent of all rural schools have had to close their doors since 1930, a total loss of more than 150,000 schools nationwide.

But statistics don't have human faces. This is our school. This is our community. These are our children.

While there is certainly no money in our town's budget, it's not impossible that emergency state funding could be made available, which is a question of political will. Or perhaps some private donations will be offered to help keep our doors open.

Various news outlets may visit the school over the next few days, some with cameras. They're mostly interested in campus shots, though I have encouraged them to return for our

255

upcoming soccer game against Devlinshire (Go, green!). If you do not want your child filmed, please let me know. That said, I do believe news coverage could help.

We are a tiny community, a tiny school. Perhaps when seen from the outside, it looks like we don't matter. We who live on the inside know that the opposite is true. We do matter. The one promise I can make to you is that I'll never, ever lose sight of that.

Your principal,
Alice C. Glebus

Canceled

When you watch a television show, it rarely changes genre mid-season. Comedies stay funny, thrillers stay suspenseful, and dramas stay...well, dramatic. Maybe that's what's so jarring about what happens after everyone finds out the school might close. Everything just shifts.

The cast shifts, that's for sure. Over the next week, there's no more chanting, no more fighting, no more laughing, no more talk about Paulie. It's like the Originals packed up the loudest parts of themselves into a suitcase, set the bag down, and forgot about it. If someone were to find it and unzip it, they'd be greeted by cries of *Caitlyn likes kickball!* and *In the name of Paulie Fink!* and *This challenge stinks!*

But I guess no one finds that suitcase, because they stay quiet.

And that's another thing that changes: Even though the competition is down to the last two contestants, it's like the Originals don't even care anymore. They don't ask about it. When I bring it up with Gabby, suggesting that maybe a really great final challenge would get everyone's mind off of the school situation, she just shakes her head.

"Not yet," she says. "I don't think anyone's in the mood. Maybe after this whole thing blows over."

But I'm not so sure it's going to blow over. Which means the competition's going to be left hanging, like a show that gets canceled mid-season, just when you were starting to enjoy it.

The story hits the local newspaper on a Saturday. My mom reads it out loud. She asks me if I'm sad, and I guess I am, because I nod without thinking.

"Aw, kiddo," she says. She kisses me on the top of my head, and then she hugs me. We stay like that for a long time.

When we return to school after the weekend, Glebus makes the rounds to speak with each class. Mostly she spends the time reassuring us that she's doing everything she can, but that no matter what happens, we'll be okay.

"But we won't be the Originals," says Diego.

Gabby agrees. "It won't be the same at all."

I watch Glebus struggle to respond to that, and it hits me: She might be the saddest one of all. I'm not sure I like knowing that. It's better to believe your principal is a witch than to know she's a real person with feelings. I guess I thought being in charge was about making rules and making other people go along with them. But maybe it's also about everyone needing things from you that you don't know how or maybe aren't able to give.

Fiona raises her hand. "The news report says this happens to lots of schools. Is it happening to Devlinshire?"

"Of course not," Yumi says. "Devlinshire's rich, so they have plenty of tax money for their school."

I look at Glebus, expecting her to correct Yumi. Because that can't be right—it doesn't seem fair for schools to work that way. But Glebus doesn't disagree with what Yumi said. All she says is, "I have not heard that Devlinshire is at any risk of closing."

So having money isn't only about what kind of car you drive, or how big your house is or whatever. It's about really basic things, like whether you get a school.

Gabby raises her hand. "So can't we do, like, a fundraiser? Like, a dinner, or a bake sale, or a car wash or something? Or all of them, as many times as we need?"

"The school needs an awful lot of money, Gabby," Glebus says. "It's more than a car wash or bake sale can—"

"Well, what about one of those online fund-raisers? We can send the link to everyone we know, make it go viral. If this were *Megastar*—"

Yumi interrupts. "*Megastar*'s not real, Gabby."

"It's sort of real," insists Gabby. "More real than other shows, anyway. That's the whole point."

Yumi shakes her head. "It's real except for the fact that the producers create absurd situations that would never,

ever happen in real life. And then directors feed the contestants lines during the filming. And after they film, editors sit around and stitch together tiny clips from thousands of hours, which means that they can tell whatever version of the story they want."

"I know all *that*," Gabby says, "but at least they start with real people, not actors."

"Real people who audition for the part in the first place," Diego says quietly. "And then are picked by casting agents."

Fiona reaches over, places her hand on Gabby's arm. "It's fake," she says quietly. "It's all really fun to watch, sure, but it's fake."

Gabby yanks her hand away. "*None* of you understand what I'm trying to—"

But before she can finish, Glebus clears her throat and tries to return to the point. "We could certainly try a fund-raiser," she says. "But you should know that nine out of ten online fund-raisers never meet their goal. You only hear about the successful ones, that's all. So it's highly unlikely that it would work."

I expect Gabby to suggest other things, like, I don't know, writing to celebrities for help, or finding out who won the lottery recently and asking them to pitch in. But instead, she just stares at a spot on her desk, her eyes open like she's trying not to blink.

Interview: Fiona

FIONA:

That morning, as we headed to the goats, we saw the first of the notes. It was stuck to the Paulie statue, between the rules and the photo of Jadelicious.

I thought maybe Yumi had left a sacrifice. She never did get the chance, since no one was in the mood for an elimination ceremony after that closet-hiding fiasco.

But when I asked her if she'd left something, she just shook her head.

We walked closer. It was the newspaper article, the one that had appeared in the *Northland Free Press* over the weekend. There was the headline: MITCHELL WEIGHS SCHOOL CLOSING. I already knew the beginning by heart: *October 21, MITCHELL, VT. The looming closure of the Mitchell School, an experimental village academy school that opened eight years ago, has sent shock waves through the community of Mitchell, population 826...* I could practically recite the whole article now. *Budget crisis. Town funding insufficient. Unsustainable. Needs influx of cash.* A bunch of boring-sounding words that all add up to one thing: we're in trouble.

Across the article, someone had scrawled with a big red marker: PLEASE SAVE THIS SCHOOL.

"Who did this?" I asked. And when nobody answered, I shouted it: "WHO DID THIS?"

To this day, I still don't know.

At recess, there was a second note, this one scribbled on lined paper: MITCHELL MATTERS. By soccer practice, there was a third: THOUGH MITCHELL BE BUT LITTLE, SHE IS FIERCE. There were more notes the next day, too. By Wednesday afternoon, two days before the game, there were so many notes Paulie's neon shirt looked like it was covered in white ruffles.

All through practice that day, it was like I heard this voice inside me. *Fiona, what if you lose? Fiona, what if you lose the school? Fiona, what if you lose the game? Fiona, what are you going to do? Fiona Fiona Fiona Fiona Fiona.*

At the end of practice, I marched over to that statue of Paulie. I grabbed a piece of paper and a marker, and I scrawled: HELP.

CAITLYN:
Did you mean help us beat Devlinshire, or help us with the school?

FIONA:
I'm not sure. Maybe both. By that point, the fate of the school and the outcome of the game felt like one and the same.

Interview: Gabby

When my dad was going through his treatment, we kept getting these bills in the mail—bills we knew we'd never be able to pay. At first we hid them from my dad, because my grandma said that he only needed to think about getting better. But after a while, when he didn't get better, there was no need to hide them anymore.

People did all these things to try to help us. There were bake sales and car washes and community dinners. I probably went to eight separate spaghetti dinners where people paid five dollars to eat pasta off paper plates. The Donut Lady put out a jar where people could stuff their change, and on three different nights, the waitstaff at Big Esther's Diner donated every penny of their tips. Even some people who had never been all that nice to my dad helped out.

Oh, and the Originals even ran a lemonade stand downtown. They only got $32, but it was still really nice. And one day when I was super sad, Paulie said he'd talk to his royal connections from the Republic of Endrisistan, which of course was so stupid but it just made me laugh so hard when I really needed it.

All of it was so nice. But it wasn't enough.

If we'd been characters on *Megastar*, here's what would have happened: The producers would have filmed us counting our money and looking at bills. And just when the audience was starting to worry, there'd be a knock on the door. We'd open the door and the judges would walk in. They'd tell us that some rich person—some celebrity or talk-show host or something—had heard about our story. And they'd decided to pay off all our bills for us. As the cameras were rolling, they'd hand us one of those posters that looks like a giant check, with such a huge dollar amount that we'd never have to worry again.

I know just how I'd react, too: I'd hold my hands up to my cheeks. I'd gasp. My grandma would cry, and then we'd hug, and the following week, *People* magazine would write a profile about the whole thing.

My grandma and I started watching *Megastar* right after the funeral. At first all we wanted was a distraction. But then it became more than that. At the start of the season, all of the contestants are regular people, just like us. I loved knowing that by the end of the season one of their lives would change completely. And if *their* lives could change like that, ours could, too.

But I don't know. Maybe Yumi's right. Maybe that sort of thing only happens on TV.

Bad Omens

The day before the Devlinshire game, Mags pulls an index card that says simply, in Fiona's handwriting: Recess.

Mags stares at it for a few long moments. The look on her face is the same one she had when she first dreamed up the index-card challenge—like she's turning something over in her mind. "I've got an idea," she says. "Let's not *talk* about the value of recess, of taking a break from work and stress. Let's immerse ourselves. What do you say we skip class today? Head outside."

Is she serious? When none of us follow, she turns around. "Well, come on!"

On the way out, Mags tells us every society has wrestled with the idea of what constitutes a good life. "The Greeks had a name for their version of the good life: *eudaimonia*. The concept incorporates all the things it takes for a person to flourish: joy, hard work, learning, and ethics. *Eudaimonia* isn't about short-term happiness. Rather, it's a way of asking the question *When I look back on my life, what will I want to have done?*"

We step outside. It's a bright, brisk day. She wraps her sweater around her and looks at us. "So. Let's live some *eudaimonia* right now. Here you are, late October of your seventh-grade year. You've been given this unexpected gift of an extra recess. How shall you spend it?"

Thomas flashes me a quick grin, then raises his hand. "I hear that Caitlyn likes kickball," he offers. I know he's talking about Zucchini Day and the world's stupidest chant: *Caitlyn likes kickball!* I was so mad at them that day.

But as they begin chanting it now, I don't feel so alone.

We divide into teams, make the Paulie statue home base. My team is first to kick. Diego's up. "Remember," he says before taking his place at home plate, "the ball is every Devlinshire kid who ever ticked us off." Then he slams it into the outfield and makes a clean run to second base.

Gabby reaches first base as Diego takes third.

Yumi's up next: a good, strong groundball. Fiona, in the outfield, grabs it as Diego moves toward home.

"Oh no you don't!" shouts Fiona. *"In the name of Paulie Fink!"* She launches the kickball toward home plate. It misses Diego by a wide margin, flies past home, and lands smack-dab in the middle of the goat pen.

The big goat walks over to the ball and nudges it with his nose, curious. Then he picks it up in his mouth and chomps down. It deflates almost instantly.

"Well," says Henry, "this doesn't seem like a great omen."

While the rest of us are trying to figure out how to spend the rest of our free class period, Yumi asks Mags for a permanent marker. She sits down at the base of the Paulie statue and begins to draw on the wilted kickball.

"I never made my sacrifice," Yumi says. "I want to make one now."

When she's done, she holds it up. She's drawn a face. One eye is noticeably larger than the other, the nose looks a bit like a snout, and the lopsided smile looks way too much like a banana.

Everyone knows exactly where this kickball head will go.

Since Fiona's the smallest, Timothy and Thomas lift her up. She slips the kickball face onto the top of the branch. The Paulie statue doesn't look like some weird headless scarecrow anymore. It looks like a lopsided, grinning, patched-together *person*, draped in pom-pom garlands. All the notes stuck to it make it look like it's dressed in tatters.

"He looks good," says Willow.

"He looks *great*," Sam agrees.

"What do you think it means when you put a bad omen on a good-luck charm?" Fiona asks.

"I don't know," Diego replies. "Something unexpected, probably."

Fiona nods like she's thinking hard about that. Then she turns to the rest of us. "We have to beat Devlinshire this year. We just *have* to. It could be our last chance."

A Rabbit in the Fort

On the morning of the game, we all show up in green T-shirts. Each of us is wearing a different shade. Henry's shirt is the color of cooked peas, with a CAMP HIGH PEAKS logo on the front, while Fiona's is more of a mint; she's even got a matching blazer over her T-shirt and shorts. Diego's is the color of a shamrock, and both of the twins are wearing camouflage.

Mine is a deep, dark green, almost black, like a swamp on a cloudy day. It has the name of the hospital where my mom used to work.

"Next time we should pick a single shade of green," I say to Henry. Even as the words are coming out of my mouth, I wish I could take them back. There probably won't be a next time.

When Mags comes in, she grabs Paulie's hat, reaches in, and pulls out an index card. She unfolds it. "Talk about the right card at the right moment," she says. Then she reads it out loud: *"How to be brave when everything changes too fast."*

My card. I wrote it a million years ago, when I was dealing with one sort of change. I was so embarrassed after I turned it in, like I was the only one who would ever ask such a question.

Mags walks to the window and stares out for a few moments before turning back to us. "I don't think I can tell you anything here that you don't already know, Originals. Being brave is what you're already doing. It's putting one foot in front of the other. As you do, try to show as much honor, as much *arete*, as you can."

Somewhere over the course of the morning, the news van shows up. They're filming everything—the goats, the statues, the playground, the portrait of Julius Oxthorpe. It's pretty distracting. When we get to recess, we can even see them at the edge of the field, filming us from a distance.

"Well." Gabby frowns. "This isn't exactly how I pictured being on TV."

At lunch, Mr. Twilling stops me as I head into the cafeteria. "Hey, Caitlyn? I could really use your help. It's about Kiera."

It takes me a second to realize who he's even talking about: Fuzzy. She's just Fuzzy to me.

"A few of my students have been asking questions about the school, about what's going to happen. We've tried to be honest with them, but also reassuring. Most of the kids are fine—next year's a lifetime away when you're in kindergar-ten. But Kiera's a sensitive soul. She left the classroom to go to the bathroom, but didn't come back. She went into the fort that Henry built, and now she refuses to come out. Do you think maybe you could talk to her?"

I tell him I'll try. Of course I'll try.

When I get to the fort I can see Fuzzy's red sneakers sticking out. I squat down. "Knock, knock." I poke my head in. Fuzzy's knees are pulled up to her chin, her arms wrapped around them. "Is there a Real Rabbit around here? I've been trying to find a Real Rabbit all day. Oh, hey look! There's one."

She doesn't say anything, so I crawl inside. Fuzzy shifts a little to the left, making room.

It's nice in here. Bigger than it looks from the outside. It's dark, with slivers of sunlight slipping in between the branches.

"Are you sad?" I ask. She moves Real Rabbit's head up and down, like Real Rabbit's the one saying yes.

"Maybe a little scared, too?" She doesn't answer, just bites her lip.

"I get it," I say. "I had to switch schools this year, did you know that?"

She looks up at me, and I can tell she's surprised.

"I forgot that you might not know," I say. "But your first day of kindergarten was my first day here, too. I was so scared."

And now that the words are finally out there, I realize how true they are. *I was scared*.

"But you're big," Fuzzy whispers.

"Well, that's true," I say. "But that didn't stop me from being scared."

It wasn't just that first day, either, I realize. I think I've actually been scared for a long time. Even when I thought I was being as strong as stone.

For a long while, we sit there, just the two of us, and Real Rabbit, in a fort and kind of scared.

And when Anna Spang's face pops into my head, I don't try to push it away. I just sit there with the memory.

The Story I Don't Tell

It happened last year, on one of those dreamy green days when the teachers open the windows and warm breezes move into the classroom, and you can just feel that summer's around the corner. We played volleyball in gym class. Every time the ball came near Anna, kids made donkey noises. I don't remember who started it—it wasn't me, but I joined right in. The teachers told us to knock it off, so we did it more quietly.

When the game ended, Anna walked straight into a bathroom stall in the locker room and shut the door. She didn't come out.

I was halfway to my next class before I realized I'd left my math notebook behind. I raced back to the locker room. Anna was on a bench, all alone. Just me and Anna for once, none of my friends nearby. She looked different—more *real*, almost like I was seeing her for the first time. Her eyes were swollen and her skin was blotchy, like the map of some distant planet.

I remember thinking, *That's what I look like when I cry.*

If my friends had been there, I'd have moved past her, pretended she wasn't there at all, maybe laughed a little too loud to show that I was too busy having fun to even notice her. Maybe if a teacher had been there, I'd have said something, like *Bell's about to ring*, or *Better hurry, we've got that math quiz*.

And if we lived in a different universe altogether, I'd have said something else. *I'm not really like you think I am.* Maybe I'd tell her *I don't know what this thing is inside me, this hard thing, I don't know where it came from, but I know it's taking over.*

Instead, I just stood there, each of us looking at the other, until finally I snatched up my notebook and hurried away.

Then summer came, and my mother told me we were moving. And now here I am, sitting with a sad kindergartner and her stuffed rabbit, wondering what to say. I can't tell her the story that's on my mind, because I know she'd ask why I wasn't nicer to Anna. And I know I'd never be able to give her an answer that's good enough.

Sometimes ordinary people do crummy things. That's just the truth of it. They do things that they'll wish later they could undo. And they'll just be stuck with them forever.

I watch Fuzzy, and I think about the way she looked at me on the first day of school: like I was someone to look up to, even though I didn't know how to talk to her, didn't even know how to open her milk carton.

Fake it till you make it, Gabby had told me.

I wonder: What if I really could be the person Fuzzy thought she saw on that first day? What would that person do right now?

"Hey, Fuzzy," I finally say. "I want to tell you a story."

"Paulie vs. the Gleeb?"

I shake my head. "Nope. This is a different kind of story."

The Story I Do Tell

Once upon a time there was a girl who felt too soft on the inside. She made a wish that she could be hard, and I guess it worked. Soon she did feel something hard inside her, like a peach pit had formed behind her ribs.

No, that's not right. The thing she felt was even harder than that, and unlike a pit, nothing would ever grow from it.

This thing was hard like stone.

Some days that stone burned like lava, and on others it was as cold as ice. And when she felt it, it was difficult to feel much else. It grew, that stone. It got a little bigger every day. The girl didn't think this was such a big deal, except sometimes she was sad, and always she was scared, and a stone isn't any sort of comfort when you're sad and scared.

So I guess it turns out it really mattered quite a bit.

The stone made her mean, too. To lots of people in small ways, and to one particular person in a very big way. The bigger it grew, the meaner she became.

Then one day, this girl wandered into the woods. She walked so deep into the woods she couldn't see her old house anymore, which made her extra frightened. That's when she met a Real Rabbit, who had big eyes and very long arms and just a tiny bit of magic inside. With his big eyes, he saw the stone. He saw how tired she was from carrying it everywhere. So with his long arms and a tiny bit of magic, Real Rabbit was able to reach down the girl's throat and pull out the stone.

Once it was out, he threw the stone away, into a river. The girl felt lighter then, and a little less tired, and a whole lot less mean.

Which meant that Real Rabbit isn't just magic. He's also kind of a hero.

How to Be Brave

"The end," I finish.

Fuzzy looks at Real Rabbit. She stretches his arms out, moves him back and forth, making him sway from side to side.

"Did it hurt?" she asks. At first I think she's talking to Real Rabbit, but then I understand.

"When the stone came out, you mean?"

She nods.

"Well." I think about that. "A little. But once it was out, she felt a lot better."

"Did she say sorry? For being mean?"

I remember standing in that locker room, eyes fixed on Anna. How frozen I felt.

"Not yet," I admit.

Her brow furrows, just a bit. "She should say sorry."

It must seem so simple to Fuzzy. Maybe it is simple. But sitting there, I can't imagine apologizing to Anna. It's like she's on one side of a rushing river, and I'm on the other, and there's no bridge to connect us.

"She probably should," I say. "Maybe someday. But this particular girl still isn't very brave."

"But she's braver than she used to be?"

I consider that. "Yeah," I finally tell her. "Yeah, I think so."

Fuzzy keeps making Real Rabbit dance, her lips moving like she's singing without noise. Even though I can't hear her, I'm pretty sure Real Rabbit can. Me, I listen to the sounds on the other side of the fort—the leaves rustling like whispers, the goats bleating in the distance, the faraway sounds of the cafeteria where everyone is but us.

She should say sorry.

She isn't very brave.

But she's braver than she used to be.

I don't know what makes Fuzzy finally decide that it's time for Real Rabbit to stop dancing. I don't know what makes her feel ready to go back into the world. But after a bit, she crawls out of the fort, then brushes pine needles off Real Rabbit.

When I come out, the sunlight is brighter than I expected, and it takes a few seconds for my eyes to adjust. When they do, I see one of those newspeople in the distance, filming the goats.

As we walk across the field, Fuzzy holds up one of Real Rabbit's paws to me, and I take it. She's got him by the other paw. Now we're three in a row. Two humans and a magic rabbit, walking hand in hand.

The cameraperson shifts. Now they're pointing the

camera right at us. I think about Glebus telling parents that nobody has to be filmed if they don't want to. And I realize I don't care. *Let them film*, I think. *Maybe someday, years from now, Fuzzy will watch the footage and remember that all of this—this ramshackle mansion, these cranky goats, this makeshift fort, and this strange crooked scarecrow surrounded by sacrifices—even existed.*

"Will it ever be back?" Fuzzy asks.

"Hmm?"

"The bad stone. Will it grow back? In the girl?"

I think about that, about how all these good ideas about *arete*, honor, have been around for two thousand years, and yet people just keep messing up anyway.

"I don't know," I tell her. "The girl doesn't want it to, but she's not sure. She's not certain about much of anything anymore."

Ahead of us, the cafeteria doors open, and the Minis come spilling out onto the playground. I look at the field where we're going to play soccer soon, and at the Paulie statue that's supposedly our good-luck charm, with the kickball head that's probably a bad omen. I look at all those notes fluttering in the wind.

Devlinshire arrives in an hour.

Surprise

Everyone's freaking out. We're in Mags's classroom, waiting for Devlinshire to arrive, all jangled nerves and raw energy. Diego's leg is jiggling up and down so fast he's practically jackhammering a hole into the floor. Fiona can't stop shifting in her seat. Next to me, she tucks her left foot under her butt. Almost immediately, she untucks. Shifts again.

Everyone's moving, actually. Yumi's drumming her fingers on her desk. Henry rakes his fingers through his hair, and Timothy won't stop cracking his knuckles. As for me, I only notice that I'm flicking a pencil back and forth when it flies across the room.

Which means I'm nervous, too.

That's when we hear the rumble of a bus engine. Getting closer. "They're here," Henry whispers.

We listen to the *hiss* of brakes, the *creak* of bus doors opening. And then we hear voices, kids' voices, coming through in an indistinct blur of chatter. But then someone shouts something, three syllables, and others follow.

They're chanting. Devlinshire is chanting. Just like the

Mitchell kids do. Except what they're saying is something altogether different.

"Ring the bell!
Ring the bell!
Ring the bell!"

Fiona's the first to get up, so fast she knocks her chair to the floor.

"Fiona," Mags warns, but Fiona's already at the window. As soon as she's up, everyone else follows.

There they are, marching toward the building: a mass of kids in sapphire-blue shirts, crisp white shorts. They're heading straight for the Good Day Bell like an advancing army of bright blue beetles.

"Ring the bell!
Ring the bell!
Ring the bell!"

"Don't you dare," Fiona snarls. "Don't you dare touch our bell."

We watch, helpless, as one of the kids in blue reaches out, grabs the rope. Next to me, Gabby sucks in her breath.

Clang.

All these weeks, I've only rung the bell one time: that afternoon with Fuzzy. The Good Day Bell still doesn't feel like it belongs to me. But for some reason I get this hot, angry feeling inside me when I hear that *clang* and the cheers that follow.

That bell is barely mine. So it definitely isn't *theirs.*

I glance at the others, expecting them to look furious. Instead, they look…confused.

"Wait," says Fiona. She squeezes her eyes shut, then opens them again. Then she shakes her head, as if trying to wake herself from a dream.

"No…," mutters Diego, more to himself than anyone else. "No *way*."

"Holy crow," Gabby says, her voice awed.

I look at the Devlinshire kids again, trying to figure out what's got the Originals so shocked. "What is it? What's going on?"

Nobody answers. I glance at Henry. He's gone kind of pale. Almost like he's seeing a ghost.

That's when it hits me. Maybe there *is* a ghost of sorts down there.

Or maybe not exactly a ghost. Maybe more like an alien. Or someone who mysteriously vanished, and now—just as mysteriously—is walking toward the building.

Wearing a bright blue shirt.

THE
FIRST GREAT
PAULIE FINK

Interview: Diego

I couldn't believe it.

I mean, I actually couldn't believe it. I kept thinking that this was a joke. That my eyes were playing tricks on me or whatever.

Paulie Fink was down there. *Our* Paulie Fink. Returned from the dead like one of the zombies that Timothy and Thomas are always imitating.

Paulie moved to *Devlinshire*?

He was one of the *rich kids* now?

The One and Only

"Which one is he?" I ask.

Fiona points, but I don't see anyone who jumps out like I always expected Paulie Fink would. It's just a bunch of kids.

"There," says Fiona. "Right *there*." But of course that doesn't help.

"Wait, *which* one?"

"Blue shirt," Diego offers, as if that helps.

"Pushing the hair out of his eyes," adds Yumi.

Oh. "*That's* Paulie Fink?" Everyone nods.

I don't know what I expected. It's not like I thought he'd have green scales and three heads and fourteen eyeballs or anything. But whatever I expected, it wasn't that totally ordinary shaggy-haired kid, sweatshirt tied around his waist just like everyone else.

"Huh," I say.

It's like he can feel us looking at him, because he lifts his eyes, right up to the window where we're all standing. Gabby screams and ducks.

Fiona yells, "Holy fudge nuggets, he sees us!"

Everyone else takes a step backward. Which, if you ask me, is a mighty curious reaction for a group of people who have literally been making offerings to a shrine they created in his honor.

Behind us, Mags commands, "Wave to him."

We wave.

Interview: Gabby

I read this story once in a *Megastar* fan forum. A girl wrote that she'd traveled from North Carolina all the way to Florida to meet Jadelicious in real life. This was just after season two ended, when Jadelicious went on her world tour.

The girl stood outside Jadelicious's dressing room for like two hours. She was holding a copy of Jadelicious's new book, *No Imitation: Winning the Jadelicious Way*. When Jadelicious finally stepped outside, the girl was so confused. It *was* Jadelicious—she had her cat's-eye makeup and silver heels and everything. But at the same time, it seemed like it couldn't possibly be the real Jadelicious. Her eye makeup was smudged, and her cheeks were a little bumpy, like she'd once had a bad case of acne. Mostly, though, the girl wrote on the fan forum, she seemed *way too small* to be Jadelicious.

And Jadelicious, she's larger than life, see?

That's how it felt when I looked at Paulie. It's weird, because I think now he was taller and maybe a little thinner, like someone had taken the Paulie we'd known and stretched him. Something about his face looked different, too. Like his jaw was a little harder, more square.

But here's the weird thing: Even though he looked taller, he also seemed much, much smaller.

In our minds, he'd become larger than life. But then there he was in front of us, just a regular kid in a blue soccer jersey who looked like he'd grown a few inches. The way regular kids do.

I wanted to punch him in the face. That's what I was thinking as we left Mags's classroom and headed down to the field. I thought it over and over again. *I'm so mad I could punch him.*

That traitor.

That rat.

That backstabbing double-crossing Benedict Arnold.

It wasn't just him I wanted to punch, it was all of them. Every stupid Devlinshire kid. Heck, I'd have punched the Devlinshire Hills School itself in the face, which is weird, because a school doesn't even have a face. But I wished Devlinshire had one, so I could punch it.

None of us said a word as we walked. Not one word. We were quiet as we marched toward the back field and saw the crowd waiting: teachers, parents, kids, and all those Minis. Everyone started cheering when they saw us, which somehow made everything feel even worse.

My hands were balled up into tight fists at my side, and my jaw hurt from clenching it so hard.

Devlinshire was warming up, doing some sort of slow-motion skip in unison with a call-and-response. Their coach shouted, "Who's gonna win?"

All together, they shouted back, "We are!"

And right smack in the middle of them was Paulie, lifting his knees and shouting "We are!" just like the rest of them.

His *we* was our *they.*

It felt like they weren't just saying that Devlinshire was going to win this game, but that Devlinshire would *always* win. Like anything that would ever matter to us in our whole lives, they'd manage to take from us. Like it's not enough to have all the money they could ever possibly want, they also had to have one of *us*.

Talk about a double whammy.

They also had a school that wasn't going to close. Triple whammy.

Not to mention they had uniforms and houses that they didn't have to clean themselves and a ski mountain and rock stars and swimming pools and an unbeaten record against us.

I'll tell you, sometimes there are just too many whammies to count.

The Kickoff

It's weird how quiet we are as we walk to the field. Unnerving, really. On the sidelines, I see my mom, wearing medical scrubs and clogs, a wool sweater as big as a blanket wrapped around her. She's talking with Gabby's grandma, and Mags, and some lady I don't know. I can pick Timothy and Thomas's dad out of the crowd; he's got the same broad face as his twins. Glebus is there, passing out donuts to the parents. The younger grades are all there, too. Some of them are holding signs. Fuzzy's sign doesn't have any words, just lots of stick figures in green.

I wave, and she waves back.

On the other side of the field are the Devlinshire kids and their parents. They look different, those parents. A little shinier, almost, like they're made from some different sort of fabric altogether. I see an older guy in a fedora and leather jacket—the rock star, maybe. But there's no time to ask, because almost right away, Mr. Farabi calls us into a huddle.

He reminds us of our positions. I'm up front with Fiona

and Diego. Henry is in goal, and everyone else is somewhere between us. By now, Devlinshire's moving into a huddle of their own, a tight circle of blue. With their heads together, I can't see their faces. For the life of me, I couldn't tell you which one is Paulie Fink.

"I want you to keep the pressure on," Mr. Farabi tells us. "Don't be afraid of passing. But if you've got the ball in your possession and the field is open in front of you, run like crazy."

It's kind of the most obvious advice in the world, but we all nod, because it's the only thing we've got. And then the pep talk is over, and we're all walking to our positions.

Devlinshire takes possession of the ball almost immediately—some tall, lanky kid nabs it and passes it to a compact little guy, all muscle, who passes it right back. Those first couple of passes are slow-motion, casual. The Mitchell kids start to spread out. Then *bam*—everything changes. Lanky Kid gets the ball again, does a little quick-step, then flicks the ball behind him to some girl, and before we even realize it's happened, the girl's sprinting toward our goal at breakneck speed.

"What the—" I hear Diego say. Then everyone's chasing the girl, but it's too late. She reaches our goal in seconds, passes the ball to an open space near the front of the goal. And that's when that little guy, Muscles, comes from out of nowhere, hurtling toward the goal, arriving in the open space exactly when the ball does.

He lifts his foot. Takes a shot.

No way, I think. The game just started. It's way too soon for anyone to score.

The ball flies just out of Henry's reach. It lands in the net with a soft *whoosh*. From the sidelines, I hear my mom shout, "It's okay, Mitchell, you'll get it back!"

But we don't get it back. In fact, it only gets worse from there.

Interview: Yumi, Diego, Timothy, Thomas, Fiona, and Willow

YUMI:

It was *brutal*. That whole first half was a blowout, just utterly humiliating. No matter what we did, Devlinshire kept advancing.

DIEGO:

Every time one of them got the ball, I'd think, *That ball is mine*. I imagined getting it back, charging down the field toward the Devlinshire goal. And then I'd remember who was waiting for me there: Paulie Flipping Fink. It was like a kick in the teeth every time. By the time I regained my concentration, the player in blue had passed me and was moving down toward our goal like I wasn't even there.

TIMOTHY:

It happened like that again and again. We had a couple of breakout moments—Diego and Fiona managed to take a couple of shots on goal. Diego actually scored about ten minutes in, evening out the score. But almost immediately, Devlinshire got another goal, pulling ahead to 2–1. And after that, Paulie stopped every attempt we made.

THOMAS:

But that's the most infuriating part of the whole thing: Paulie was good in goal.

FIONA:

The kid deflected, caught, threw his body on the ball. Paulie
Fink! Like, what the heck?

WILLOW:

That's actually the very question Mr. Farabi asked after
Paulie's third stop. He threw his hands in the air and shouted,
"Why the heck couldn't he do that when he played for us?"

FIONA:

The whole thing made me feel like an idiot, I'll tell you that.
Like Paulie's whole life here had been one giant prank. We
thought that we'd been in on the joke. Instead, the joke was
on us. I just got more and more furious. And when Devlinshire
got a third goal just before the halftime whistle, I was the
kind of mad where you just want to hurt someone.

Shark Attack

"Doing great, Mitchell," Mr. Farabi calls as we come off the field at halftime. He's applauding, as if we're not getting thrashed. "You're really looking good out there."

"We're getting crushed," mutters Diego. "In case you hadn't noticed."

I'm expecting Fiona to start shouting at everyone, but when I look around, she's nowhere near us. Instead, she's marching fast to the far end of the field, past the goal.

Something about the way she's moving—with a determination that's almost menacing—reminds me of a small, bloodthirsty shark.

"Hey, Fiona," calls Mr. Farabi. "Where are you—?"

But by the time the question's out of his mouth, Fiona's arrived at the Paulie statue. She pulls her foot back and kicks it. One of the notes flutters to the ground.

She pulls her foot back again.

No, Fiona. Not in front of them. You can't let Devlinshire know they're upsetting you. I sprint toward her, and Gabby and Henry follow.

"Jerks," Fiona mutters as we arrive. *Kick.*

"You stupid..." *Kick.*

"Rich..." *Kick.*

"Spoiled..." *Kick.*

"Jerks." *Kick. Kick. Kick.*

The rocks that had been resting on the basketball hoop base, keeping the whole thing stable, tumble to the ground. The kickball face flops sideways, and the whole statue tilts precariously to the side.

"Uh, Fiona?" Henry tries to make his voice sound light, like this is all sort of funny. "It's kinda early in the game to break your foot, you know."

Gabby's laugh is nervous. "Right? I mean, there's a whole second half."

Fiona stops kicking. She takes a deep breath. In a very small voice, she says, "He's not even looking at us. We're out there on the field with him and he won't even *acknowledge* us, did you notice?"

Gabby nods. "I noticed."

"He's embarrassed by us," Fiona says. "He's got his new rich friends, and now we're nothing to him. It's like he thinks we're *nothing.*"

I could tell Fiona it might not be like that. It could simply be that he doesn't know what to do, that he's afraid of saying anything at all. But I have no idea what Paulie's thinking.

"And besides," she continues, "what makes him such a

genius, anyway? How come *he's* a genius and *I'm* just a girl who gets in trouble?"

Fiona gives the statue one final, hard kick. "*I scorn you, scurvy companion!*" she shouts.

And now the statue isn't leaning. It's falling. A thought flashes into my head: *Somebody had better prop that thing back up, or it's going to come crashing down onto the goat pen.*

By the time the words are in my head, it's already happening.

The Paulie statue knocks out a section of the fence when it lands. The kickball face slides off, landing in the middle of the pen with a *splat*. The goats leap back, startled.

For a moment, everything's still.

Then one of the baby goats takes a few curious steps forward. He nudges the deflated kickball-face, then takes it in his mouth. He wags his tail, like a pleased dog.

That's the last moment of calm before all hell breaks loose.

Chaos

If you'd asked me a few months ago what I expected to learn in seventh grade, capturing escaped goats wouldn't have made the top five things on my list. It wouldn't have made even the top five thousand.

But that's exactly what I learn to do next.

As soon as the goats realize the fence is down, they're off and running. They leap out of their pen and onto the soccer field, sending kids and parents and a retired rock star scattering.

Glebus jumps into action. She points at Mr. Farabi and shouts that he needs to get the fence back up, fast. Then she starts commanding everyone else. "Toward the building!" she shouts. "Single-file line! Orderly, please! Younger kids first!"

Then she whirls around to us. "Originals, you stay here."

Devlinshire players take off running toward the building, cutting in front of the little kids. Their parents follow, holding arms out like bodyguards.

Only one kid in blue hangs back: Paulie. He watches

us until his coach yells for him to follow. And then Paulie's moving toward the school, too.

Glebus runs over to us, out of breath. "Originals, I'm going to need your help catching the goats, okay? They know you. They *trust* you."

But by now, the animals are everywhere. On the playground a baby goat tries to scamper up the slide; he makes it up a few feet, slides back down, and then tries again. Another roots around in the sandbox. Two goats romp through the field, side by side, each holding part of a GO MITCHELL sign. Another bounds toward the statues, a strip of neon-green fabric between its teeth.

So much for good luck.

"You want *us* to chase the goats?" Gabby asks. "Now? In front of *Devlinshire*?"

Glebus smiles. "You think those kids could catch a goat if they tried? Come on, let's prove you know some things that they don't."

Interview: Willow, Sam, and Lydia

WILLOW:

The next half hour was pretty much the most humiliating experience of my life.

SAM:

All our lives.

LYDIA:

At first everyone ran around chasing the goats without much luck. I caught the one who kept trying to scramble up the slide. But most of the goats ran away as soon as we approached them. So when Mr. Farabi finished fixing the fence, he called us over. He was like, "Originals, we're going to have to work together."

WILLOW:

Here's what we had to do: One at a time, our class had to make a wide circle around each goat. Then we moved in slowly. Finally, when the circle was so tight the goat couldn't escape, Mr. Farabi slipped a rope around the goat's neck and walked it to the pen. Then we had to start all over with the next goat.

LYDIA:

We caught a baby goat near the sandbox, then a goat who was tearing up Paulie's T-shirt, then another goat chowing down on one of our posters at the edge of the woods. We caught goats rummaging through the trash, nosing around through gym bags, and chomping up the notes from the Paulie statue. Even Henry's fact book that he'd sacrificed was shredded.

SAM:
And the whole while, the news cameras were there, filming away.

WILLOW:
After who knows how long, the place was trashed, and there was only one goat left: the big ugly guy—for the life of us, we could not catch him. He crashed through Henry's fort, knocking sticks everywhere. He ran into one of the goals, dragging it across the field. It wasn't until he got his head stuck in a bucket that we could finally capture him.

LYDIA:
But by this point, we were exhausted. I remember Diego looked around and was like, "This place is a war zone."

WILLOW:
And then Gabby was all, "And I think the goats won."

SAM:
And that's when we started to laugh.

The Final Challenge

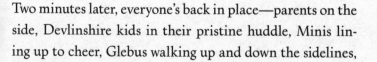

We're still cracking up by the time the Devlinshire kids are back on the field. It's uncontrollable laughter, the kind where you don't make any sound, where all you can do is hold your stomach and shake.

The Devlinshire uniforms are unruffled. Their white shorts are still clean.

I imagine what the scene must look like to them—all of us muddy and shaking amid all that mess—and it only makes me laugh harder.

"New reality show." Yumi's laughing so hard she can barely get the words out. "The Next Great Goat Escape."

"It's goat-geddon all over again," Fiona says, doubled over.

And instantly I know how to turn this game around.

Two minutes later, everyone's back in place—parents on the side, Devlinshire kids in their pristine huddle, Minis lining up to cheer, Glebus walking up and down the sidelines,

303

apologizing to everyone for the interruption. Mr. Farabi is over by the fence, making sure it's solid enough to hold the goats for the second half, which means that we're without a coach. So I call everyone in for a huddle.

"This is it," I tell the other kids. "*This* is your final challenge." They stare at me, not understanding.

I glance over at the Devlinshire kids, a ring of sapphire. "The competition for the Next Great Paulie Fink is officially back on," I say. "And the final challenge begins right now."

"*Now?*" asks Fiona.

"Right now."

"In the middle of the game?" asks Diego. "No way."

"Most of us aren't even in the competition anymore," Sam says. "It was down to Fiona and Diego."

I glance at Gabby. "That happens, doesn't it? The old contestants return to help the final contestants?"

She nods. "Definitely." But the Originals just look at me skeptically.

"You put me in charge," I tell them. "In fact, you *begged* me to be in charge. So I'm telling you: I'm *going* to get this school a new Paulie Fink, one that's not a traitor. Someone who's all ours. And I'm going to do it based on what happens in the next half of this game."

Nearby, the kids in blue shout, *"Devlinshire!"* before jogging onto the field.

"Don't you see?" I say. "Those Devlinshire kids think they know how this story goes: They think that they'll win, just like last year, and just like the year before that. And they expect we'll just go along with that story, play the part of the losers. But what if we refuse to play that role?"

Suddenly it feels urgent, like there's more than a soccer match at stake. "What if we decide to play a different game altogether?"

"So we...don't play soccer?" Yumi asks.

"We play soccer," I say. "But we play it *our* way. On our terms."

The ref blows her whistle. It's time to take the field.

"So what do you want us to do, Caitlyn?" That's Diego.

"Okay," I say. "Do you remember Mini-geddon? The way Paulie won team tag when you were all so certain he was going to lose? He used the element of surprise. That's...your challenge. Use the element of surprise in this second half."

Mr. Farabi's done with the fence, and he's jogging over now. "Originals, *get out there.*"

"Just—create some *chaos*," I tell them. "That's literally what you all do best! It's like, part of your—your *arete*, or something. And as for these Devlinshire kids..." I take a deep breath.

"Caitlyn," Mr. Farabi urges me. "Field! Now!"

My words come out in a rush. "I know they have more of everything. But just because they *have* more doesn't mean they *are* more. I mean, maybe all they are is..." I squeeze my eyes shut. I want to say something about how things aren't always what they seem, how something can seem like strength when it's really the opposite. Like a stone in your chest, or a fancy uniform, or a list of rules.

"All they are is...," I repeat.

It's Timothy who finishes my sentence. "Fusty nuts!" As soon as he says it, I realize it's exactly right.

"Fusty nuts!" his brother shouts, and takes off toward the field.

Then everyone's sprinting toward their places, chanting together, "*Fus-ty nuts! Fus-ty nuts!*"

But where's Fiona? I glance around. For some reason, she's rooting through her gym bag. "Come on!" I yell at her.

She's barely on the field when the whistle blows.

Interview: Fiona

Everyone has their thing, you know? The thing that makes them feel more like themselves. Every time you see Shakespeare, he's got a quill pen. Every image of Athena, she's got her shield. Artemis has a bow and arrow, Zeus has a thunderbolt.

I have the power of the blazer.

Just before I took the field, I slipped it on. Instantly, I felt more powerful. So when the second half started, I shouted, "I am Fiona!" I saw a couple of the Devlinshire kids glance at me, then at each other, like, *Ooookay, what's the matter with this girl?* Which just made me scream even louder, "And I am a strong and powerful woman!"

And here's an interesting thing. Already, Devlinshire had taken control of the ball, just like they did in the first half. But as soon as I shouted the thing about being a strong and powerful woman, the kid with the ball lost his focus. Just for a second. A nanosecond, even. But a nanosecond was all Diego needed. He swiped the ball out from under that kid. Then he charged forward.

I ran down the field alongside Diego. He looked so confident. Weren't those gods and goddesses always coming down to earth in disguise and giving temporary powers to the mortals? That's what Diego looked like: like he'd just been given superpowers by Zeus or whatever.

"Artemis, goddess of the hunt!" I shouted, thinking maybe she'd want to give *me* some powers. And then I thought, why stop with some made-up goddess? Why not ask for help from *real* strong and powerful women?

So when Devlinshire got the ball back, I ran at them screaming "Mae Jemison!" She's a really famous, great astronaut, and I know about her from a book that Henry gave me filled with facts about great women in history.

And it worked! I got that ball, and I managed to pass it to Diego. So that's when I started trying to remember other names—women who weren't "well-behaved," and who made history because of that. "Nellie Bly!" I shouted, thinking of the reporter who rode around the world in a hot-air balloon. "Komako Kimura! Shirley Chisholm! Frida Kahlo!" An activist who fought for women to be able to vote. The first woman to run for president of the United States. An artist who turned painting inside out.

Disruptors, Gabby might call them.

It felt good, shouting those names. But even better than that: It flustered Devlinshire every time.

That's when I realized, Caitlyn: You were on to something. The element of surprise really works.

It Gets Weird

It's the craziest thing. How Fiona manages to break their concentration so quickly. And then it's not just Fiona. Like when the little muscular guy powers the ball up the center of the field toward our goal, Gabby hollers, "Fake it till you make it!" She sprints straight at him, doesn't swerve or anything. Which you can tell he isn't expecting.

Gabby grabs the ball and sends it over to Yumi. And Yumi...oh, man, the girl leaps toward it. And when I say *leaps*, I mean like a ballet dancer flying across the stage. As she moves through the air, she makes this singing sound—kind of an *opera singer meets dying coyote* noise. Yumi crosses the ball to Fiona, who shouts, "Uhhhh, that lady who discovered radiation!"

Then get this: From the sideline, Glebus shouts to Fiona, "Marie Curie!"

Fiona looks over, kind of confused.

"She's also the first person ever to have won two Nobel Prizes!" Glebus adds.

Fiona's shock—Glebus is helping her out!—lasts only

an instant. She flashes a quick thumbs-up, repeats the name, then passes the ball to me. I take a shot. Paulie catches it, so it's a miss. But already I sense the game changing.

I guess everyone else senses it, too. As Paulie punts the ball toward the center of the field, Sam shouts, "Do the Fiona!" Every player in green—including me—starts jumping up and down.

I barely even notice the news cameras rolling.

The game shifted. At first I figured it was because we'd managed to throw Devlinshire off. We'd broken their concentration. I thought they'd get used to the antics after a few minutes and then we'd be right back where we'd been all along.

Except they didn't get used to it. They started getting *annoyed*. And the more irritated they got, the better we got. I can't explain it. But we were faster, tighter, more accurate. Like we were a *unit*.

It's almost like the way Mr. Farabi described it: We were the ultimate ecosystem.

And that made me think about the whole competition we'd been through. Shakespeare. The goat-food fight. The Minis. The fight over banana peels. Getting stuck in that closet, then realizing that our lives were going to change.

The real Paulie hadn't been there for any of that. Yet every bit of it was just as memorable as that stupid, hilarious, ridiculous chicken suit of his.

Now it was the last challenge, and we were getting under Devlinshire's skin, and if this was really the ultimate ecosystem, I was going to have to go all-in.

So the next time the ball came to me, I decided to release my inner chicken. I just ran toward the thing screaming, *"Caw-caw-caw-CAW!"*

Which isn't even a chicken sound, really. I think it's more like a crow. But who cares about the exactness of my chicken imitation? Not me.

The thing I cared about was that we were all in this together.

Do the Caitlyn

That's how the second half goes, more or less: with Diego making some crazy bird noise, and Yumi leaping across the field, and Gabby quoting Jadelicious, and Fiona shouting about people I've mostly never heard of, occasionally looking to Glebus for help, and all the rest of us dancing around doing the Fiona, the Yumi, the Diego.

The twins even start their zombie-werewolf game, calling out things to each other like *Ninja! Rabid raccoon!* and running across the field all funny.

On the sidelines, a few parents start doing the wave. My mom joins in, and then so does Mags. I notice that the two of them are cracking up together, like they're already best friends.

About ten minutes into the second half, I pass the ball to Diego. He catches it, makes a run toward the goal, zigzagging around some blond Devlinshire kid.

He pulls his foot back, and *bam*. He pockets it right into the upper-left corner of the net.

The score is 3–2. Not much time left.

He turns around and points at me. "Do the Caitlyn!"

And everyone looks at me, because I still don't have my own dance.

I don't even think about it. I start wagging my pointer finger in an exaggerated way, like I'm scolding someone, or telling them what to do.

Behind me, I hear Gabby cheer, "This is the best reality show ever!"

Flying

One of the Devlinshire kids shouts to the coach in blue: "Tell them to stop!"

But their coach just lifts her hands, helpless. There are no rules against singing on the field. Or against dancing while you run. Or calling out the names of historic women. Or laughing so hard your stomach hurts. There might be *conventions*, but that's not the same thing as *rules*.

The ball pings around the field until a Devlinshire kid makes a breakout run toward goal. He's got a clean shot.

Henry leaps, catches the ball. No goal. Still 3–2.

Mr. Farabi shouts from the sidelines, "A minute left, Mitchell! One minute left in the game."

Henry sends the ball to midfield. I watch it move closer—from Sam to Yumi to Fiona.

Paulie's in ready position: knees bent, eyes on Fiona. Behind him is the Paulie statue, nothing now but a fallen branch and a chewed-up T-shirt.

I have no idea who Paulie Fink is. I will never really know

who he is, or anyone else for that matter. There is so, so much I don't know.

But I do know a few things.

I know about Plato, and his cave. I know that everyone has a cave of their own, and that walking out of it, into the light, is one of the scariest things there is. I know about Mount Olympus, and about how people used to make up stories to try to make sense of their world. I know how to design a competition, and how to keep it going when everyone around me is falling apart. I know the difference between funny and mean, and I know how to make a shy Mini smile.

Fiona flicks the ball to me. By now, my legs are so exhausted that running feels like slogging through mud. But my insides are light as air.

Is the girl braver than she used to be? Yes. She is.

Less than a minute, and we're down by a goal. We can't possibly win this game. There's not a chance in the world.

But I'm running anyway. Because that thing Mags was talking about before? *Arete*? Being your best self? I know what it feels like now.

It feels like flying.

Everything—my teammates, the spectators, the goats—all of it just kind of vanishes. There's nothing but the ball and the goal ahead of me. Paulie's waiting for me there, and he's already proven that he knows how to make a save. Maybe he knew it all along.

My kick is perfect: the force, the lift, the angle.

I watch the ball sail toward Paulie, watch him stretch. Leap. Reach.

Miss.

There's no sound. Nothing but that *whoosh* of the ball hitting the net, tying up the game.

The world returns: the grass and the cheers, and my mother's voice on the sidelines, mixed in with all the others. My classmates barreling down the field toward me.

Paulie looks at me, and one side of his mouth curls upward. "New kid's got game," he says.

I don't have a chance to respond. Fiona slams into me. "Caitlynnnn!" she hollers, wrapping her arms around me. And then Diego's there, and Willow, and Yumi, and then there are so many green T-shirts surrounding me that I can't even tell who's who anymore. It's like we're a single creature—one giant breathless tangle of relief and joy.

They're still hugging me when the ref blows the final whistle.

In all the excitement of the last-minute tie, I just plain
forgot about Paulie Fink. That isn't something I ever
expected. It was only after we'd caught our breath, and
finished dumping water over our heads, saying stuff like "Can
you believe it, I just can't believe it," that I even looked over
at him.

There he was: Paulie Fink, all by himself, taking his cleats
off. That's when it all came rushing back.

Paulie was a Devlinshire kid now. And he never even
told us.

The Devlinshire players were zipping up their bags,
walking toward their coach, one by one. Paulie stood. Put on
a sweatshirt, zipped it up.

There he goes.

Then I was on my feet, moving toward him. "Paulie,"
I said to his back.

He turned around. Blinked a couple of times. "Oh. Hey,
Fiona," he said sort of awkwardly.

I looked over to where the teachers were walking the
Minis back toward their classrooms.

I wanted to say, *Give the signal*. I wanted him to call
out to the Minis, exactly the same way he did during Mini-
geddon. I wanted to say, *They'll come. They'll remember. They'll
come if you call.*

I wanted to see it so badly—the Minis hearing
that siren sound, then sprinting toward him with their
short little legs and their light-up sneakers and their
glittery, falling-down tights. I wanted to know that they
remembered his infamous *Whoop-whoop-whoop-WEEE!
Whoop-whoop-whoop-WEEE!*

But I didn't say anything. I just stood there and looked
at him.

*His hair is shorter he is taller his eyes are sadder he used
to have a disco ball spinning around behind his eyes but where
is it now?*

I could tell him about the competition, all the stupid
stuff we'd been doing. I'd catch him up on everything, and
then we would laugh and the disco ball would be there to
stay.

But I didn't even know how to begin telling him all of
that, and before I figured it out, his coach was shouting.
"Mr. Fink, let's GO!"

Paulie's eyes flicked to his coach, then back to me. "I
wanted to help," he said. "Before, when you were all chasing
the goats. I wanted to come out to help. My coach wouldn't
let me."

I could picture that. Paulie running around with us,
cracking jokes, wrapping his arms around a goat and leading
it back to the pen.

"You'd have had fun," was all I said.

Just before he turned away, he grinned. And there it was: just a glimmer, but real. The old disco ball.

I watched him get smaller and smaller. A minute later, I heard the Devlinshire bus start up and roll away, taking Paulie Fink with them.

We're on TV

The story airs late that night, on the ten o'clock news. Mom and I watch it together.

It was a lively afternoon at the Mitchell School, the newscaster says. *First, the school—which has been threatened with closure due to budgetary constraints—had some…unusual happenings.*

Then there are goats running across my screen, and we're chasing them. A goat with the Paulie head in its mouth, the big guy barreling forward and dragging the net with him. It's all right there, as if Yumi's Next Great Goat Escape reality show had become…well…actual reality. Then it cuts to us on the field, all of us doing my finger-wag dance in our mismatched shirts.

I stare at the screen. "Oh wow. Oh no. We look ridiculous."

"You look like you're having fun," Mom tells me. "That's what you look like."

The shots from the game are just a lead-in for the bigger story: the one about the school closing. The segment ends with that shot of me and Fuzzy walking across the field, away from the fort, with Real Rabbit between us. *The community remains hopeful*, the voiceover says. *But they're running out of time.*

It's the strangest thing: I recognize everything they're showing on-screen, but it doesn't look right somehow. The clips they're showing aren't *wrong*, exactly. They're just... incomplete.

The segment doesn't show me afraid to get out of the car at the start of the year or standing in front of the classroom with those dumb rules tucked into my pocket, or getting knocked down by the mean old goat and trying not to cry. It doesn't show me barely knowing how to talk to Fuzzy on the first day, or fumbling for words in the fort. It doesn't show me with Anna Spang, or anything about my old life. It doesn't show what came before, or what will come after, or what my insides feel like.

It's just this one moment out of thousands, seen from the outside, with someone else picking the angle, the lighting, the frame, the view.

WXTE posts the story online the same night. I remember Gabby saying we just need the story to go viral, and for a few hours, I'm hopeful. When I go to bed, we're the number-three news story on the WXTE website. By morning, the video's had 290 views, and some comments have appeared:

LOL, funny!

Shouldn't these kids be learning math or something?

I know, right? Good luck holding a job someday, kids.

Wish I'd gone to a school like that.

Me 2.

Me 3.

By the following morning, there are even more comments:

Most pathetic thing I ever seen!!!!

Face it: nobody cares about rural folk anymore.

I wish my son could go to a school like that.

Oh, this is one of those everyone-gets-a-trophy places.
Just wait till these kids enter the real world.

But it's as if none of those commenters even read the story. Or if they did, the story doesn't matter. Like people decided what they believed about the world long ago, and now whatever they see or hear is just proof that they were right all along.

Anyway. No one starts an online fund-raiser, like Gabby had hoped.

Then other news replaces the Mitchell School on the WXTE home page. Over near Burlington, a rescue dog saves a toddler from a fire. In Springfield, a woman comes home to find a bear rummaging through her refrigerator. Nationally, some famous Hollywood actress gives birth to twins. The next day, a disgraced banker goes on trial. Then the day after that, Rexx Rowdy—Jadelicious's archenemy—announces he's running for Congress, which sets off an around-the-clock media blitz.

Just like that, Mitchell's not in the news anymore. Which means Glebus was right: We're going to have to figure things out on our own.

Interview: Gabby

After the game, I kept thinking about that thing that Yumi said to me: about how nothing on *Megastar* is real. I understood what she meant, but my point was that Jadelicious the persona began as an idea, dreamed up by an ordinary person. Maybe she faked it...but she did make it.

Now Jadelicious is a fragrance. Jadelicious is also an instantly recognizable line of footwear. And factories all over the world are pumping out T-shirts and jackets covered in purple sequins. Jadelicious the ultimate Megastar is already on her third world tour, and she's selling out the biggest stadiums in London and Sydney and New York.

Those audiences are real. So are those factories. So are all the people who slip on a pair of Jadelicious shoes or a purple-sparkle sweatshirt and maybe feel just a little more inspired to step into their own spotlight.

I'm just saying: Something doesn't have to be exactly, literally true to be *real*. Just about everything real in this world began as a flicker in someone's imagination. You don't have to believe in reality TV to understand *that*.

Something I Don't Send,
and Something I Do

A few days after the game, I take out a blank piece of paper and begin to write.

> ~~Dear Anna~~
> ~~Hey, Anna, Remember Me?~~
> ~~Funny, I was just sitting here thinking about you, Anna~~

I tap my pen against my teeth a bunch of times and try again.

> Anna,
>
> Probably you don't want to hear from me. And I'm not even sure why I'm writing exactly.
>
> Believe it or not, at my new school we have goats, and we have to take care of them. They're actually kind of cute—sort of like puppies. The baby goats are cute, anyway. We also have to take care of little kids. It's

not bad. I don't know how long I'll be going to school here after all though. I wonder where I'll go next.

If you get this, say hello to everyone at school for me. Or don't. It's okay if you don't. I guess I just wanted to say I hope you are having a good year.

Caitlyn

I fold up the letter, hold it in my hand for a while. Then I open up my desk drawer and shove it inside. It's not even the things I want to say. Not really. And even still, I'm not brave enough to send this. Not now. Maybe not ever.

But I do have an idea for something I can send.

Not to Anna, but to someone else.

You Are Invited

**SEASON FINALE
THE SEARCH FOR THE
NEXT GREAT PAULIE FINK**

**The Mitchell School
Friday, November 10
4:00 PM**

PLEASE RSVP TO MS. GLEBUS

Season Finale

From Mags's window, Fiona and I watch the car pull into the driveway.

"He's here," whispers Fiona. She adjusts her tunic—really just a striped sheet, wrapped around her like she's in ancient Greece—then smooths it. I glance down at my own tunic, white with little yellow flowers.

The passenger door opens, and there he is: the First Great Paulie Fink. The Unoriginal original. The legend.

He looks just the same as he did two weeks ago, when we saw him walking up the path in his blue uniform, except this time he's wearing jeans and a sweatshirt.

"Go!" I tell Fiona. "Tell everyone to get into place!" Fiona dashes out of the classroom, toward the field.

I walk down the stairs to that heavy front door—the one I opened from the other side just a couple of months ago, when I had no idea what lay ahead.

Paulie's standing there, hands in the pockets of his jeans. "Uh, hi?" he says. He swallows, meets my eye, then looks away again.

He's nervous. That's so weird.

I remember Fiona kicking the Paulie statue and saying *He's embarrassed by us.* He wasn't, I realize. He just didn't know how to act. I wonder if most people walk around feeling that way all the time.

I take a deep breath. I do what Jadelicious would—what Paulie might have, if he were still a student here and he happened to be standing where I am now. I sweep my arms out to my sides, grandly.

"Welcome"—I'm using my Speech Voice, the one I didn't know I had until I got to Mitchell—"to the final episode of the Search for the Next Great Paulie Fink."

He flashes a confused half smile, like he has no idea what's going on, but he'll roll with it.

This whole thing was my idea. I thought of it a few days after the news story ran, which was right around the time the town council decided to schedule the vote about funding the school for January 10, two months from now.

I didn't say anything when I first thought of it, but the next day it still seemed like a good idea, so I knocked on Glebus's door. Standing in her office, I realized I couldn't explain my plan without telling her about the whole competition. My voice shook a little as I told her why we'd been doing everything that had gotten us into so much trouble. She watched me, expressionless. When I got to the part about what I wanted to do next, she surprised me.

"Okay," she said.

"Okay?"

She nods. "Goodness knows we could use a little bit of luck around here."

I wanted it to be special, so I decided to make handwritten invitations. Before Glebus mailed Paulie's, everyone—kids, teachers, and Glebus—signed it. I signed it, too.

Beneath all the signatures Fiona scribbled two sentences in her chicken-scratch handwriting: You better be there, Paulie Fink. YOU BETTER BE THERE.

Now here he is.

"So . . . what's this all about, exactly?" he asks.

I don't answer. Instead I hand him a chain we made from vines, like a long necklace. "Will you please put this around your neck before the ceremony begins?"

He eyes me quizzically, like he's wondering how much he should ask. Then he shrugs, places the chain around his neck, and waits for his next instruction.

"Now," I say, "follow me."

HENRY:
You know something I only just learned, Caitlyn?

CAITLYN:
What's that?

HENRY:
All those stories about the Greek gods and goddesses, they're all just sort of cobbled together, like patchwork. Back in ancient Greece, there wasn't a single source that told the whole story of any one god, or anything else, for that matter.

So all those mythology books on the shelves today? They're pieced together from scraps of information that showed up in lots of different places over many centuries.

CAITLYN:
Wow. Sort of makes you wonder what got lost, doesn't it?

HENRY:
That's the thing. Almost everything you know will disappear. Just like it did for the Greeks. Just like it does for everyone.

And when it does, maybe you'll wish you'd written it down.

That's what I thought as I watched you and Paulie walk toward us at the ceremony. I noticed the vines around his neck, the way he squinted toward us and scratched his temple. The air was cold, and I blew on my fingertips for warmth, and even as it was happening I felt the moment slipping away.

And an idea started forming inside my head, an idea for the humanities project. And it involved all of us.

The Final Countdown

I explain the basics as the real Paulie and I walk toward the place where the Paulie statue used to stand.

"A competition," Paulie repeats. He's squinting at the Originals, standing statue-like in the distance.

"Yup."

"For a new..."

"Paulie Fink. Yup."

"Because..." He turns to look at me, and he scratches his temple. "Why exactly?"

"Because you're a megastar. Totally legendary, you know?"

There's no hilarious comeback. No joke or anything. So far, the most surprising thing about Paulie Fink is there's nothing surprising about him.

The whole class is waiting for us near the goat pen, wrapped in sheets. They're standing in two neat rows. Beside them stand Ms. Glebus, Mr. Farabi, and Mags. Everyone is silent and very still.

Everyone except the goats, of course. Those goats are doing what they always do: charging back and forth in the

334

pen, bleating at everyone. *Are you going to feed us or what?* they seem to be saying.

"The First Great Paulie Fink has arrived!" I declare. "Let us begin the final elimination ceremony. Let us crown, at last, the *Next* Great Paulie Fink."

Ms. Glebus and the teachers all look like they're trying to stifle smiles, but the kids stare straight ahead, completely serious.

"Fiona and Diego, will you please step forward?" I command. They look at each other, nod seriously, and then step forward together.

"For as long as I've known you two, which admittedly has been only about two months, you have been fierce competitors. And as we searched for the Next Great Paulie Fink, you fought...valiantly. You fought with honor. I will be honest: *Kleos* rightfully belongs to you both."

I take a deep breath. "This has not been an easy decision," I say. "But the moment of reckoning has arrived at last."

Final Interview: Diego and Fiona

CAITLYN:
Okay, you two. This is the last interview. Tell me what you were thinking during the final elimination.

DIEGO:
You know what I was thinking? I was thinking how accidental it all is. Where you happen to be born. Who you wind up with in school. Whether you have stuff in common or not. It's just dumb luck, and yet for your whole life, you share the same memories with this tiny handful of people...

FIONA:
Oh, puh-lease! You were thinking that you wanted to win. Just the same as I was.

DIEGO:
Well, of course I was thinking *that*. But I was thinking other things, too. Weren't you?

FIONA:
Well. I guess I was also thinking that I missed Paulie. He was standing there with us, just like he used to, but everything was different. I wished he'd never left, you know?

DIEGO:
Yeah. That. Big-time, that.

FIONA:

I knew that whichever one of us won, I was going to have to keep missing the real Paulie. I hated that. I hated that there'd never actually be a new Paulie, not really. We weren't going to be able to go back.

DIEGO:

That's sort of what I was trying to say. For the rest of our lives, we'll meet other people. And we'll tell them our stories, but none of them will ever really get it. You only understand how things were if you were there.

[*Twelve seconds of silence*]

FIONA:

Darn it, Diego. Why'd you have to give me the feels?

DIEGO:

Yeah, sorry. I kinda have a case of them myself.

[*Pause*]

Anyway. I wish there was more to say, but I actually can't think of anything else.

FIONA:

Me neither. I know, that's shocking, right? Anyway, I guess you can stop recording now, Caitlyn. But...thanks for all of this, okay? It was pretty cool. The whole thing.

[Recording off]

We Have a Winner

"Fiona Fawnstock?" I begin. Fiona takes a deep breath, stands a little taller. "Fiona, you are an original in every sense of the word. You don't always follow the rules, but maybe this world doesn't need more rule-followers. Maybe it needs more people who aren't afraid to just jump in and try things. That's what you do, Fiona: You jump in. Every time."

By this point, she's beaming. Which is why it's so hard to say the next part.

"The thing is," I start, "I think the world needs the original Fiona Fawnstock more than it needs Fiona to become someone else. So I'm sorry, Fiona. You are not the Next Great Paulie Fink."

Fiona lets that sink in. Then she turns to Diego, extends her hand as if to congratulate him.

"But wait," I say. "I'm not done. Diego? You are a fierce competitor who also manages to celebrate others' victories. I'm pretty sure that means you have real *arete*. But I'm afraid that you, too, are too much of an original to lose. Diego, you are *also* not the Next Great Paulie Fink."

Diego does a quick double take as Gabby, behind him, murmurs, "Oooh, plot twist!"

Only Mr. Farabi, Mags, and Glebus don't look surprised. They know exactly what's coming.

"Thanks to Fiona, we no longer have a Paulie statue as a good-luck charm," I continue. "Instead, here in front of us, we have a real-life Paulie. The original. Diego and Fiona, please give to the real Paulie Fink whatever sacrifice you've brought."

Fiona hands Paulie a brown paper bag. Diego gives him a small box. Paulie glances at me. "Should I open these now?" he asks.

"Later," I say.

"So after this *whole* competition . . ." begins Yumi.

"There's no Next Great—" Thomas follows up, but I raise my hand to stop him.

"I said that neither Fiona nor Diego is the Next Great Paulie Fink. But there is a Next Great Paulie Fink, and this individual stands among us now. It is someone who has demonstrated a remarkable ability to disrupt us, to surprise us, to make us laugh, and—most important—to unite us."

I glance at the original Paulie Fink quickly—just long enough to see him staring at his sneakers, listening intently. For the life of me, I can't tell what he's thinking.

Then I nod at Mr. Farabi. It's time.

Mr. Farabi goes into the goat pen. He wades through the bleating goats until he reaches the one he wants: the big goat.

The stinker. My archenemy. Mr. Farabi ties a rope around his neck and leads him out of the pen.

As he does, the old goat lets forth a giant belch, which cracks everyone up. Even I smile. Here I am, doing my best to look like a solemn, serious leader, and that dumb goat is showing me that I'm not.

The old beast really is a Shakespearean Fool.

I sweep my hand toward the animal. "Citizens of Mitchell, I give you: the Next...Great...Paulie Fink!"

As everyone breaks into applause, Gabby shouts, "*Ohmahgah!* The scapegoat wins! But it's *perfect!*"

Paulie looks around, confused. "Hang on," he says. "Did you just name a goat after me?"

Katharsis

I tell Paulie to place the vines around the old goat's neck. When he does, the Originals go wild. There's no more seriousness. Fiona starts running around and hugging everyone, and the class is basically just a cluster of high fives and hugs.

But the ceremony's not over yet. I hold up my hand until everyone is quiet.

"We all know this community can use a little luck these days," I say. "And Mags, how did the ancients try to improve their luck?"

"*Pharmakos.*" She smiles. We've already talked about this part.

"And what did *pharmakos* bring them?"

"*Katharsis.*"

"Thank you, Mags," I say. "*Pharmakos* brings *katharsis*, which is a way of chasing away bad luck. Now, I like to think that this would be obvious, but just in case: There will be no beating anyone with branches. Instead, we'll just all take a moment to touch this goat, our Next Great Paulie Fink. As you do, please imagine yourself transferring whatever bad luck you'd like to cast out."

Mr. Farabi walks the goat past the line of Originals. Each kid reaches out to touch the goat. Even Mags and Glebus do it.

I'm the last to touch the goat. I close my eyes, feel my fingers running through the hair on the back of his neck. When I finish, Mr. Farabi begins to lead the animal across the field. We follow. And we chant.

Of course we chant.

At first we chant "*Pharm-a-kos, pharm-a-kos, pharm-a-kos!*" Then we change it to "*Ka-thar-sis! Ka-thar-sis! Ka-thar-sis!*" By the time we're rounding the front of the school, we're all chanting "*Paul-ie Fink! Paul-ie Fink! Pau-lie Fink!*"

Paulie—the human Paulie, that is—shakes his head. "I am so totally confused," he says. But he's grinning, and I see what Fiona was talking about. I see the disco ball.

There's a truck waiting in front of the school. The side says LEAPIN' GOATS FARM. There's a woman leaning against it. She's got long gray braids and loose overalls and a blue baseball cap that says I'M KIND OF A BIG DEAL IN VERMONT.

Mr. Farabi hands her the rope.

"Back to the farm for you, troublemaker," she says, giving the old goat a scratch on the head. She leads the Next Great Paulie Fink up the ramp and into the truck. She gives us all a wave as she pulls away, rolling past the Good Day Bell and down the driveway in a cloud of dust.

Then the class begins cheering again. *"Cait-lyn! Cait-lyn! Cait-lyn!"*

It's the same thing they chanted back when this whole competition began. When they were trying to convince me to be in charge, and I thought the whole thing was ridiculous. Maybe it *was* ridiculous. But that doesn't mean it didn't matter.

Now it's over, and everyone looks at me.

"That's, uh, kind of as far as I planned," I say. So they all turn to Paulie Fink.

"Don't ask me," he says. "I don't know what's going on here."

We stand there for a few awkward moments. I guess we could all just go home now, but I realize I'm not ready. Not yet. So I turn to Mr. Farabi.

"Do you have another kickball around here?" I ask.

FROM THE DESK OF PAULIE FINK

Well. You probably figured I'd poke my head into this story eventually. Took me a while, but I guess it's about time I said hi.

Hi there. If we haven't met before, it's nice to meet you. I'm Paulie Fink. The real one, that is. Not the goat.

I'm writing to you from Devlinshire Hills—where, for the record, not everyone has a pool or a fortune waiting for them when they turn eighteen (or even twenty-one). Not by a long shot.

But a few of us are very lucky.

If you've gotten this far, you probably don't need me to spend too much time on small talk. You already know way more about me than you ever wanted to know. Instead, I thought I'd take a cue from the Greeks. Tell a couple of stories, see what becomes of them.

Here's one:

> A kid shows up to a new school at the start of fourth grade. Kind of a loser. Drives his teachers and classmates bonkers. Gets in trouble nearly every day, and sometimes the whole class is punished for his actions. Also, he can't kick

a soccer ball to save his life. Never even has anyone over to his house. He figures lots of people will be relieved when he finally just disappears.

Here's another story:

A confident god of chaos dominates a school. He's brave and witty. He outsmarts foes, hosts banquets, leads an unlikely army to a stunning victory using the element of surprise. After he's gone, people build statues in his honor. People compete to see who will fill his shoes, but of course no human ever can.

And, just for the heck of it, here's a third:

There once was a spoiled rich kid. Has everything he ever needs, plus his mom makes big donations to whatever school he happens to be attending. So how much trouble can he ever get in, really? He never fits in anywhere, though. His mom ships him from school to school in California, and then decides to move back east to send him to a school operating out of his family's old estate. Eventually, his mom grows tired of getting letters and calls from the principal.

She moves him to a different school district. A better one, she says. He assumes everyone will be glad to see him go. In other words, he might be legendary, but he's hardly a hero.

Every one of these stories is different. And every one of them is true.

Long story short: My great-great-granddad was Julius Hewitt Mayberry Oxthorpe, who had a thing for velvet suits and who built a textile factory on a river in northern Vermont. Julius built an estate on the edge of town, where he surrounded himself with books and statues. He was followed by a few more generations of Oxthorpes: Paul Jarvis Oxthorpe, who made that mill a little bigger and decided to keep some pet ostriches on the grounds of the estate. Then Forrest James Oxthorpe, who cared more about his collection of decorative tapestries than either the factory or the town. After a couple of decades of declining revenues, Forrest sold the whole business off to some multinational corporation for a buttload of cash, then moved to Boca Raton and spent the rest of his days visiting auction houses. It didn't take long for that corporation to transfer the whole business overseas.

Forrest's daughter was Beatrice, who ran off to art school in California to become a sculptor. She married a gallery owner there named Gilbert Fink, then divorced him nineteen months later. But not before they had a kid.

That's me. Paulie Fink.

Today, Mom is Beatrice Oxthorpe Masterson, wife of Mark Masterson, who used to work at a bank in Boston but now manages other people's money from a brick-walled office above the Foxhollow Café in downtown Devlinshire Hills, Vermont.

One of his clients is a retired rock star.

All of which is to say that (a) I come from a long line of eccentrics, and (b) I might be a Fink, but I'm also an Oxthorpe.

I told that to the other kids once. They were looking at Julius's portrait, and I said: *That's my great-great-granddad, you know.* They were all, *Yeah right.* I guess Julius seemed about as real to them as Glebus smuggling vanilla-scented candles, or the Republic of Endrisistan.

It just so happened that on this occasion I was telling the truth.

If you've read this far—and hey, nice job if you have—you're probably asking, *What the heck is this about?*

That's exactly what I asked a few weeks ago—after the ceremony that everyone kept calling a season finale—when a random email from Henry popped up in my in-box. Attached was a class project: PLATO'S CAVE, KLEOS, PHARMAKOS, AND KATHARSIS: GREEK CONCEPTS IN MODERN-DAY VERMONT. It included Caitlyn's "Official Record of the Search for the Next Great Paulie Fink," with excerpts from interview transcripts and a bunch of her own stories, too. I read every word.

I've got to hand it to Caitlyn: She did a great job pulling it all together. But there's one story she didn't have: mine.

Don't worry, I'm not about to insist you sit here for another three hundred pages. Let's face it: Silence is golden (and duct tape is silver). I just want to complete the story of the competition by telling you what happened that night, after I got back to Devlinshire and opened up the gifts that Fiona and Diego had given to me.

In Diego's box was a scrap of fabric, neon green, and chewed at the edges, with part of a word visible: WINNER. There was a note:

Stay legendary, Paulie.
Your buddy, D.

In Fiona's bag was a different scrap of fabric. It was the same color as Diego's, and just as chewed. Her scrap also had a word on it: PICK.

I hope you always pick the element of surprise.
And remember, it's not trouble until
they say your name three times.
Your friend, forever and ever and ever,
Fiona

When I realized they'd both given me pieces of my old shirt, I laughed out loud. But I guess I liked the way Fiona signed her note best of all.

Here's what I keep wondering: What if I actually *was* the person that they described? The powerful trickster who influences everything. The one people were leaving notes for at the tree, asking for help.

What would *that* version of Paulie do right now?

I'll tell you what I think he'd do: He'd turn this whole stinking situation, the school closing, on its head. He'd figure out some way to make *pharmakos* real.

So. Mom and Mark, Uncle Teddy and Aunt Cynthia, Auntie Alex and Uncle Geoffrey, Aunties Laura and Genevieve, Uncle Russ, Cousins Jennifer and Toby and Hannah, Great-Uncle Cecil, and Great-Aunt Susan, and everyone else who gets this email, which is to say literally every single Oxthorpe I could find an address for (including, I suspect, even a few that I'm not related to):

What if we were to pull the ultimate trick?

What if *we* were to save the school?

What if we became the people Gabby wants to believe are real—the ones who see a need, and step up?

I mean, talk about the element of surprise.

It's a long shot, I know. But you know what? We Oxthorpes kind of hit the jackpot. In the scheme of, like, all of history, we're pretty lucky. So what should we do with this good luck?

I guess we could keep it to ourselves. We could also pretend we don't have it in the first place—not talk about it, maybe even go out of our way to hide it.

But there's something else we could do: We could use it. Not to buy velvet suits, or decorative tapestries, or pet ostriches.

Instead, we could use it to save a school.

Anyway, I'll turn this back to Caitlyn one last time. It seems only fair to let her have the last word. When we left off, we were all at the Mitchell School. They had just loaded a goat with my name on it onto the back of a truck and watched it drive away. Remember that? Great, let's get back to it.

From the heart of my bottom,
Ciao for niao,
Flatulently yours,
Your nephew/grandnephew/cousin/random stranger/
whatever,

Paul Julius Oxthorpe Fink

It Won't Last, but We Play Anyway

The sun is sitting low on the horizon as Mr. Farabi disappears into the school.

It's strange, seeing the school at this hour. The shadows are longer than I'm used to, and everything is glowing with this ridiculously golden light. My mom would like how everything looks right now: the mountains, the last leaves fluttering to the ground, the way everything feels kind of glowy and dreamlike.

Mr. Farabi comes jogging out of the building carrying a kickball. "Who's up for a game?" he says.

As we walk toward the field, I glance around. In this light, you can't quite see how falling-apart everything is. You can't quite see the missing patches of paint on the building, or the cracked windows, or the encroaching brambles and weeds that are everywhere the goats aren't.

I mean, I guess you can see those things if you look. I could choose to look, and some part of me even wants to.

But I don't. Not right now. Right now, I'm looking at

the way Sam and Willow and Lydia are linked arm in arm, three across. I remember how I assumed on the first day that there'd never be room for a fourth. But Fiona runs up and wiggles right in between Lydia and Willow, as if it's no big deal. Four across. Then Diego joins them. Five across. Yumi joins in, too. Six. Then others. Seven across. Ten.

In our tunics, you could almost imagine that we've been transported to some other moment in time. Like this is a part of history, rather than the present day. That's when it hits me: We *are* history. This, right here, is all history ever has been: regular people living their lives, making things up as they go, hoping they get it right.

Now the line in front of me is eleven across: every kid in my class, plus the original and totally legendary Paulie Fink.

"Wait," says Gabby. She's got one arm draped over Henry and the other over Yumi. "Where's Caitlyn?" She turns around, takes her hand off Henry, and waves me over.

I step into place between Gabby and Henry. And then I'm part of the line, too.

It won't last long, this light. Soon, the sun will dip below the mountains. When it does, dark will fall quickly, and we'll all scatter to our different homes and our different lives, and eventually everything that's happened—the ceremony, the competition, probably even this school—will fade away forever.

But not yet. Not just yet.

Because right now, I can feel Gabby's and Henry's arms against my shoulders, and Mr. Farabi is just a tiny bit ahead of us, and he's bouncing that red kickball up and down.

Right now, we've got a game to play.

Author's Note

At the heart of *The Next Great Paulie Fink* is Plato's allegory of the cave, a 2,400-year-old thought experiment. While I've simplified Plato's argument a bit for younger readers, the essence comes down to this: We might be wrong, even about the things we "know" for sure. Millennia later, this is still a pretty radical idea.

If you're interested in Plato's allegory of the cave, check out Alex Gendler's TED-Ed video and related discussions. Interested in philosophy? A good beginner-friendly starting place is Stephen West's podcast, *Philosophize This!* At the conclusion of each episode, West thanks listeners for wanting to know more today than they did yesterday—a pretty good goal, I'd say.

Leaving our cave requires examining the stories we've been told, and the way these stories shape our understanding of and our experiences in the world. It's my hope that this book can serve as one small example of the power of opening ourselves up to new stories. The book itself even parallels the history of storytelling: There's a moment, for example, where the characters move from oral storytelling into written form. The book also explores several storytelling genres and elements (tall tales, parable, allegory, primary sources, newspaper accounts, and rhetorical speech), ultimately veering into an examination of narrative itself.

I've taken the epigraph at the start of this book from Emily Wilson's gorgeous, groundbreaking translation of Homer's *The Odyssey* (New York: W.W. Norton & Company, 2017), the first into English by a woman. Wilson's translation, along with works like Madeline Miller's incredible *Circe* (New York: Little, Brown and Company, 2018), demonstrates the power and potential of exploring ancient tales with new eyes and with new voices. Other contemporary scholars, writers, and thought leaders whose work has helped me think more critically about the version of the story of ancient Greece I was taught include Kwame Anthony Appiah, Mary Beard, Joel Perry Christensen, Curtis Dozier, Yung In Chae, Daniel Mendelsohn, Dan-el Padilla Peralta, Erik Robinson, and Donna Zuckerberg. You'll find several of these writers at the website Eidolon and the blog *Sententiae Antiquae*. I'm especially grateful to Christopher Lovell, PhD, my go-to person for all things related to ancient Greece, for his expertise and guidance.

Fiona uses the phrase *Well-behaved women seldom make history*. The expression was first used by historian Laurel Thatcher Ulrich, who was writing not about the value of misbehaving per se, but rather about who gets left out of our historic narrative—and who, ultimately, gets *kleos*.

Mr. Farabi's name was inspired by Abū Naṣr al-Fārābī, circa 872–950, a Muslim philosopher who both helped preserve ancient Greek texts and expanded on them. Among other accomplishments, al-Fārābī was a Neoplatonist who wrote about the power of philosophy to inspire souls, promote justice, and create more virtuous societies.

This name is a small nod to the fact that ancient Greeks are part of a wider human exchange of ideas and cultures—one that transcends borders, religion, and ethnicity.

Acknowledgments

A few thank-yous are in order: First, to the entire team at Little, Brown Books for Young Readers, for your patience and hard work, and for having more faith in me than I had in myself. Special thanks to copyeditors Chandra Wohleber and Jen Graham, and to my epically heroic editor, Andrea Spooner. You are wise, steady, and mighty, and totally legendary.

Thanks, too, to my agent and friend, Mollie Glick (what a blessing you are); my beautiful Mojos Molly Burnham, Leslie Connor, Jacqueline Davies, Lita Judge, and Grace Lin; readers Amie Bui, Lisa Cushman, Marisa Daley, Darlie Kerns, Molly Kerns, Emma Mathews, Piper Mathews, Rebecca Tucker-Smith, and Tom Wade; the students and faculty at Pine Cobble; and Joe Bergeron, guru of all things related to school policy.

A huge thank-you to the individuals who inspired a few of the antics in these pages: Eric Printz, the original Box-Man, who was once trampled by a goat; Aidan White, who successfully escaped his own goat trampling; Daniel Currie, no stranger to fruit-fly infestations; the Crugers gang for all those epic games of team tag; Beau Leahy, who found his inner bird during a game of capture the flag; and Patrick McGarrity, who livened up a mundane workday by hiding beneath my desk.

And, of course, to my family, especially Blair, Merrie, and Charlotte.

Here's to wanting to know more than we did yesterday. Here's to each of us venturing out of our cave.

Discussion Questions

1. Mags defines *kleos* as "Renown. Glory. Being remembered" (page 140). What qualities do you think make someone worthy of glory or renown? Who are some examples of people who will be remembered? What would you want to be remembered for?

2. How does Caitlyn's treatment of Anna Spang influence your view of Caitlyn as a person? Why do you think Caitlyn treats Anna the way she does?

3. In order to navigate her daily life at school, Caitlyn creates many lists of rules. Discuss how these rules impact her. Do they help, hurt, or limit her? Do you have unwritten rules in your own life?

4. The chapters switch back and forth between Caitlyn's perspective and the interviews she conducts with other characters. How do these two formats differ from each other? What kind of information does each format reveal?

5. What is the significance of the name the Originals? Is it appropriate? How do the Originals turn their uniqueness into strengths? Is Caitlyn able to do this, and if so, how?

6. What are some of the differences between Caitlyn's old school and the Mitchell School? Are there any parts that stay the same between the two schools?

7. How does the story Caitlyn tells Kiera about the girl "who felt too soft on the inside" reflect Caitlyn's own experiences (page 275)?

8. Henry tells Caitlyn that "Back in ancient Greece, there wasn't a single source that told the whole story of any one god, or anything else, for that matter" (page 332). What are some examples of characters not telling the whole story about an event or character?

9. How does Paulie's letter change your perception of him? How does the way he describes himself compare to how his classmates view him?

10. Do you think you can ever really know what someone else is going through? How can your assumptions about someone else's life impact them? How do your assumptions about others limit yourself?